Jane Sleight is an author fas　　　　　...ionships in the modern age. Her first books were the *Tales of a Modern Woman* novel trilogy and the novel *Sasha* - a tale of womanhood in the 21st century. Her first novella was *Walking Back Toward Myself* - a tale of self-rediscovery set in Cumbria. *Like Father, Like Son* and *The Secret of Contentment* are both romantic intrigues exploring reasons why people hide secrets from their partners. She has also written *Crumbs from the Bread of Life*, a collection of contemporary poetry and short stories, and a three-act play called *Womanipulation*, that examines the nature of friendship between women.

You can find updates from Jane on Twitter **@janesleight**, on Facebook **@JaneSleightAuthor** and at her website **janesleight.com**.

By Jane Sleight

Novels

Tales of a Modern Woman series

Part 1 - Teen Rebel to Woman
Part 2 – From Woman to Wife
Part 3 – Happy Ever After?

Sasha

Novellas

Walking Back Toward Myself
Like Father, Like Son
The Secret of Contentment

Short Stories and Poetry

Crumbs from the Bread of Life

Plays

Womanipulation

Jane Sleight

Faking It

A contemporary novel

Jane Sleight Publishing

First published 2023 by Jane Sleight Publishing

Acknowledgements

Thank you to my amazing husband for not complaining about the amount of time I spend scribbling in notebooks.

Thank you Gary, Penny and Alice, my beta-readers, as well as Rushmoor Writers, whose responses and invaluable advice gave me the confidence to share Juliet with the world.

Chapter 1 – Juliet

Juliet stood alert, holding up a name card at the T5 Arrivals Hall at Heathrow as she scanned the faces of the arriving passengers. Travis McBride nodded at her in acknowledgement as he came through the automatic doors.

'Travis, I'm Juliet, Daniel Cross's PA. Come this way.' She steered him out of the terminal and into the short stay car park. 'How was your flight from Atlanta?'

He shrugged. 'Fine. Dull. Shit movies.'

She put his suitcase in the boot of her VW and drove out of the car park and onto the motorway. 'I'm going to take you to your hotel and get you checked in so you can have a rest after your journey. I've some sightseeing planned for this afternoon, if you're interested, before the theatre and supper with Daniel and his wife, Giselle. Does that sound acceptable?'

'Sounds great. Are you my companion for the weekend?' He put his hand on her knee.

'I'll be looking after you,' she said, trying to sound polite. 'Probably best if I focus on driving for now.' She firmly removed his hand.

'Whatever you say.' He sat back and half-closed his eyes.

She took him to a hotel in central London, asking him about his life, his family and about America, getting him to recommend places to visit, all the time negotiating her way through the London traffic. She pulled into the hotel drop-off point and guided him to the reception desk, where she was warmly greeted. 'Hallo, I'd be so grateful if you could look after Mr McBride for me,' she asked the nearest receptionist. 'His room's been booked on the Executive floor and it should be available now.'

The reception staff dealt with Travis efficiently. As they should, thought Juliet, given the amount of business Cross International put their way. Juliet handed Travis his key card along with her business card. 'I'll pick you up at 3pm if I don't hear from you. Earlier or later is fine. Just let me know.'

'You're great. Ever thought about working Stateside? I'd take you on like that,' he said, clicking his fingers.

A lot of the businessmen she met offered her a job. 'Thank you. It might be nice to work abroad one day. I'll give it some serious thought. See you later.' She went back to her car and drove to her flat. She'd worn a dress to meet him but he was rather too tactile for her liking, so she'd wear trousers for the rest of the day. She laid out fresh clothes, ready for later. As she changed into her running gear, she realised she hadn't made a note of the access code for Travis's phone. He'd mainly used his fingerprint to open it but it had asked him to tap in the PIN a couple of times and she'd managed to see what digits he'd entered. It would be handy later.

She went out into the damp of the morning. A light drizzle had settled in, which was great for cooling her on her run but less good for sightseeing with Travis. If it was raining too heavily, they'd have to do the tour by car, but it was so much nicer to walk and the guests tended to behave better out in the open. Her legs felt sluggish as she ran along the Embankment. She'd rest in the morning. There'd be no early Sunday morning run as she usually did, not when she had Travis to organise. The thought galvanised her into running faster and she found her stride.

She sprinted the last few hundred metres then walked slowly up the stairs to her flat to cool down. Showered and freshly made up, she felt ready to face the rest of the day.

The rain began just after 2pm so Juliet drove to Travis's hotel and waited in reception. He appeared just after 3pm, looking weary. She took him on a loop of the city before showing him the different parks. He'd visited before but had never realised how much green space London had. She took him to a funky café in a back street near Trafalgar Square, where she bought him a strong black coffee. They braved the rain to look at the second-hand book shops in Cecil Court, more for her pleasure than his, before queuing at the Lego shop in Leicester Square, where Travis bought an enormous *Star Wars* model for his son, uninspiringly named Travis Junior. Juliet took him back to his hotel and told him she would see him at the theatre. Daniel's driver was picking Travis up that night, so Juliet went home to relax. She'd been thankful Travis had behaved himself.

She left her flat at 7pm on foot. It was still damp but she dodged the showers and arrived in good time. She found Daniel, his wife Giselle and Travis in a bar opposite the theatre. She declined a drink before steering them across the road and into their seats in a box in the Royal Circle. They were seeing a play, a good play, but Juliet had seen it several times with other visitors and zoned out during the first half. Travis was engrossed but still let his hand wander onto her upper thigh every so often. She left it there but made no attempt to reciprocate and he lost interest before the interval.

After supper at a French restaurant, during which Travis and Daniel discussed business while Giselle and Juliet made polite small talk, Daniel and Giselle went home, leaving Juliet to take care of Travis.

'Shall I walk you back to your hotel? London's pretty special at night,' she said, trying not to sound as though she'd said the words a hundred times before.

'That would be awesome.' His white-toothed smile dazzled.

She took him down to the Embankment and walked across Waterloo Bridge and back along the south side of the river. When she was near the entrance to her apartment block, she stopped. 'I live just in here. Would you like to come up for a nightcap?'

'You live here? Holy moly, Daniel must pay you big bucks.'

'It's a company flat. Apartment.'

She pointed out the lift but he said he was happy to use the stairs. He'd boasted that he kept himself fit but his breathing was heavy by the time they reached the top floor. He made a grab for her as soon as she closed the flat's front door but she managed to avoid it.

'Let's have a drink first.' She opened a bottle of champagne, poured him a glass then, out of his sight, added a tiny tablet to it. It dissolved quickly. She made herself a tonic water with bitters and took the drinks over to where he was pacing in front of the sofa, as he admired the river view. He reminded her of an animal on heat, prowling for a conquest.

'Cheers, Travis. I do hope you've had a nice evening.'

He tasted it delicately. 'Is this Bollinger?'

'It is.' She took a long drink from her glass, hoping he would do the same. All animals, humans included, couldn't help but mirror the movements of others they were with, particularly if they liked them, she'd found.

'You are spoiling me.' He sunk the contents of the glass and licked his lips.

'Let's go and relax in here.' She topped up his champagne and he followed her into the bedroom.

He climbed onto the bed beside her and she saw him reel slightly then frown.

'What's the matter?' she asked.

'God, I feel weird,' he said. His head flopped to one side. He was out cold.

Juliet began to undress him. From his trouser pocket, she extracted his phone and opened it, making sure the unlock code she'd seen him use was correct. She took it to the main room, connected it to her laptop with a USB lead then opened it so she could start copying data. Contacts, messages and photos were all downloaded in a matter of minutes. She began checking the other apps he had on the device, to see if there was any other information Daniel might find useful.

Once satisfied she'd got everything, she removed the wire and opened the phone up with a tiny screwdriver she kept in her laptop bag. She placed a chip device into the phone that would let Daniel listen to Travis's voicemails and calls as well as download text messages. It had limited benefit, she knew, as people like Travis updated their phones almost as often as they changed their underwear, but while Daniel was negotiating with Travis, he'd get the inside track on what Travis was thinking and who he was plotting with. Often, they would discover someone having an affair, which could be a useful bargaining tool.

Now the phone was set up, she wiped it clean of her fingerprints and put it back in Travis's trouser pocket. She took the hotel key card from his wallet and finished undressing him, before stripping naked. She manoeuvred Travis into the middle of the bed and climbed on top of him, using cameras that were hidden in the corners of the room to take pictures that looked as though she and Travis were having sex. She checked the results to make sure the fact that Travis was comatose wasn't obvious from the angle of the shots.

Happy with the results, she put on her all-black running gear, along with a dark baseball cap and wrote a note to Travis that she left by the bed. "Just gone to late night pharmacy, be back soon, Tiger. Jx" It was very unlikely Travis would wake up, but her going to pick up condoms for their night of passion was a good excuse for her absence if he did.

She jogged to his hotel and let herself into his room with the key she'd taken from his wallet. She took a picture of his open suitcase, so she could put it all back exactly as it was when she'd finished, and went through everything methodically. Finding nothing of interest other than some prescription drugs, she repacked it and went through his flight bag. She couldn't find a laptop which meant he'd probably put it in the room safe. There'd be an opportunity when he visited the office to download data from it, she was sure. She found his notebook, and took a photo of every page which she would review later. It would be a struggle to read it all, as Daniel would want a summary before he met Travis the next day. She'd have to do it as soon as she got back to the flat, hoping Travis wouldn't wake till the morning. As long as the tablets were their usual strength, it should be fine.

She returned the bag to its previous state and made her way back to the flat. She made a coffee, wedged a chair under the bedroom door handle as a safety mechanism and began to go through the data she'd gathered. It took a couple of hours and she garnered precious few nuggets of information that would be useful. She emailed everything to Daniel then made herself comfortable on the sofa with a blanket and a pillow, setting an alarm for 7am.

When the alarm went off, Juliet felt as though she'd only been asleep a few moments. She perked herself up with a shower, got dressed and made a cafetiere of coffee. She poured a mug for Travis after drinking some herself and went to wake him. She noticed she'd left the pharmacy note on the bedside table and hastily screwed it up as he opened his eyes. 'Morning,' she said, trying to sound as bright as possible.

'Goddamn, I feel like shit. What time is it? What happened?' He rubbed his right temple.

'It's 7:30am. We…had a nice time together after the theatre but I think you might have had one glass of champagne too many. You fell asleep afterwards.' She smiled and handed him the coffee as he sat up.

'I don't remember anything.' He was shaking his head slowly.

'I'm sure it'll come back to you. You certainly seemed to enjoy yourself.'

'Did I? Did we…?' He looked to her for answers.

She touched his hand. 'As I said, we had a lovely time. Now, I need to get you back to your hotel. You've a full day ahead.'

'God, yeah, going out on that boat trip.'

'You'll have a brilliant time. The Thames is great.'

'Will you be there?' he asked.

'Unfortunately, I have a prior commitment. Do you want to shower here? Or shall I take you back to your hotel?'

Juliet dropped a dazed and confused Travis at his hotel. She drove home and washed up from the night before, scrubbing the champagne flute to ensure there was no trace of the contents. She'd found it harder than usual to spend time with Travis, because he bore a passing physical resemblance to her late father. She tried to think about something else to dislodge thoughts of the one man in her life she'd truly loved. Her love for him had been eroded over a number of years, drop by drop, like water from a leaking bucket, as his alcoholism had worsened. She'd shunned relationships since his death until she'd met Cameron. She'd finally dared to open her heart to him but her trust in him after cautiously dating for eighteen months had been a mistake. He'd betrayed her almost as badly as her father. Or that's what it had felt like at the time.

She settled on the sofa and picked up a book she'd been promising herself for some time. A good novel helped her leave behind the sadness of her life as well as the pressures of her job. The thriller's opening description of suburban housing reminded her of her childhood, as it described the lives and stories that were hidden behind each front door. She remembered the day she'd left home, the smell of new paint heavy in the air where she'd tried to smarten the place up. Her father's debts were considerable when he died, so the house had to be sold to pay them off. She'd walked away with just enough money for a rental deposit on a studio flat.

She'd slowly built up some savings but had never felt secure until she joined Cross International. When Daniel took her on as his PA, her life had changed. Her salary wasn't vast but she had no living costs. She got a bonus in shares every year which had been building up. She cleared enough money to buy nice clothes, some beautiful shoes and the best food. She had access to theatre, art galleries, museums and exhibitions, often as a VIP, at no cost to herself. She was lucky, she knew. And yet sometimes, she felt an emptiness. Why, when her life was so full, she couldn't fathom.

Chapter 2 – Daniel

Daniel was irritated. He could always tell when something was irking him. There was a niggle in his stomach, a grumbling feeling that wouldn't go away. His usual response was to tackle it head on, to confront the issue. But something was stopping him.

He re-read the report Juliet had written on Travis McBride. It had all the usual headings and there was information in each section yet it seemed to lack any real value. Was Juliet losing her touch? Was her interest waning in her work? Or was she getting complacent?

He finished the coffee his wife had brought him and sat back. He had plenty of dirt on Juliet. If she forgot who paid her wages, he had enough evidence of her doing things she shouldn't. But he didn't want to be in that position. He liked her, probably more than he should. He'd talk to Giselle about it, get a woman's view on what might be wrong with Jools. And he'd keep an eye on her. Make sure she was still giving him value for money.

He called Juliet before he left for his boat trip with Travis. 'How's everything?'

'All fine. I've got the final copy of the new contract for Mandarin House for you. The meeting's on Tuesday for the formal sign-off with their people, but I thought you might want one last review. Your Monday's pretty much full with Travis. I'll send the contract across now.'

'Can we talk about Travis?' he asked.

'What about him?'

'Not much of use, was there, in your report. Is everything OK?' he asked.

'Fine. He just didn't have anything I could uncover. It happens sometimes, Boss.'

'Do you need a break?'

She snorted. 'What does that mean?'

'You don't seem your usual self.'

'In what way?' She wasn't giving anything away.

He regretted starting the conversation. 'No, you're probably right. It just happens, sometimes. I was expecting more dirt on him. He's a pretty low-level player. They're usually the ones that don't hide a trail of what they're up to.'

'Maybe he's a bigger player than you give him credit for.'

'It's possible.' He wasn't convinced.

Patrick, his driver and right-hand man, came into the room, tapping his watch to remind his boss it was time to leave.

'I'll speak to you later, Jools.'

'OK, Boss. Enjoy your Sunday.'

Daniel returned from his day with Travis just after 7pm. After dinner, he sat with his wife Giselle in their TV room. Giselle laid on one of the sofas with her head on Daniel's lap, as had been her habit since they'd first got together as teenagers in the 1990s.

'Shall we watch the rest of that Peaky Blinders episode?' she asked.

'Whatever you want, love. Can I talk to you about something first?'

She sat up. 'Course. What's worrying you?'

'Who says I'm worried?' he asked.

'You're asking to talk.'

'I'm getting predictable in my old age.'

'I see it as consistency. Nothing wrong with that. What's on your mind?' she asked.

'It's Jools.'

Her face showed annoyance. 'What about her?'

'She just seems to have lost the fire in her belly to do her job.' He described the lacklustre report and what he felt was a general malaise.

Giselle shook her head. 'Let's face it, the way she runs around after you, she doesn't have much of a life of her own, does she? Maybe she's getting stale. Too focused on her job. Does she have many friends?'

He shook his head. 'None that I know of. But then, no reason I should know.'

'How much time does she spend away from the office?' she asked.

'She's there till 7pm or 8pm most nights, unless we're out for the evening.'

'But how often is she not looking after your guests or attending events with you or whatever else it is she does for you?' she asked.

'Well, she didn't come on the boat today. She had most of the day to herself.'

'And what did she do?'

'She said she was relaxing at home,' he said.

'And she doesn't have any close family, does she?'

'She doesn't have any family at all.'

'And no boyfriend?' she asked.

'Not since that toerag Cameron dumped her. Still, he got what was coming.'

She looked at him for a while without saying anything. 'Do I want to know?'

'Best not.' His instructions had been mistaken and the beating Cameron had received was more severe than he'd intended.

She shrugged. 'She must get lonely sometimes, Dan.'

'That's makes her ideally suited to the job. The lack of people around her. No-one to blab to, to let slip what I've been up to.'

'Must be pretty miserable for her,' Giselle said. 'I can't imagine what I'd do if I didn't have my girlfriends to confide in.'

'She's never given any indication she's unhappy,' he said.

'But she wouldn't, would she? Not to you. She's always trying to look unflappable and in control to you. Do you want me to talk to her?'

He thought for a moment. 'No, you're alright. I'll try and encourage her to get a bit of a life for herself. Maybe it'll perk her up in her job.'

'Yeah. Let's get the TV on and disappear into Tommy Shelby's world for a while.'

The next day, Daniel asked Juliet to come into his office. They both noticed a man hovering at the outer door.

'Harvey's right to look nervous,' Daniel said. 'What are you doing tonight, Jools?'

'I'm going to the Savoy with Jeremy Harrison,' she said.

'Of course. Do what you can. He's going to go far. Quite a switched-on guy, so he may not go for the usual routine.'

'He's a man. He'll go for it,' she said.

'You know, Jools, I'm a bit worried I make too many demands on you, that I don't give you enough time for your own life.'

She sat up, like a meerkat on alert. 'What do you mean?'

'Well, you spend so much time with me at work and entertaining my business associates. You don't get much time to see friends or family. Giselle's worried about you.'

'Giselle? Why would she be worried? Unless you've said something to her.'

'When was the last time you did anything for yourself?' he asked.

'Last weekend, I went to that Pre-Raphaelite exhibition.' Her voice sounded chippy.

'On your own,' he said.

'What's wrong with that?' She looked uncomfortable.

'Are you lonely?' he asked.

'No,' she said. 'I have a great life. I don't…what point are you trying to make, Daniel?'

'You're always on your own.'

'I'm rarely on my own. I'm here with everyone in the office, I'm out at events with loads of people. I'm out with your guests. And I'm here with you. All of which means, I like my downtime to myself.'

'Giselle thinks it's unnatural you don't have any friends.' She hadn't said that, but now Daniel thought about it, it was a bit odd.

'Friends are over-rated,' she said.

'No family either.'

'Family is definitely over-rated.'

'Your relationship with Cameron was a while back. Haven't you wanted to get yourself a new boyfriend?' he asked.

'No.'

He couldn't help but feel pleased. He rather liked having her all to himself.

She stood up. 'If there's nothing else, I'll send Harvey in.'

'Don't change the subject, Jools.'

'Daniel, I don't want a new boyfriend. And please tell Giselle not to worry. And don't you worry about me either. Unless…do you think it's affecting me here? That I'm not doing my job properly? Though what that would have to do with my private life is a fucking mystery.'

'Course not.' Her casual swearing gave away her annoyance. 'We just worry about you, Jools. You're like family to us. I just, well, I wouldn't want to be the reason you have no life outside work.' He regretted his choice of words. It sounded like criticism.

'I have all the life outside work I want, thank you, Daniel. Don't judge me by other people's standards. And if you have any issues with my work, just tell me.'

He put up his hands in mock surrender and said nothing.

'I'll send Harvey in now.' She left the office and Harvey swaggered in.

He wouldn't be swaggering out, Daniel decided.

Chapter 3 – Juliet

Juliet met Jeremy Harrison at the American Bar in the Savoy. He was a lawyer, representing a company that Daniel was asking to join a consortium. Daniel was convinced Jeremy had some inside information about the target organisation and would have some secrets to divulge, either under the influence of drink or by Juliet searching his phone.

'Juliet. Nice to see you.' He didn't stand up when Juliet arrived at the table. 'I'll take another glass of this.'

He's all charm, Juliet thought. She bought him a glass of his champagne of choice, along with a tonic water for herself and sat down on the semi-circular leather seat opposite him.

'Have you been here before, Jeremy?' she asked.

'Of course. Though I'm keener on the Rivoli at the Ritz.' He took a sip of the champagne. 'What's it like being Daniel Cross's skivvy?'

She couldn't decide whether to rise. 'Oh, as skivvying jobs go, it's one of the best. He's very generous and we get on well.'

'But he's still a wide boy, a market trader made good.'

'Is there something wrong with that?' she asked.

'No class, these people.'

It was going to be a long night. 'What's your background?'

'The usual. Colet Court, Eton, Oxford.'

'And yet you work for quite an insignificant organisation. What went wrong?' She wasn't sure if he was the sort of person who would like being challenged.

'You cheeky bitch.'

Clearly not keen on being challenged then. 'Well, you've obviously done well for yourself if you're familiar with the Savoy and the Ritz. But then so am I and I'm just a skivvy.'

'A six-figure salary and an easy workload suits me right now. Means I have plenty of time for fun. But I'll end up running my father's law firm when he retires, unless something more tantalising comes along.'

'Are you an only child?' she asked.

'No, but I'm the eldest and the only decent lawyer, so I'm the only real choice.'

'Lucky you.' She noticed he'd already finished his champagne. 'Do you want to eat or are you happy drinking?' She was thankful she hadn't booked dinner. The less time she had to spend with him, the better.

'Not hungry. Well, not for food anyway.' He leered and she tried not to shudder.

She bought them more drinks and decided to get him to talk about himself a little. 'What do you like to do outside work? You obviously keep yourself fit.'

'I cycle. I've several racing bikes. Like to get together with friends and cycle as a group.'

'Are they the bikes with the very thin wheels?' she asked.

'That's the ones.'

The wankers who always hog the road and ride several abreast without a care for anyone else, she thought. 'I run,' she said.

'Right.'

God, this conversation's hard. 'Do you like the theatre?' she asked.

'Not really. Like a good action movie.'

'Any you'd recommend lately?'

He half-shrugged and drank down the rest of his champagne. 'Shall we go?'

'Where?' She took a sip more of her tonic.

'Back to your place?'

'OK.' She pulled on her jacket and led him down the stairs and out into the cool of the evening. 'Are you happy to walk? It's just over the river, not far at all.'

He shook his head. 'Let's get a cab.' He waved one down and got into it, leaving Juliet to speak to the driver. She climbed in and sat on one of the pull-down seats that faced backwards, keen not to sit too close to her companion. He pulled out his phone and checked his emails until they arrived at the apartment building.

Juliet got out and paid the driver.

'Have a nice evening, love.'

'Thanks.' She rolled her eyes and gave him a flat smile.

The driver gave her a quizzical look in return. 'Dump him and come out for a night with me if you want. No strings.'

'Thanks, but this is a work meeting. I'm sure you'd be much better company,' she whispered. She led Jeremy to the lift and waved to the concierge. As she opened the flat door, Jeremy lunged at her and began to kiss her, running his hands up and down her body, grabbing her breasts.

She pulled away. 'Slow down. Let's have a drink first.'

'I don't want a drink. I want you to get naked and suck me off.'

He pulled her down toward the sofa and began to unbuckle his belt, all the while kissing her, more to keep her from speaking, she sensed, than from any desire to be intimate.

She twisted away from him. 'You need to shower first.'

'I had a shower before I came out tonight.' He was holding her wrist and using his strength to make sure she couldn't pull away entirely.

'You're hurting me,' she said.

'Only because you're squirming,' he said.

She made a decision to do what he wanted. It wasn't the first time she'd been in this position, but it hadn't happened in a long time. She blocked out the feeling of self-loathing for not fighting back.

After he'd climaxed, she left him on the sofa and opened a bottle of champagne, putting two tablets in the glass before handing it to him. He took a small sip then grimaced. 'Tastes like shit. You drink it,' he said and pushed the glass onto her lips.

'I don't drink,' she said, taking the glass away from him.

'You were drinking in the bar.'

'Tonic water. I'm teetotal,' she said.

'What the fuck for?'

'Because my father was an alcoholic.'

'People who can't control themselves are pathetic.' He picked up the crystal flute and downed the contents.

She refilled his glass and he started to drink but she noticed him moving his head from side to side as the drugs began to take effect. She knew two tablets wouldn't kill him but it would knock him out for a good many hours. He'd have a stinking headache when he did wake up but she wasn't in the least bit sorry.

After he fell into a deep sleep, she took his phone from his pocket and used his index finger to open the screen. She checked the settings to make sure there were no security features that could catch her out then worked her way methodically through the apps. After a few minutes, she went to the bathroom and brushed her teeth, keen to get the taste of him out of her mouth. She made a coffee and settled down to the job in hand. After she'd finished with his phone, she opened his wallet and found a small pouch of white powder. She kept it to one side and took pictures of the business cards and credit cards. With nothing more to search, she put his phone, wallet and drug pouch back where she'd found them, threw a blanket over him and went to her bedroom, taking her laptop with her. She wouldn't be able to get any pictures of him in a compromising position on the bed-cam, so the evening had provided limited benefit.

She emailed Daniel with the information she'd been able to glean and included details of what had happened.

He rang her back straight away. 'Are you alright?'

'Yes.' In reality, she felt like crying but Daniel wouldn't want to be subjected to an emotional outburst. She heard Jeremy's phone ringing. 'Hold on a minute, Boss.' She dashed into the main room, concerned the phone might wake Jeremy up, but he hadn't stirred at all. The screen was flashing with the word "Mummy" so on a whim, Juliet took the call.

'Jeremy?' An educated, slightly drunken woman's voice echoed in Juliet's ear.

'I'm sorry, Jeremy's asleep. I can take a message.'

'Is that you, Fenella?' Without waiting for Juliet to respond, she continued. 'Listen, darling, I need you to remind Jeremy about his appointment with Doctor Latimer tomorrow. I spoke to him on Friday morning and he's sure he can help cure this bed-wetting issue. Poor Jeremy, he used to do it as a child but apparently it can come back in adulthood. I don't want him to be late. It's at 10:30am.'

Juliet made a murmuring noise to signal assent.

'Goodnight then, Fen.'

Juliet stared at the phone. She wasn't sure how Daniel could use the information but was sure he was better off knowing it than not. If Jeremy had been a nicer person, she'd have kept it to herself. She covered him back over with the blanket and went to her room, where Daniel was still hanging on. She told him what she'd found out.

'Now that is pure gold, Jools. I could kiss you. Are you sure you're alright? With him having been a bit frisky?'

'Yes, I'm fine.' She wasn't sure at all. Frisky hardly covered what she'd had to deal with. The vulnerability she'd felt was disconcerting. 'Is that everything? I need to wash up from tonight. Can't have him finding any evidence in the morning.'

'Off you go, then.'

'See you tomorrow, Daniel.' She went to the kitchen and washed the glasses extra carefully then put them in the dishwasher and turned it on. The noise of the water splashing around would be unlikely to wake Jeremy if his phone hadn't. She set her alarm for 5am and went to sleep.

The alarm broke through a dream where Jeremy was raping her. She woke up, sweaty and damp. She peered into the sitting room and could see Jeremy had barely moved from where she'd left him. She showered, put on make-up then tried to wake him.

He groggily came to life. 'What did you do to me?' He moved his head from side to side, as if he was trying to dislodge the muzzy feeling.

'You drank a fair bit then passed out.'

He blinked rapidly a few times and rubbed his face. 'That's bollocks. I can hold my drink. You did something.'

'I pleasured you, at your insistence, then you had several drinks and fell asleep.'

'You're a liar. Something happened.' He tried to get up but was still woozy enough to be unsteady on his feet.

'I've arranged for someone to take you home. They'll be here shortly.' She'd been worried he might get violent or aggressive, so had called one of their regular drivers to come and take Jeremy home.

'Where's my phone?' He padded his jacket and found it in his inside pocket. His wallet was in his trousers, where he'd left it. 'I will remember, I always remember what happened eventually. Then you'll be in trouble.' He was staring wildly at her.

The entry phone rang. 'That'll be your lift.' Juliet got up, pressed two buttons on the intercom and opened the door. Relief flooded over her at the sight of Bill, one of the taller, more muscular drivers. He was good with his fists and would soon sort out Jeremy if he got difficult. 'Bill, come in. This is Mr Harrison. He's not feeling too well. Can you drive him carefully to wherever he needs to be?'

Bill walked into the main area and smiled at Jeremy. 'No problem, Jools. Sir.' He gestured towards the front door.

Jeremy looked at him then at Juliet and shrugged. 'You won't get away with this,' he said, directing his words at Juliet.

'Come on, Sir. Let's get you in the car.' Bill's touch on his arm, combined with his polite yet menacing stare, left Jeremy no choice but to leave.

Juliet watched the door close then burst into tears.

On her way back from a working meeting that night, Juliet walked along the Embankment from Westminster Bridge, in a break from her usual routine. She noticed a small crowd ahead and looked to see what was the cause of everyone's interest. It appeared to be a man in a wheelchair, having an argument with a skateboarder. As she drew closer, she realised the man shouting at the skateboarder was her ex-boyfriend, Cameron.

Shortly after Cameron had left her, he'd been mugged and badly beaten, leaving him unable to walk. She'd heard about what had happened from Cam's sister and had not seen Cam since then. As she came into earshot, she heard the skateboarder apologise to Cam. The crowd melted away.

'Hi, Cam,' Juliet said and offered a smile in his direction.

He looked twice. 'Jools. Hi. It's been ages. This is Billie, my girlfriend. Billie, this is Jools. An old friend.'

Juliet noticed a young girl who hadn't left the scene. She was attractive in a fragile kind of way. 'Hi, Billie.'

Billie pushed the edges of her mouth up for an instant, in pretence of a smile, but said nothing.

'What are you doing here?' Cam asked.

'Just on my way home from work. Been with Daniel to a reception at one of the Government departments.'

'You're still working for him then?' he asked.

'Why shouldn't I be?' Juliet asked.

'No reason, I guess. You…alright?'

'Yes.' Juliet felt the ice in Billie's stare.

'Cam, we need to get going or we'll miss the train.' Billie began to turn Cam's wheelchair so he wasn't facing Juliet.

'Sorry, Jools, gotta go. Nice seeing you.' He gave her a half smile before he was wheeled away.

'Bye. Nice to meet you, Billie,' Juliet said. She didn't mean it.

Juliet felt rattled by the encounter, for the entirely selfish reason that she didn't want to be reminded about the end of her relationship with him. He'd left her, citing her lack of honesty about herself as the reason. "You never let me in, Jools. I'm never allowed to see the real you. I always feel at arm's length," he'd said. Later on, she'd found out he'd already started seeing someone else and the betrayal Jools felt was all-consuming. All that bullshit about her not letting him into her life or her heart. It was just about him having found someone new, something different. There was no point in trying to get him to change his mind, not when he'd already started sleeping with someone else. She'd felt such a fool.

She walked towards the metal barrier that ran along the water's edge and stared into the middle distance for a long time. That was what happened when you let someone get too close. It hurt like hell when they left, like someone slowly ripping out your insides. She missed having someone to share her life with, someone to hold hands with as she marvelled at the beauty of the sunset over the Thames. But she'd learnt her lesson and now only shared the sunset with her Instagram followers. It was safer.

Juliet was at her desk extra early the next day, having been woken by another bad dream about her encounter with Jeremy. As she tried to focus on proofreading a report, she looked up as one of the security guards at Cross International hovered by her office door.

'Hey, Bernie, what's up?' she asked.

'There's a copper downstairs, wanting to see you.'

'To see me?' She frowned. It was 6:30am. 'At this hour? I'll come down.' She slipped on her high-heeled shoes, put on her suit jacket and walked with Bernie down the stairs to the reception area.

A man in a dark suit was waiting by the front desk. He was well-turned out, Juliet noticed, with polished shoes, combed hair and an ironed shirt. He stood tall and alert.

'Can I help you?' she asked and the policeman's head swivelled towards her as she approached him. As she got closer, she was struck by the blue of his eyes. They were mesmeric, such a pure colour and somehow, they enticed her to gaze at him.

He was staring back at her with a similar expression and it felt to Juliet as though the world stopped for a tiny moment, as though their eyes were sharing a conversation, a "How do you do?". She smiled at him and the moment was broken. She repeated her question.

'I'm Detective Inspector Haywood. I'd like to ask you and Mr Cross some questions,' the policeman responded. He showed her his ID card while offering his hand. She shook it, noticing the smoothness of his skin and the neatly filed nails. His grip was firm and the smile he gave her reached his eyes.

She took the ID card, studying it carefully. 'Detective Inspector Philip Haywood,' she said. She looked back up at him, nodded and handed it back. She noticed a stiffness in his body, a hardness set into his jaw, as though he knew she was going to fob him off and was bracing himself for the knock-back. 'You're very early this morning, Detective Inspector. I'm afraid it won't be possible to speak to Daniel without an appointment. His time is extremely precious and his diary is full most days for the next month. Let me see if I can answer his questions too. I'm Juliet Russell, Daniel's PA. Though I assume you know that already.'

'Is there somewhere we could go, Ms Russell?'

'Of course. Come with me.' She led him to one of the smaller meeting rooms on the ground floor, mouthing at the security guard to keep Daniel away from the area. Bernie nodded back.

'In here, Inspector.' She waved towards one of the chairs and he hovered, waiting for her to sit down before relaxing into a seat.

'Can I get you anything? Tea? Coffee? Some water, perhaps?' she asked.

'No, thank you.' He took his phone out of his back pocket and laid it on the table.

Chapter 4 – Phil

Phil looked at Juliet without speaking, marshalling his thoughts as he decided how to play the conversation. People like her, people with that level of self-confidence, usually made him feel uncomfortable, yet she was beguiling. Her voice was warm, yet firm. There was no trace of fear in her expression, more curiosity. Her soulful eyes made her look heartbreakingly young and somehow sad.

He shook his head a little to dislodge the thought. He was being fanciful, letting his overactive imagination see things that probably weren't there. Given who she worked for, he didn't want to feel any sympathy towards her and certainly didn't want to give her an easy ride.

He cleared his throat. 'There are two things I need to find out. Firstly, to establish Mr Cross's whereabouts on three dates earlier in the year.'

'Well, I'm sure I can help with that,' she said. 'What's it in connection with?'

'An ongoing enquiry into some rather serious offences.' He looked at her and she held his gaze, to the point where he found it difficult to maintain eye contact and looked away.

'Serious offences?' she asked. 'I assume you wish to speak to Mr Cross as a witness?'

When he didn't respond, she put her hand in her jacket pocket and took out a business card, placing it on the table. 'You'll find my contact details on there. If you email me the dates you're interested in, I can let you know exactly where Mr Cross was.'

'I can send them over now.' He picked up his phone but couldn't get a signal. 'Can you give me access to your Wi-Fi?'

She shook her head. 'There's a whole process I have to go through to get you a password. Our Security team are real sticklers for making sure we follow it without exception. Best to wait till you're outside.' She wasn't going to make it easy for him.

'OK. Of course, you may not know where Mr Cross was, so perhaps I should just wait and speak to him,' he said.

She smiled. 'Detective Inspector, I know where Daniel Cross is every hour of every day. And what he's doing.'

'I hope not. That could make you an accessory.' He could hear his voice was short; could she?

She looked bemused, almost playful. 'An accessory? To what? I'm sure Daniel doesn't do anything he shouldn't. He's too busy running his empire. How much do you know about Cross International?'

'Why don't you tell me about it?' he asked. He wasn't really interested but maybe in the telling, she might give something away. He'd long desired to put Daniel Cross behind bars, convinced he was a criminal masquerading as an upstanding businessman.

'Daniel started working at the age of sixteen, selling hair products from a market stall. He set up a company, selling the products to salons, then began to move into manufacturing hair and beauty products. He kept growing the business, creating new lines and expanded into Europe. His wife came up with the Bad Hair Day range, which increased the company's footprint worldwide when it was hailed in America as the new wonder product. Since then, there've been a number of acquisitions of other beauty ranges as well as the joint venture with the Wellington Pharmacy chain here and the Pharmarkt group in Europe. And we're growing still.'

'Impressive,' he said.

'Between you and me, Daniel's a little aggressive on the golf course. I've heard tales of clubs going flying, but I'm guessing you're not here on account of that,' she said.

He felt she was playing with him now and he gave a frustrated snort as he shook his head. 'You don't seem to be taking this very seriously, Ms Russell.'

Her demeanour changed. 'I assure you I am taking this very seriously, Detective Inspector. Why don't you send me those dates and we can sort this out? If that's everything?' She stood up and he couldn't stop himself getting to his feet.

'No, actually.' He picked up her business card. 'Can I just tell you the dates and you look them up now?'

'I think it would be better for both of us if we had an audit trail, don't you? Then there's no comeback, no mistakes. Oh, I thought you said the 17th, not the 16th, that sort of thing.'

He knew she was right. 'I'd appreciate a quick response to my email. This is an urgent police matter.' It wasn't that urgent but she didn't need to know that.

'I will deal with it as soon as I receive it. I promise you.' She gave him that stare again, challenging him not to believe her.

'Thank you.'

'So, what was the other thing? Did you mention two things?' she asked.

'It's about…well, a more delicate matter, Ms Russell.'

'Please call me Juliet.'

'Juliet, I'm not officially asking, yet, but I gather on Sunday, you spent the night with a Jeremy Harrison?' He thought he noticed a flicker of fear cross her face.

'I did, more's the pity.'

'What happened?' he asked, hoping the open question would elicit a detailed response.

'What does he say happened?' she asked.

Jeremy Harrison was a friend of Phil's superior, Detective Chief Superintendent Pidgeon. While no official allegation had been made, Phil had been asked to speak to Juliet to see what he could find out. He felt uncomfortable being put in this position.

When he didn't respond to her first question, Juliet asked another. 'Has Mr Harrison made a complaint?'

'Not officially. Not yet, at least,' Phil said.

'So, there's nothing to discuss, really.' She stood up again and he caught the smell of her perfume.

'Well, I think if I could hear your description of the evening, it might help to make the unofficial grumbling go away. To stop there being a formal complaint.'

She looked him up and down, then sat back on the steel-framed chair. 'Well, Detective Inspector, some men wrongly assume if I'm entertaining them, that sex is part of the package. They don't get the 'No' signals. Mr Harrison got…difficult. Started ranting when I wouldn't respond to his sexual demands.'

'And what did you do?'

'I'd rather not go into the sordid detail. Let's just say I performed a sex act when I didn't want to, just to stop him becoming unpleasant.'

'Did you force alcohol on him?'

She laughed. 'Have you met him? He's six foot two.' She gestured with her hand held above her head. 'I'm five foot two and probably, what, half his weight? How the hell would I force anything on him? I kept offering him a drink because he was getting aggressive and I thought some champagne might mellow him out, but he was having none of it.' She pulled back the sleeves of her blouse and jacket to reveal the finger-shaped bruises on her wrist. 'If anyone has cause for complaint, it's me, rather than him.'

She was right. It didn't make sense, the way Harrison told it. Phil couldn't work her out, whether she was Miss Vulnerable or Miss Feisty masquerading as vulnerable. He decided to change tack. 'If you start work this early, what time do you finish?'

She frowned. 'Not sure I see the relevance of that information or that it's any of your business, but usually around 7pm, unless I'm attending an event.'

'Long day,' he said. 'You must be very loyal to Mr Cross.'

'Not sure it's anything to do with loyalty. I work hard, but that's just who I am. And I'm well rewarded. Now, I do have a very busy day ahead of me.'

'Of course. Perhaps we could talk some more after work.' He looked directly at her. 'I mean, it would be unprofessional of me to ask you out for a drink tonight but...'

She looked surprised. 'Tonight? My diary's almost as busy as Daniel's, Inspector. And given you seem to be investigating both me and him, would it be appropriate for you to fraternise with me in that manner?'

He grimaced. What was he thinking? 'You're right.' He felt himself beginning to blush. 'I'm sorry if I caused offence.'

'No offence at all.' Her smile seemed genuine.

'Do you ever feel uncomfortable, working for someone like Daniel Cross?'

It was her turn to grimace. 'Uncomfortable? Why?'

'Because of his reputation. Alleged reputation,' he corrected himself.

'Are you aware that Daniel has a very close friendship with Chief Constable Collinson? If Daniel had a reputation, as you call it, surely Michael Collinson wouldn't, couldn't be his friend.'

He bit the inside of his lip but said nothing.

'I know there are some disreputable business people out there who are jealous of Daniel's success, so maybe they're the ones spreading baseless rumours and ridiculous lies about him. I wouldn't set too much store by them.' She stood up again. 'Let me see you out.' She opened the meeting room door and he followed. She walked to the revolving door at the entrance and offered her hand. 'I'll respond as soon as I can to your email, Detective Inspector Haywood. It was nice to meet you.'

He clasped her hand and the handshake was just as firm the second time around. 'Thank you for your time, Juliet,' He pushed the nearest face of the revolving door and found the murk of the late summer morning hadn't disappeared. He walked back to his car, hoping he'd put enough money in the parking meter.

Chapter 5 – Juliet

Juliet returned from her encounter with DI Haywood to find Daniel standing by her desk, looking impatient. Her boss was an attractive man, all designer grey stubble and Armani suit. His eyes were a piercing steel-grey.

'Who was that?' he asked.

'Detective Inspector Philip Haywood,' she said, enjoying the sound of his name.

'What did he want?' he growled at her.

'To see me about that bastard Jeremy Harrison. And to ask about your whereabouts, he said.'

'When?'

'Don't know yet. Told him to email me the dates and I'd check your diary,' she said.

'Why did that take such a long time? Bernie said he was in here at half-six.'

'Just the stuff about Harrison, though it's unofficial as yet,' she said.

'Do you think he's doing a serious investigation about me?'

She gave a small shrug, slightly annoyed at his lack of interest in her position. 'Difficult to tell at this stage. Don't worry about it. I'm sure it's nothing we can't handle.'

'Depends what dates he's asking about.' He nodded towards his office. 'Let's get on.' They walked into the adjoining room. It was three times the size of Juliet's work space, with an original Hockney on the wall as well as an antique desk, rumoured to have belonged to the original Duke of Wellington. There was a small dressing area behind the main office, where his dinner jacket was hanging up, ready for his evening out.

Juliet sat down with him for their usual morning catch-up, taking him through his diary and running through the supporting documentation she'd prepared.

'Remind me what's on tonight?' Daniel asked.

'You're going to the opera, remember, while I entertain the guy from Taylor's? You're seeing *The Love for Three Oranges*. Prokofiev, I think. Royal Opera House.' she said. 'A light supper afterwards at that bistro you like across the road.'

He rolled his eyes.

'I know, but Giselle loves it,' she said.

'And I must keep my wife happy.'

'She doesn't ask much of you, Daniel. And she's loyal.'

'You mean, she's discreet.' He looked over his glasses at her.

She shrugged. 'Same thing,' she said.

'You know that copper came to the house last week. Told Gizzy she needed to escape my evil clutches or she'd end up going down with me.'

'I assume Giselle didn't bite.'

'She told him to piss off and frogmarched him out of the house. I was so proud of her.' He gave a deep chuckle. 'Are we done?'

The email from DI Haywood was waiting for Juliet when she got back to her desk. She typed up a draft response to the Inspector's request, giving the details of Daniel's movements on the days in question, with names and contact information for everyone he'd seen.

Daniel called her in just before lunch. He was in an especially bad mood after his morning meetings.

She perched on the edge of his desk, holding a copy of her response to the DI's email. Daniel always checked out her legs when she sat there, so she waited until his gaze reached her face before speaking. 'What's up?' she asked.

'Sales figures for the northern region are shocking for that new range. Harvey's fucked up again.'

'Are you going to sack him?' she asked.

'I'm gonna put his nuts in a vice for a few weeks then sack him,' he said. He looked at the email in Juliet's hand and his face transitioned from annoyed to angry. 'Oh, fuck. You seen these dates? Someone must have been talking. Too much of a coincidence.'

'You forget, Daniel. I don't know what you get up to when you go off on one of your secret jaunts. I've no idea if it's something you want to hide from the police or Giselle,' she said. She didn't know precisely but she thought there was a correlation between Daniel's disappearing hours and someone suddenly changing their behaviour towards him from awkward to amenable. She put the printout of her draft email on the desk. 'Here's the response. There's nothing on there that can't be verified by someone the police will think is reliable,' she said.

He read it carefully. 'Thank you,' he said. 'Have you sent it?'

'No, just wanted to check you're happy with the content before I did. I'm sure the police will leave you alone after this.'

She went back to her desk and pressed the send button on her response to the DI's email, watching it disappear from the screen. His acknowledgement of its receipt arrived within minutes, telling her he would corroborate the information and get back to her with any further queries. Juliet forwarded the note to Daniel's lawyer, then put it and Detective Inspector Philip Haywood out of her mind. Daniel had a hectic schedule planned and she had some foreign trips to organise. It took all her concentration to make sure she met his exacting demands for airlines, seats, transfer times and preferred airports.

She left the office just before 7pm and walked the twenty minutes along the Embankment to her apartment. She said hello to the concierge before walking the six flights up to the top of the building. The apartment was open plan, with one large living space that overlooked the Thames. She walked out onto the balcony and watched the city twinkling in front of her. It was a sight that never failed to move her. Coming back to the moment, she realised she was going to be late for her evening, so showered, applied some make-up and dried her hair as quickly as she could. She put on some mid-height heels and walked the ten minutes along the river to the bar where she was meeting her companion for the evening.

When Daniel arrived in the office the next morning, Juliet made him his usual coffee then went in to talk to him. 'Morning, Boss. Need five minutes.'

He gestured with his head towards a seat opposite him. 'What is it?'

'This business with Jeremy Harrison and the guest last night. For the first time, I'm feeling a bit concerned, scared even. I've always been fine with it all, but when they start misbehaving in the apartment, it makes me nervous. And it's putting me off my stroke. Can't settle with them. Which makes them suspicious.'

'Did last night's guy…?'

'No, he didn't, not exactly, but it was hard to persuade him to drink the champagne. If Harrison went to the police, albeit unofficially, what if one of the others goes officially? And they find the drugs in his blood?

However hard I wash the glasses, they could find some residue there too, if they chose to look hard enough.'

'God, you are spooked. It's never bothered you before,' he said.

'I know. I just don't know if I can do this anymore. I don't want to let you down, Daniel. But it won't work if I'm not confident with them. What can we do?'

'We?' He raised his left eyebrow as he said it.

She watched him thinking it through and knew better than to interrupt when he was considering his options.

'Let's draft in a couple of ladies to help out with the evening work. Though we'll have to use your apartment. Can't do this in a hotel. Maybe you could shut yourself away till the drugs have kicked in, then help with the photos.'

Was it any better if guests were entertained in her home, even if she wasn't meeting them, she wondered?

'We could certainly look at that,' she said.

'Have you thought about what I said, about getting yourself some friends, people to hang out with? So work isn't your sole focus?'

She let out her breath slowly, through closed lips. 'Maybe I just need to get myself a guy.'

'I said friends,' Daniel said.

'But if I had a boyfriend, people like Jeremy Harrison wouldn't loom so large in my world. In fact,' she said, 'you know that policeman that came calling? He wanted to take me out for a drink.'

'Did he?'

'He was easy on the eye. Maybe I should take him up on his offer. I'm sure it was only so he could pump me for information about you, but it might be nice to spend a bit of time with him.'

'You sure that's wise? There's a lot to lose if the police start investigating us. Or if they find out more than they should.'

Was he questioning her loyalty? Did he think she'd indulge in pillow talk? 'I've been loyal to you for a long time, Daniel and I'd never let you down. I know how much I owe you. You've been there for me through some tough times. You're the closest I've got to family.'

He looked as though he believed her. 'Sorry,' he said. 'I'm getting a bit paranoid in my old age.'

'Don't worry. One other thing, and I don't want to stoke your paranoia, but I think you need to be a bit wary of Harvey.'

He felt his hackles rise. 'Harvey?'

'I overheard something yesterday. His PA mentioned a meeting he had, but it's not in his calendar. I searched her desk a little while ago and I think he's been meeting Sir Ashley Flint.'

Daniel balled up his fist. Ashley Flint ran Cross International's biggest competitor and had friends in high places, from whom he'd bought his knighthood, it was rumoured.

'Do you want me to get Pat to tail him? So we'll know who he's meeting?' she asked.

'Yeah, let's find out where the bastard goes.'

She stood up. 'Is that everything for now?'

'For now.'

She rang DI Haywood the next day. 'It's Juliet from Cross International. Given you've now got confirmation of Daniel's whereabouts, I was wondering if we could have that drink. Unless you need to speak to me formally about Mr Harrison?'

'I don't think we need to discuss Mr Harrison anymore. And I'd like that very much.'

'My first free evening is a week on Wednesday, I'm afraid. Does that work for you, Inspector?'

'Good with me. Please call me Phil.'

She could hear he was smiling from his tone of voice. She gave him her address. 'Why don't you pick me up there around 7:30pm?'

'Sure. I'll see you then,' he said.

She ended the call and found his imagined smile was infectious.

Her good mood didn't last long. Daniel had arranged, without telling her, for a couple of women to visit Juliet for a training session in the art of keeping the clients happy, so she wouldn't have to entertain in future. As she explained how she looked after people, how they needed to be flattered and cossetted, she couldn't stop it sounding like she was a cheap escort who'd do anything to keep guests happy.

She'd ignored the discomfort she felt about the things she did at work for a long while. Maybe she was being soft by worrying about it, given these women were comfortable to do it. When she'd asked how they felt about it all, they seemed elated. "Nice to have one up on men for a change" and "They'd do the same, and worse, to us if they had the chance" were their responses. Of course, allowing others to do this part of the job meant Juliet had to spend time away from her flat, but she hoped she might be able to stay with Phil when it was necessary. Assuming she and Phil got on. But she had a feeling they would. Or was it just that now she had a good reason to make sure they did?

Chapter 6 – Phil

Phil stared dispiritedly at Juliet's email again.

'What's up with you?' Phil's right-hand man, Detective Sergeant Tom Boyd, asked.

'Cross appears to have solid alibis for all those dates. I've checked the information and it's all kosher.'

'Fuck, are you sure?' Boyd picked up a stress ball from his desk and squeezed it hard repeatedly.

Phil nodded.

'What's she like, his secretary? Beauty or the beast?'

'Definite beauty. Fit, attractive and bright. I'm taking her out to dinner next week. Figured she could prove an ally in trying to nail Cross,' Phil said.

'You don't miss an opportunity, do you?'

'I can't believe he's got away with it for so long. There's got to be a way to get him.'

'Probably not without ruffling Collinson's feathers,' Tom reminded him.

'Yeah, well, I'm not bothered about that. He should choose his friends more carefully,' Phil said.

'Who? Cross or Collinson?' Tom laughed. 'I know it pisses you off, Cross getting away with violence, intimidation and God knows what else, but come on, Guv, don't get obsessive about it. We've enough to do on the Johnstone case.'

Phil sighed. 'You're right. I'm probably chasing shadows with all this. Let's run through what we've got on Johnstone's attacker with the team this afternoon. Talking of which, where are they?' He noticed the room was devoid of other people.

'Court, dentist, co-ordinating the house-to-house and searching out CCTV,' Tom said, counting on his fingers the four other colleagues that made up their core team.

Phil nodded. 'Tell 'em to get back here by 2pm. We need to start back at the beginning again.'

'OK, Guv.'

Phil spent the rest of the morning checking again the information about Daniel's whereabouts. The corroboration came from people with no criminal record and no reason to lie. Of course, he could be under-estimating the reach of Daniel Cross, of who was in his pay, his influence or his friendship circle. But maybe he was wrong about Cross and he was just a successful businessman with enemies who were happy to muddy the water of truth with unprovable allegations. It wasn't what his gut told him, but he took Tom's warning to heart about obsession. He'd done it a few years back with an alleged paedophile and that hadn't ended well, scuppering Phil's chances of promotion for probably the remainder of his career. Well, not unless he could nab a high-profile criminal to make people forget his past mistakes.

He drove home just after 9pm. He rented part of a large house in Woking. His landlady, Elsie, let him pay what he could afford after his divorce left him badly off. His children lived in Malta with their mum, her boyfriend and her parents, so opportunities to see them were rare. He flew to Malta twice a year and the kids would travel to London in December so he could have an early Christmas with them. Though he felt Sal had been unreasonable to him throughout their split, she did seem to value him as the father of her children and had been more flexible than he'd expected when it came to visitation arrangements. Probably because her new man was such a dick, he told himself.

He got a bottle of lager out of the fridge and sat down in front of the TV in his bedroom, flicking through the Freeview channels until he found a programme about the English Civil War. He half-listened to it as he pondered his next move on Daniel Cross. He wondered whether he'd asked Juliet out because it gave him access to information about Daniel or simply because he fancied her. He acknowledged in the privacy of his own home that he was aroused by both the sight and the thought of her. She came across as intelligent, articulate and independent, things he'd come to value in a woman as he'd got older and understood himself better. He'd known, when he met Sal, that she was more of a homebird, a woman who was not ambitious for herself other than wanting to be a good mother and wife. It was unfashionable for a woman to be happy with that today. Modern convention meant they had to have a separate career and be independent but Sal had never been that person. Juliet struck him as the opposite, at least, that's the impression he'd got from his brief meeting with her. He wondered if she wanted children. Why the hell are you thinking about that? You don't even know her. There was something about her he found intriguing and alluring. And that didn't have anything to do with her employer.

There was a tap on his door.

'Come in, Elsie.' He hadn't gone in to see her in case she was asleep. She was in her early eighties and Phil helped her with the garden and allotment that she'd tended for years but could no longer maintain. In return, he got a lot of free fruit and veg, a reduced rent and a reason to get out of bed when he wasn't working. It was getting close to autumn now and the days were starting to shorten. He knew he'd need to spend part of his next day off clearing out the summer plants and thinning out the winter vegetable seedlings Elsie had raised that summer. He opened his door. 'Everything OK?' he asked.

She leant heavily onto her walking stick. 'Mustn't grumble. You'd only roll your eyes,' she said.

'What can I do for you?' he asked.

'Could you be a love and change the battery in my TV remote? Fingers won't work tonight.' She suffered from arthritis that had left her with hands gnarled like an old tree.

'Sure. Have you got new batteries out of the cupboard?'

She nodded.

He walked out in his stockinged feet to her bedroom door. They shared the ground floor. The upstairs was full of furniture she no longer used but couldn't bear to sell. Her husband had been an antiques dealer and she'd hung onto some of the more precious pieces. Phil had suggested to her she cleared it out but she wouldn't entertain the idea. Once a month or so, he'd help her up the stairs so she could look at the pieces and reminisce about where George had bought each item and what he'd liked about it. Phil had heard the stories multiple times but tried to look as interested as he had the first time she'd told him.

Elsie opened her door and Phil went into the room. She'd left the batteries next to the remote control and it was the work of moments for him to swap the old ones out. He pointed the remote at the TV and the channel changed.

'Oh, thanks, lovey. Thought I was stuck watching ITV3 all night.'

'Anything else I can help with?' he asked.

'Kitchen bin could do with emptying, if you don't mind,' she said.

'No problem.' He went into the kitchen and got a new bin-liner from under the sink. As he tied off and pulled out the full bag, Elsie joined him.

'You busy at work?' she asked.

'Got that rape case on the go.'

'I saw about that on the news this morning. That poor girl,' she said. 'Still, I'm sure you'll get him.'

'I hope you're right, Else. And before he does it again.' He put the new bag into the bin. 'I'll put this one in the dustbin when I go to work. Anything else?'

'No, you're alright, dear. Thanks.' She leaned over to him. 'Are you courting?' she asked.

'No, still footloose and fancy-free, Else. Why? You offering?'

She gave a fruity laugh. 'Oh, in my day, I'd have jumped at the chance. No, I just got a feeling you were thinking about someone. Can see it in your aura.' Elsie had long thought herself something of a psychic and a clairvoyant, she'd confided to him. When her friend's husband had passed away, she'd held a seance in an attempt to contact him. Phil had been pleased he had the excuse of work to avoid having to attend.

'Nothing like that, Else. I did ask someone out for dinner but that was in a professional capacity, sort of.'

'Most people meet their partners at work these days,' she said, peering closely at him as if to divine his level of feeling. 'Sorry, lovey, I'm making you feel awkward, I can tell. You get off now.' She waved her stick towards the hallway and he picked up the bin bag.

'Night then, Else. I'll lock the front door.'

'G'night, dear.'

He put the bin bag by the front door and double locked it before returning to his room. He'd missed most of the history programme he'd been watching so switched off the TV and picked up an old biking magazine, flicking through the pages, looking enviously at the motorbikes. His own bike had long been sold; a casualty of the economy drive he'd had to go on when the divorce had been finalised. He hoped one day he'd be able to buy another one, something powerful he could ride across the UK and into Europe. There was no freedom like it. He closed his eyes momentarily, enjoying the memory of the rush of speed on an open road, snaking around bends on quiet country lanes.

He decided to go to bed and as was his habit, showered before he got under the covers. Often, he'd be woken by an urgent call that meant he had to dash into the office or to a crime scene, so being ready to get dressed and out in minutes was an advantage. He picked up his latest library book, a weighty tome on the history of the Plantagenets, and read it until his eyes felt heavy. He switched off the light and fell asleep within minutes.

The 6am alarm pierced his dream and he slapped the snooze button with venom, sensing a pleasurable dream had been in progress. He'd been on a boat with his children, he remembered, puttering around the Norfolk Broads. It was an evocation of a holiday they'd had. Sal hadn't been keen on getting on the boat, so had lazed on a grass verge by the water, while Phil, Billy and Max had watched the world go by, seeing ducks, dragonflies, moorhens and even a glimpse of a kingfisher. The boys had been awe-struck at each new sight. It did his heart good to remember his children's delight at the simplest of things.

He pulled on his work clothes after his morning ablutions and drove to the police station.

Boyd was already in. 'Morning, Boss.'

'Any developments?' Phil asked.

'Freya picked up some interesting stuff on the CCTV footage in the High Street.'

Phil went to stand behind Tom's desk so he could see his laptop screen. He watched as a man wearing dark clothing appeared, apparently following their victim, whose short jacket and high-heeled ankle boots made her a distinctive figure on the grainy footage.

'The Tech Team are going to try and enhance that image on the back of the jacket.' Tom rewound the footage to the point it was clearest. 'Though it looks familiar. Just can't figure out where from.'

'It's that building firm, Black Circle,' Phil said. 'The one that did the refurb of the shopping centre last year.' The Black Circle vans had kept parking in his road and he'd used his ID card to give a warning to the foreman to find somewhere else to park. Technically, it was misuse of his authority as there were no parking restrictions in place, but both he and the foreman knew there would likely be something wrong with one of the vehicles if Phil chose to have them inspected more closely.

'That's right, yeah. Shit. There could be hundreds of those in circulation. Any beggar who's ever worked for them probably has one,' said Tom.

Phil could hear a tinge of defeat in Tom's voice. 'I doubt that. Most casual guys wouldn't be there long enough to warrant getting one. Let me pick that one up, talk to someone in their office to see if we can find out anything. And there's a bit of a limp, isn't there?' They watched the footage again.

'Yeah, it's just slightly off, his stride pattern. Good spot, Boss.'

They both looked up as the main office door banged against the wall.

'Sorry, don't know my own strength.' Lewis Deacon, a Detective Constable who was on his way up in his career, blushed slightly as Tom and Phil stared at him. He was slightly built and both his colleagues chuckled.

'You're not exactly the world's strongest man, Lew,' said Tom, as he nudged Phil. 'Dee beat him at arm-wrestling in the Alexandra last week.'

'Dee weighs about as much as a Pot Noodle. You need to get down the gym, mate.' Phil ribbed the DC gently, wanting to include him in the banter but not wanting to dent his youthful ego. Phil remembered from his own experiences just how harsh it felt when the older guys in the station had taken the mickey out of him. The newer generation seemed even less resilient than he'd felt at that age.

By 8:30am, the rest of the team were in and poring over the CCTV footage to see if anything else could be discerned about the man following the victim. They now spread their search for CCTV footage out in the direction from which the hooded man came, to see if they could work out where he'd started from.

The rape case took all of Phil's head space that day and his gardening duties kept him physically busy on his day off. His back ached from working on the allotment. But his mind kept drifting to thoughts of Juliet.

Chapter 7 – Juliet

Juliet got back to her apartment at 6:45pm and dashed into the shower. She put on fresh make-up, dried her hair, all the while wondering what to wear for her night out with Phil. He'd dressed smartly for work so she figured even if he was in jeans, they'd be smart ones. She decided on a simple black dress and put on a delicate diamante necklace and earrings with pale lip gloss. She didn't want to vamp it up too much, feeling he was likely to be someone who thought less is more. She wondered why she'd accepted his offer of a drink, half-wishing she could have a quiet night in. Yet she knew there was something intriguing about him and she wanted to work out what it was.

She was ready with only a few minutes to spare and sat on the sofa, watching the clock, till at precisely 7:30pm, the entry phone rang. She got up and looked at the video screen and could see Phil holding a small bouquet of flowers. He was moving from foot to foot impatiently.

'Come up to the top floor,' she told him and pressed the two buttons on the entry system that allowed him to come into the front door and use the lift. Once she heard the ping of the lift arriving, she opened her front door.

As she suspected, he was immaculately turned out in pressed chinos, a plain mid-blue shirt and a dark jacket. His shoes were, again, polished.

'Hallo.' She smiled and gestured for him to come in. He followed her into the main room.

'Holy crap,' he said as he took in the view of the river and city from the large picture windows. 'Sorry, nice to see you.'

She moved towards him and gave him a continental peck on each cheek.

He handed her the flowers. 'For you.'

'How beautiful. That's very kind of you. I'll just go and get a vase. Would you like a drink before we go out?'

'It's up to you. Is this your own place?'

She fished the only vase she possessed from the back of the cupboard under the sink. 'Goodness, no. It belongs to the company. I get to live here in return for certain duties,' she said.

He looked suspiciously at her. 'Duties?'

'I entertain visiting clients.' She watched his face. It was so expressive she could almost hear him speaking. 'No, Phil. I'm not a hooker.'

He looked sheepishly at her.

'I make sure the clients have everything they need for their trip. Hotel, food, entertainment. I take them on tours of the city. I've always loved London because there's such diversity available in food, art, theatre, you name it. And it's a hassle sometimes, babysitting these people but look where I get to live.' As she spoke, she did a poor job of arranging the flowers.

'Shall I?' he offered.

'Be my guest.' She watched in bemusement as he picked up each stem in turn and arranged them in a bouquet in his hand before placing them in the vase. They sat beautifully.

'Well, aren't you full of surprises?' she said.

'My landlady gave me a few tips. You look lovely, by the way.'

'Thank you. I'm going to put these in the bedroom. They're so fragrant. Shall we go? Do you have anywhere in mind?'

'I've booked a restaurant under the arches along the river. It's Mediterranean, if that's OK.'

'Great. I didn't realise we were eating. You said a drink.'

'Sorry. Is that alright?' he asked.

'It's fab. I didn't get lunch so I'm really hungry. And I'm teetotal, so drinking's not really my thing.'

'Teetotal?' he asked. 'Have you never drunk alcohol?'

'Oh, I did as a teenager. But in this job, I need to be on top form all the time, particularly when I'm entertaining drunken businessmen. It's easier to stay sober. And, well…' She shook her head. 'That's a story for another time.' She picked up her coat from the back of the sofa. 'Let's go.'

He followed her out of the apartment and down the stairwell out onto the Embankment.

'I hope Phil, that you're going to tell me all about yourself over dinner. You're very intriguing.'

'Is that what you say to all the guests you entertain?' he asked.

She felt her hackles rise. 'Well, if I do, they accept the compliment more graciously than that.'

'I'm sorry. I think you're making me nervous,' he said.

'Are you the nervous type?'

'Not usually,' he said.

'I'll do my best to put you at your ease while you're eating. I wouldn't want you to get indigestion on my account.'

They walked in silence between commuters and tourists until he stopped at the door of a restaurant. 'This is the one,' he said.

'Excellent choice.'

'Have you eaten here before then?' he asked.

She grinned. 'Once or twice.' She opened the door and the nearest waiter greeted her.

'Hey, Jools.'

'Hi, Mehmet, how are you?' she asked.

'Hi, Jools,' the barman shouted.

'Any news on that grandchild?'

The barman shook his head. 'Still waiting.'

The restaurant manager came from the back of the restaurant to see her. He held out his hand. 'Miss Juliet, welcome. I didn't know you were dining with us tonight.'

'I didn't know either, Tarkan. My friend happened to book us in here. Clearly a man of excellent taste.'

Phil touched her on the shoulder. 'Is this your second home?'

'It's one of my regular haunts,' she said.

'Sir, you have a reservation?' Mehmet asked.

'Haywood, 8pm.'

'Can you spare us a booth, Mehmet?' she asked.

'Of course, for you.' He led them to a booth at the back of the restaurant, handed out menus and left them alone.

Juliet took off her coat and put it down next to her.

'Sorry if this is a bit dull for you,' Phil said and started to look at the menu.

She shook her head. 'It's perfect. One of my favourite places. You're acting like you're on the back foot again, apologising. There's really no need. Just relax. I don't bite.'

Mehmet hovered.

'Do you know what you want to drink, Phil?' she asked.

'A gin and tonic would be nice.'

'A G&T for my friend and I'll have my usual, please.' She smiled and Mehmet nodded wordlessly before disappearing.

Phil waved the menu. 'Is it worth me looking? Or do you have a recommendation?'

'It depends on what you like or don't like. I can get them to do a meze for us and they'll bring a selection of what's good tonight.'

'I'm not keen on squid.'

'Noted. Do you like olives? Only I don't, so they won't bring them unless I specify.'

'Love 'em,' he said.

'Great. Now, at the risk of sounding like an escort, tell me all about yourself, Phil.'

Before he got the chance to answer, Mehmet returned with their drinks and Juliet gave him their food order.

Phil took a sip of his drink. 'What do you want to know about me?'

'Start with the basics. When and where were you born?'

'1989, Guildford. Probably.'

She frowned. 'Probably?'

He ran his tongue around his bottom lip. 'Do you know what a foundling is?' he asked.

'Yes. Wow.' She felt a pull in her stomach.

'I was found in Guildford, so I was probably born there too.'

'So, you're adopted. But the adoption paperwork doesn't help at all with your origin.'

'No.'

'Have you thought about getting a DNA test?' she asked.

'Thought; yes. Acted; not yet.'

For a split second, she hesitated and then did something she'd not done for a long time. She dared to be open with a stranger. 'It's a gamble, finding out your heritage. It didn't pay off for me.'

His eyes widened. 'You're adopted too?'

'I am.' She wondered if she'd sensed that connection with him, but that was silly. She couldn't possibly have known. 'Did you have a good adoption?'

He smiled. 'Great. Really loving parents. Both sadly gone. One to cancer, one in an RTA,' he said. His eyes sparkled with moistness and he rubbed the corner of his left eye to take away the start of a tear. 'They were so precious to me. Understandable really, having never been able to track down my real parents. I wanted to look after them as they got older, pay them back for taking me in and looking after me like I was their own. But I never got the chance. Both taken too soon.'

'What did you do after you left school?' she asked, anxious to get him onto what she hoped was a happier topic.

'Went into the military at eighteen for five years then decided to join the police. Been in over ten years now.'

'How very public spirited of you. And what do you do for fun?' she asked.

'Fun? Well, I love spending time with my kids, but they live abroad, so that's a rare treat.'

'How old are they?'

'Billy's ten and Max is eight.' He pulled his phone out of his pocket and showed her the picture on his home screen. The eldest boy had dark hair and an olive complexion. The younger one looked very like Phil.

'They live with their mother?' she asked.

He nodded. 'In Malta. She didn't like being a military wife so I left. Then it turned out she didn't like being a policeman's wife, either.' He took a large swig of his gin and tonic.

'Do you resent leaving the military?' Juliet picked up her glass and sipped her lime and soda.

'No, I feel as though I found my vocation in CID. Doubt I'd have ever discovered that if it wasn't for Sal. Not that I'd ever tell her.'

'Was it not amicable, your split?'

He didn't respond immediately. 'It was er…strained. Better now.'

'Why strained?' she asked.

'I was a bit over-protective.'

'What do you mean?'

'I've always worried about something happening to the people I care about, so I try and protect them from bad things. When Sal and I first got together, she liked it, me caring. But I think she found it stifling after a while. Particularly during the split, when I suppose I was trying hardest to keep hold of her.'

Juliet admired his honesty and self-awareness, but sensed he didn't want her to delve further from the way he folded his arms defensively. 'What do you do when you're not working?' She was interrupted by a delivery of food to their table. A tray of hot and cold starters was placed between them. 'Thanks. I warn you, Phil, this bread's addictive.' She picked up a piece of the soft, warmed Turkish bread, which was lightly oiled, with sea salt and sesame seeds sprinkled on top. 'It's lovely with the dips.'

Phil followed her lead and spooned some tzatziki onto a piece of bread. 'It's not very rock and roll but I spend a lot of my spare time gardening. It's a bit like you babysitting clients. It helps with the rent.'

'Flowers or edibles?' she asked.

'Edibles in the allotment. Flowers and shrubs in the garden.'

'I miss having garden space. Not that I knew anything about what I was doing, a bit like the flower arranging, as you saw. But it's quite rewarding, planting things and watching them grow.' She picked up a stuffed vine leaf and took a bite.

'Tell me about you, then. How have you ended up at Cross International?'

She hoped he wasn't going to start questioning her about Daniel. 'Various admin jobs since college, where I did a secretarial course with business, law and finance training. I was going to go to Uni but er…life got in the way.'

He stabbed at a fat green olive with a toothpick. 'Life?'

She felt comfortable enough with him to answer honestly. 'I wasn't as lucky as you for adoptive parents. We lived in a lovely little place called Lullaby Cottage in a village in Sussex and it was as idyllic as it sounds in so many ways. But Mum left Dad when I was ten, he carried on drinking and died from cirrhosis when I was eighteen.'

'That must have been tough for you. Was he ever violent?' he asked.

'He was towards Mum.'

'But not you?'

'Only once.' She felt herself shiver at the memory.

'What happened, if you don't mind me asking?'

'I hit him back, twice as hard. He was a coward. Never tried it again. Even when he was completely wrecked.'

'That was brave of you. Have you got any siblings?' he asked.

She shook her head.

'And your mother?'

Juliet felt the sucker punch at her adoptive mother's abandonment of her. 'She never came back. I think she had to get away for her own

54

sanity.' She still felt disappointed, rejected by the lack of contact, even all these years later.

'And did you search out your birth parents?' he asked.

'Got the paperwork just after Dad died. They were heroin addicts when they had me. Both dead from it before my fifth birthday, it turned out.'

'That's hard.' His face was full of sympathy and she felt herself warming more towards him.

'It's all I've known, so I'm not sure it feels hard. It's just my reality.' She picked up another piece of bread, tearing a little piece off and eating it neat. She could easily have wolfed the lot but knew the best food was to come and the bread would spoil her appetite.

'So, what do you like to do for fun?' he asked.

'Touché. Mainly I enjoy this fair city. Theatre, cinema, walks, art galleries, all sorts of things. Maybe at some point, I'll get bored of it. But even in lockdown, this city was one of the best places to be.'

'Is it walking that keeps you fit?' he asked.

'Running mainly. Some gym work when I feel inclined. Which isn't often. Running frees my mind.'

'When do you get the chance to do that?' he asked.

'Early. I try to get up and out around five-ish. Though it gets harder to motivate myself, as the days get shorter.'

'You put me to shame. Though I guess I do a fair amount of exercise at the allotment. Blimey.'

She followed his gaze and saw Mehmet and another waiter carrying several dishes of warm food. 'If I'd known we were coming here, I'd have told you to skip lunch,' she said. 'Though, I have to admit, I often ask for doggy bags. They put it away for me so I don't have to take it when I've guests and I pick it up later. It keeps me in food for a week.'

'Is that a roundabout way of telling me not to eat it all?' His eyes were twinkling with mischief.

'Absolutely. Make sure you leave me some chicken. That's my favourite leftover,' she said and winked.

'What with the flat and all this food, you do alright out of Cross International,' he said as he picked up a baby lamb chop and bit into it. 'Mmm, that's lovely.'

'I do. The pay's a bit stingy for London but I don't have travel costs. I'm in the pension scheme, so it makes sense to stick with it. And, of course, I have access to a heavy mob if I want to put the frighteners on anyone who irritates me.' She watched as he processed her words then laughed loudly as his face went from shock to disbelief. 'Gotcha.'

'You certainly did,' he said. He helped himself to some Greek salad and the skewered chicken. 'I'll buy you extra chicken to take away if I eat too much, which I could easily do. This is so good.'

'It was a happy coincidence you chose this place,' she said. 'Do you like art?'

'I'm quite a traditionalist. Constable, Turner. What about you?'

'I love the Pre-Raphaelites. Must admit I struggle with the abstract stuff. I've not read that book about how a three-year-old couldn't have painted that but that's the feeling I get when I see blocks of colour or random splodges on canvas,' she said.

'I'm that level of Philistine, too. Actually, I'm worse. Not sure I'd recognise a Pre-Raphaelite if I saw it.'

'Let me show you. I'm sure you'll recognise the type when you see some examples.' She wiped her hands on a napkin, pulled out her phone and showed him images of Waterhouse's *Lady of Shalott*, Rosetti's *Proserpine* and Millais' *Ophelia*.

'Beautiful. There's something ethereal about them. Rather like you,' he said.

'Flatterer. I just love the allure of their works. I've gone to the Tate and stared at the *Lady of Shalott* so many times but it always takes my breath away. I can't draw anything, just don't have any ability in that area, so I admire their achievement of capturing something so gloriously.'

Juliet sat back and let the conversation wash over her for the rest of the meal. She had a fascination for her dinner companion. He was so different from the people she usually spent time with, who were all obsessed with image and veneer. They were usually big fans of reality television and its stars. They liked to party with plenty of drinking and sometimes drugs to oil their mood. Most weren't keen on art or books or theatre unless it involved celebrity of some sort. She'd long given up on meeting people who were interested in the things that moved her and had accepted it as the price she paid for her London lifestyle. But the idea of having a relationship with a policeman unnerved her. It would make parts of her life very difficult. She was sure Phil would disapprove of some of the duties she carried out for Daniel. Maybe it would be safest to stick to one date.

'Have you had enough?' she asked, after Phil sat back, looking defeated.

'More than enough, thanks. I should have stopped twenty minutes ago, but it tasted too good.'

'I always have to practise restraint here.' She looked around and Mehmet appeared so quickly that she wondered if he'd been watching them. 'Can you pack up what's left for me, please?'

Mehmet looked surprised at how little was left. 'I get you some extra,' he said and winked.

'You're very kind to me.' She directed her gaze at Phil. 'Do you want a coffee? Another drink?'

Phil shook his head. 'No, thanks. I'm done for.'

'Can we just have the bill, please?'

Mehmet nodded and disappeared.

Phil paid the bill and Juliet picked up her doggy bag and walked out into the cool of the evening. 'Which way are you going?' she asked.

'Back to Waterloo,' he said, 'but let me walk you home.'

She shook her head. 'It's not necessary, though you are kind to offer.'

'Right, then. OK.' The corners of his mouth dropped momentarily. 'Well, thanks for coming.'

'Thank you for dinner. I've really enjoyed our evening,' she said. She leant forward to kiss him on the cheek. On instinct, she turned her head and kissed him full on the lips. It was a surprise to her just how much she enjoyed it. It had been a long time since she'd had a proper kiss. She pulled away and could see he was surprised, too.

'Wow. Gosh,' he said, before pulling her towards him and kissing her back.

She didn't want it to stop and they remained locked together, kissing gently, till he moved back.

'Thank you,' he said, gazing directly at her. 'Are you sure I can't walk you home?'

She shook her head and felt obliged to explain. 'It's been a long time since I've been…intimate with anyone.' She remembered he knew about the Jeremy Harrison encounter. 'I mean, intentionally intimate. I…' She felt herself colouring.

'God, no. I wasn't expecting…I was just thinking about your safety. I understand.' He gave her a gentle smile. 'Can I see you again?'

'I'd like that,' she said, ignoring her earlier one-date-only decision. 'Maybe I could come and see your place, your garden and the allotment?'

'How about this weekend?'

'Let me check.' She looked at the calendar on her mobile. She knew she was entertaining what she hoped was her last client on Saturday night – a theatre trip and a late supper – but had nothing in her calendar for Sunday. 'Sunday? I can catch the train and meet you at the station or if you give me your address, I can walk.'

'It's about a twenty-minute walk from Woking station,' he said.

'Easy, then. Postcode? House number?' She typed the data into her phone. 'What time do you want me?' A smile played on her lips. She couldn't remember the last time she'd genuinely flirted with anyone.

'Whatever suits you,' he said.

'Shall I come over in the morning? Say 11am? Then I can buy us Sunday lunch somewhere. Bound to be some nice pubs around.'

'Let me cook,' he said.

'That'll be lovely.' She never cooked in her flat. It was too easy to pick up a meal on the way home from work in London. Easier still to skip proper food altogether.

'I'll see you then. Are you sure about that police escort home?' he asked.

'Definitely. You get off to the station. And I'll see you Sunday.' After a last kiss, she watched him walk quickly along the pavement, veering around hesitant tourists and revellers before he went down into the subway network that led to the station concourse.

She turned and set off in the opposite direction, getting back to her flat just before 11pm. She sent Phil a thank you text then responded to a message she'd had from Daniel, who'd asked about her date.

Daniel rang straight back, without so much as a hello. 'Did he ask anything awkward?'

'Your name was barely mentioned. It was a genuine date.'

'You think?' he asked, not hiding his sarcastic tone.

'Yes, I do,' she said.

'Are you going to see him again?'

'I am.'

Daniel snorted down the phone.

'I'll see you in the morning,' she said, irritated by his reaction. She didn't wait for a response and ended the call. It was none of his business who she dated, though sometimes it felt like everything she did was under Daniel's scrutiny.

She went to her bedroom and decided to text Phil again. "Let me know when you're in."

He came back fifteen minutes later. "Just in now. Did you think I might get lost?"

She assumed he was joking. "Pardon me for caring." She added a winking emoji afterwards, just to make sure he knew she was being light-hearted, then added "You're a very good kisser".

"Years of practice", he replied.

She smiled as she readied herself for bed. "I'm up for more practice if you are".

"Definitely. I hope I get to kiss you in my dreams. Goodnight, sweet Juliet x".

"Goodnight. Looking forward to Sunday x". She felt herself grinning before switching off the light.

She got up early the next morning and went for a run along the river before work. Thoughts of Phil were still floating in her mind as she arrived at the office.

Daniel was already at his desk so she made some coffee and took him a mug. He looked up as she put it down in front of him. 'Look at you, all loved up.' His tone was mocking. 'Did you enjoy your snogfest last night?'

She stiffened and looked at him with venom. 'What?'

'Tarkan mentioned it. You and the Inspector playing tonsil tennis outside his place.'

She bit back her anger. If Daniel sensed something riled her, he'd make something of it, so she tried to make light of it. 'I did enjoy it, thank you. Did you remember to sort out that gift you were talking about for Giselle?'

'Damn.' Daniel picked up his phone and stabbed at the screen. 'Wim, morning. Those diamond necklaces we discussed. I want the heart-shaped one. Yep. Can you drop it off Sunday? Great. I'll get someone to meet you off the flight. What time? 10:30 in the morning, OK.' He raised his eyebrows as he looked at Juliet.

She shook her head.

'It'll be Patrick, most likely. Cheers, Wim. Appreciate it.' He put down his phone. 'Ask Pat to meet him at Heathrow.'

'Sure,' she said.

'You got plans, then?' he asked.

'Yes, off to see someone.' She walked towards the door, hoping he wouldn't ask who.

'You keep me posted on your progress with the copper,' he said.

Juliet sat down at her desk and felt her jaw harden. She'd do no such thing.

Chapter 8 – Phil

Phil realised he'd messed up. Juliet was coming around to his place the next day at 11am. He always took Elsie to church on a Sunday morning. He had to admit, he enjoyed going too, not so much for the religion as for the peace, the beauty of the church and the occasional sermon that made him think about a topic in a different way. Even if it was a dull sermon, it always made him count his blessings.

He couldn't decide whether to let Elsie down or change the arrangement with Juliet. It sounded stupid when he thought about it, that he was concerned Juliet might hold it against him if he changed the plan but he'd got the impression she was super-organised, so would see him as a bit of an idiot if he couldn't make a simple arrangement without getting it wrong.

He decided to ask Juliet to come at 12pm instead. He sent her a text with no explanation. She surprised him by ringing straight back.

'Hi, Phil. Midday's absolutely fine. Do you want more of a lie-in?' she asked.

He explained his mistake.

'Why don't I meet you at church? If you don't mind. If your landlady won't mind.'

The thought delighted him, that she seemed keen to spend more time with him, not less. 'That'll be great. It's St. Mark's, just off Baverstock Road. 10:30am start.'

'Hold on.' She waited till the bing-bong announcement behind her stopped. 'I'll find it.'

'Where are you?' he asked.

'Heathrow. Just picking up a businessman, making sure he has everything he needs for his visit to Cross International.'

'You're kidding. You're never off duty.'

'I am tomorrow. See you then.' She hung up.

Was she annoyed with him for making a comment about her job? It just seemed weird to him that she spent so much time working. Though he was hardly in a position to criticise, given his own hours. But that was to be expected in his line of work. He didn't see the duties of a PA in the same league as a Serious Crime Squad detective. Why did a businessman need babysitting from the airport?

He decided he should tell Elsie about Juliet coming to church, so went to her door and knocked.

'Come in, love,' she said.

He went into her room, where she was reading the newspaper. 'Just off out. Do you need anything?'

'No, lovey, I've got enough in from that last shop you did. You getting the lunch things for tomorrow?'

'Yeah.'

'What have you decided to cook?' Elsie leaned forward with interest.

'I thought I'd go for roast pork. And an apple crumble. She looks like she needs feeding up.'

'She a skinny Minnie then?'

'She exercises a lot. But she seemed to enjoy her food, so hopefully she'll like it.'

'And you'll plate me up some for later?'

'You can eat with us, you know.'

'No, you want to spend time with her alone, get to know her better,' she said.

'She's going to meet us at St. Mark's. That's all right, isn't it?'

'You mean she's coming in for the service?'

He nodded.

'Of course. Give me a chance to check her out.' She gave him a fruity wink. 'Is she religious, do you think?'

'Dunno yet. She certainly didn't mention anything.'

'It's not really a subject for a first date, is it?' said Elsie. 'You said she was younger than you?'

'Four years younger.'

'And she's got one of those high-flying careers?'

'Yeah, kind of.' He was inclined to think it wasn't, despite the fancy flat, but maybe he was doing Juliet a disservice. She was certainly bright and capable of a lot more than she did for Daniel Cross, he suspected.

'What else are you going to do with her?' Elsie asked.

'She wants to see the garden, so I'll show her that and take her up the allotment.'

'Doesn't sound very romantic.'

'I'm out of practice. I'm just doing what she's asked,' he said.

'You could take her for a walk out to one of the pubs along the canal. Buy her a nice drink or two,' she said.

'She doesn't drink. Her father was an alky so it's put her off.'

'That's good, I s'pose. At least if you take her out, you don't need to worry about her getting out of control and making a spectacle of herself.'

'I don't think she's the out-of-control type,' he said.

'Is she a bit dull?' she asked.

'Far from it. Very sparkly, if that's a good way to describe it. There's something about her. Maybe she's just good at conversation, easy to talk to. She's always out and about in London, going to the theatre, art galleries and museums.'

'A culture vulture, arty then. Well, it's nice to see you smiling about something other than your courgettes, love.'

He laughed. 'It comes to something when I'm apparently more enthusiastic about veg than anything else. Right, better get to the shops. See you later, Else.'

'Be lucky,' she said.

He drove to the supermarket and eventually bagged a parking space. He took a small trolley from the shelter near the entrance and went inside. There was a limited selection of roasting joints so he went to the butcher's counter and found one that was just right. It was organic and the price made him blench, but he wanted to make a good impression on Juliet. He would save on vegetables, having plenty in the allotment and would make a crumble with some early season apples he'd been given in return for some carrots and runner beans. He picked up a small tub of good quality vanilla ice-cream and a bottle of non-alcoholic fizz, both of which were on special offer. Pleased with his choices, he picked up the other things on his list – toilet rolls, washing liquid and milk – and joined a checkout queue, trying not to be too nosy about the purchases of the shopper in front.

After driving home and putting the shopping away, he changed into his gardening clothes and spent the afternoon at the allotment. He felt at peace, surrounded by things he'd grown. The sense of achievement was huge, he'd found, as well as everything tasting better. He dug up enough potatoes for the week, took the first of the season's cauliflower, some large carrots and a few young parsnips. The beans were just about finished for the season, so he cleared the plants from their canes, putting them into his composting bin. The new autumn lettuce variety he'd tried hadn't been a success – it was too bitter – and had now bolted, looking very sorry for itself after a couple of cooler nights. He pulled up the remaining heads and put them into the wormery he'd started earlier in the year.

'Wanna cuppa, Phil?' The man in the next plot waved a mug at him.

'No thanks, Al. Better get on. Got to clear out the bedding plants in the front garden today.' He knew a tea break would mean a long natter in Al's shed and the day would be gone.

'Suit yourself.' Al spoke good-naturedly and went back into his shed.

The potatoes and veg he'd picked were heavy and Phil felt weary by the time he got back to the house, so he made himself a coffee and sat down in the kitchen, alone with his thoughts. Elsie had gone out to a friend's house for a game of cards. He must have fallen asleep, he realised, when he woke up with a start at the sound of the front door opening. He put his hand around his mug. The coffee had gone cold and the light was already fading. So much for getting the borders tidied up.

He felt old before his time, worrying about the garden's appearance when he was entertaining a young, vibrant woman the next day. Though it was her who'd suggested a daytime meeting, who wanted to see the garden and had volunteered to attend a church service with him and his elderly landlady. And it was her who'd fired up a passionate response in him when they'd kissed after their first date. Even the thought of it stirred emotions in his body and soul. She was intriguing, this woman of opposites. And he liked a mystery.

Chapter 9 - Juliet

Juliet took one more look at the directions on her phone. The church should be around the next bend and along the road in less than half a mile. The service started in fifteen minutes so she'd be there on time. She saw others walking in the same direction and a few people chatting outside. She couldn't see Phil so went into the church, where the early birds had already claimed the best seats near the front. She walked around, reading the wall plaques and picking up a pamphlet about the restoration fund from a small table near the entrance. The smell of the place was an odd mixture of damp mustiness and fresh flowers. She leaned forward to smell a solitary pink rose that was surrounded by other, less beautiful blooms and copious amounts of foliage.

'Does it smell?'

She straightened up on hearing Phil's voice. 'A little. Nice to see you.' She gave him a chaste peck on each cheek, which felt appropriate given their surroundings.

'Let me introduce you to Elsie.' He led Juliet to a pew at the back, where Elsie had taken a seat.

Elsie gave her a broad smile. 'Hallo, lovey. Glad you turned up. He'd have had a monk on if you hadn't. You're very pretty.'

Juliet smiled at Elsie's East End accent, so like her mother's. 'Thank you. Do you come here every Sunday?'

'Only if I don't get a better offer.' Elsie gave a ripe cackle.

The vicar swept in and took her place at the lectern, catching many of the congregation off guard. There were moans and shuffles as people hurriedly sat down. 'Good morning. At the risk of confusing everyone, let's do something different and start with hymn 247.'

The congregation stood up, mostly. Elsie stayed in her seat, as did some other older worshippers.

The hymn was vaguely familiar to Juliet and she sang along. She noticed Phil was mouthing the words but no sound emanated from him. He must have noticed her watching him because he leant over between verses and whispered 'Tone deaf' in her ear.

They sat down when the hymn was over and the vicar began to speak. 'Welcome to you all. I know starting with a hymn is not what we usually do, but I thought I'd give us all a chance to have a nice sing-song and get some oxygen in our lungs. Wake us up on such a lovely morning. It's good to see so many people here and a few new faces too.'

Juliet kept her eyes downwards, not wanting to catch the vicar's eye as one of the newbies. She listened to the sermon and Bible reading while glancing across at Phil. He looked smart in a pair of ironed trousers and a crisp, open-necked shirt under a jacket. He turned towards her, as though he'd been aware he was being scrutinised, and smiled. He gave her a tiny wink and there was such friendliness in the gesture, such warmth behind the smile, that she felt as though she was bathing in sunshine, rather than sitting in a draughty church in September. She returned the smile and tuned back in to the vicar, who was now on to parish news and plans for the Harvest Festival. She read out a new idea to host a Christmas dinner for the homeless, with a request for volunteers and food donations. Juliet saw Elsie look at Phil and he nodded, presumably meaning he would donate either his time or some food.

Their generosity of spirit gave Juliet a warm feeling and she imagined what Christmas might be like at Elsie's house. She had loved Christmas as a young child. She'd spent one Christmas with Cameron and his family after they'd been dating a few months, but there was so much emotional tension in the house, it had reinforced all Juliet's negativity about the festive season. In the last years before her mother had left, Christmas had come to mean raised voices, clenched fists swinging in anger, endless tears and piles of empty bottles followed by guilt, remorse and apologies on an endless loop.

Juliet was brought back to the present as the congregation stood up for the second hymn. She sang out, hoping the sad thoughts about her past would be displaced by the massed voices. Phil was mouthing along again and Juliet bit back a laugh at his silent participation.

After some prayers and a final blessing, the service concluded. Juliet saw Phil nod at Elsie to make sure she was alright. It was sweet how he looked after her, even if it did make his rent cheaper. Phil helped Elsie negotiate the steps of the church and the short walk to the car. Juliet followed and was invited to jump in the back of the three-door hatchback. She got in with ease and pulled the front passenger seat back into place so Phil could guide Elsie into it. He didn't rush her or give any hint of impatience, at least that Juliet could see, despite the traffic being busy and the roadside being filled with departing churchgoers.

It was only a short drive to Elsie's house, an imposing Victorian detached property. The entire frontage was protected by yew hedges. Phil helped Elsie out of the car and took her in. Juliet found the button to release the car seat and got out. She followed the pathway to the house. There was a small fountain in the middle of a gravel bed and flowerbeds either side. Everything that Juliet could see looked well-tended, with the shrubs and hedges neatly trimmed and an absence of weeds between the plants. She walked up to the open front door and tentatively went in.

The house had lovely proportions both inside and out. Juliet hovered in the hallway.

'In here, Juliet.' Phil popped his head out from one of the doors and Juliet joined him in what turned out to be Elsie's living room and bedroom. Phil made Elsie comfortable in the main seat in the room, a big faded armchair with a worn floral chintz cover. There was a small table within arm's reach that had a television remote and an empty tumbler next to an almost full bottle of single malt whisky.

'I'm alright, Phil. You get on with your day with Missy here,' Elsie said.

'You got everything you need?' he asked.

'Yep.'

'I'll bring you a tray with your lunch when it's ready,' he said.

Juliet frowned. 'Are you not eating with us, Elsie?'

'Sit with you two lovebirds? I'm not playing gooseberry.'

'It wouldn't feel right, you sitting in here while we're somewhere else. Sorry, Phil. I'm not being rude about your company, but this is Elsie's house.'

'I agree. Told you, Else.'

Elsie sighed. 'Well, all I can say is courting ain't what it used to be. Shout me when it's ready. I won't disturb you before then.'

Phil led Juliet into the kitchen. She noticed that everything was tidy and a lot of preparation had already taken place.

He took a roasting joint out of the oven. 'I've got it on a low heat, should be ready about one-ish.' His face dropped. 'You do eat pork, don't you?'

She nodded. 'I was going to pretend I didn't but I do. I love it. Though you're on your own with the crackling. Never liked the stuff.'

'Elsie'll be pleased. It's her favourite and she didn't fancy having to share. Can I get you a drink of something?'

'Have you got any diet drinks?'

'Lemonade, tonic, Coke.'

'Tonic'd be nice, thanks.'

He busied himself pouring her drink then took a half-empty bottle of white wine from the fridge. 'You don't mind if I have a drink, do you?'

'Not at all,' she said.

He poured himself a glass. 'Cheers.'

'Cheers. What can I help with?' she asked.

'I think all the prep's done.'

'Shall I lay a place for Elsie?'

'Good idea. That was kind of you to insist on her joining us,' he said.

She felt a sudden desire and didn't fight it. 'Can I kiss you, Phil?'

He nodded.

She stretched on tiptoe so she could reach his lips. 'Thank you,' she said.

'Thank you. We've got an hour before I need to get the potatoes into the oven. Do you want to see the garden?'

'I'd like that.' She'd been afraid he was going to ask her to go to bed with him.

They walked out of the kitchen door and he took her around the side, front and back gardens. He explained in detail the plants and flowers.

It reminded her of a stately home's garden. 'Phil, it's stunning. Are you behind all this?'

'Lord, no. Don't give me any credit. Elsie is the genius. She took a bare plot fifty years ago and worked with her husband to make all this.

I've just picked up the maintenance from her since she's found it too hard to keep on top of it, with her arthritis.'

'It's beautiful,' she said.

'Like you,' he said. He stroked her face and kissed her softly. 'I need to go and sort out the lunch. Do you want to sit here and relax?'

'No, let me help you. I promise I'm better at cooking than flower arranging.'

He laughed. 'I'm glad to hear that.'

They went back inside and the pork had filled the house with roasty aromas, reminding Juliet of Sunday lunches at Lullaby Cottage.

'Can you fry the chorizo and onion that's in that pan, then add the sprouts?' he asked. 'You'll need a splash of water in there to cook the sprouts right through.'

'It's quite early for sprouts, isn't it?'

'They're Elsie's favourite veg, so I grow an early variety specially for her. Though I don't think they're as good as the standard varieties.'

She focused on her task while Phil put some fat on a tray in the oven and parboiled some potatoes.

'Why am I cooking this now? Surely it won't take nearly as long as the potatoes?' she asked.

'I've found if the sprouts sit for a while, the flavour of the chorizo really gets into them, much better than if you cook them at the last minute. And it's one less thing to do.' He took the pork out of the oven, as well as the tray with smoking fat for the potatoes. He turned the oven up to high, put the pork joint onto a warmed carving dish and asked Juliet to cover the pork in foil. 'Top drawer, over there,' he directed. He put trays of prepared carrots and parsnips into the oven while she placed a double layer of foil onto the meat. He put the covered joint onto the

73

back of the hob so it would stay warm then rolled the drained potatoes into the hot fat. They sizzled and spat but he used a spoon to make sure every edge was covered in the silky liquid before putting them on the top shelf of the oven. 'I'll just make some gravy.'

'Will it put you off if I watch?' she asked.

'Not at all.'

She was fascinated by the process, as he added flour to the meat juices in the roasting tray, cooked them on the hob, scraped off all the crusty bits where the meat had cooked, and added some water from a pan on the stove.

'It's the potato water. The starch helps thicken it,' he said.

After ten minutes of alchemy, a glossy, mahogany-coloured gravy had been created. He tasted it, then offered her a clean teaspoon so she could do the same.

'That's lush,' she said. 'Now, tell me where the cutlery is so I can put some out for Elsie.'

He pointed her to a lidless coffee pot in the corner that had cutlery standing upright in it. 'She likes the bone-handled ones in there. She keeps them in the pot so I don't mix them up with the rest.'

Juliet watched Phil potter around, checking the progress of the vegetables, putting the plates to warm and washing up dirty dishes. She was feeling hungry and willed him to declare it was time to eat.

Just before 1:30pm, he said he was ready to carve and picked up a large serrated knife. His phone rang and he checked the screen to see who it was. 'Bugger. I've got to take this.' He held his phone in front of him and answered. 'Hi, Billy.'

'Hey, Dad, wassup?'

'Just cooking Sunday lunch. How are you and your brother?'

'Alright. Maaaax!'

Juliet heard Billy bellow at his sibling.

'Dad's on now.'

Phil gestured to Juliet that he'd go to his room to finish the call.

She wondered how long he'd be. Deciding she'd make herself useful, she picked up the carving utensils and cut off the string holding the joint together, then took the crackling off in a single piece. She began to carve, not knowing if he wanted thick or thin slices, so aimed somewhere in the middle. When a bit fell off the edge of the slice, she picked it up and tasted it. It was good but made her hungrier for more.

After a few minutes of watching the meat go cold, she tore off some fresh foil and covered it up. She turned the gravy off so it didn't get too thick and turned the oven to low, not wanting the potatoes to overcook.

Phil came back with a look of concern. 'Sorry. Couldn't not take that. I don't always know when they're going to call.'

'It's fine. Hope I did the right thing.' She lifted the foil off the meat. 'I've probably made a mess of it but I did my best.'

'Thanks.' He sounded less than enthusiastic as he peered at her efforts.

'Sorry.' She felt compelled to apologise.

'It's OK. I usually do thin slices but...no, thanks for trying to help.'

Talk about damning with faint praise, she thought. 'Shall I fetch Elsie through while you do whatever else is needed?' she asked.

He nodded.

She went into the hallway, tapping gently on the open door before going in. 'Hi, Elsie, time for lunch if you want to come through.'

Elsie was staring at the mantelpiece. Juliet could see she'd been crying.

'What's the matter?' Juliet asked.

'Just an old lady, remembering. Take no notice of me, love. Not all memories are happy.'

'It's always best to look forward,' said Juliet.

'It is when you're young, but I'm eighty-three, love. Not too much life ahead of me.' Elsie wiped her eyes on a cotton handkerchief. 'I'm a silly old cow. Can you pass me my stick and I'll get myself into the kitchen.'

'Let me help.' Juliet gave Elsie her arm so she could pull herself up and steady herself before walking.

'Right. Onward. Let's see what the Galloping Gourmet has done for us today,' Elsie said.

Juliet waited for Elsie to walk out of the room, not wanting her to feel rushed. She saw a black and white photograph of a man on the mantelpiece above the fireplace. It was the one Elsie had been staring at when Juliet had interrupted her. She picked up the frame and went into the hall, where Elsie was walking slowly towards the kitchen. 'Elsie, is this your husband?'

Elsie looked up. 'No, dear. That's Allan. He was the love of my life.'

'Seriously?' asked Juliet.

Elsie nodded. 'Should've run away with him when I had the chance. I was happy with George, don't get me wrong. But Allan was the one.'

Juliet didn't know what to say. 'I'll put him back where I found him,' she said. She noticed there was a lot of dust on the frame as well as on the mantelpiece and made a mental note to ask Elsie if she needed help keeping the room clean. She heard Phil calling so went back to the kitchen.

Chapter 10 - Phil

Phil was surprised at how nervous he felt, cooking for Juliet. He wanted to make a good impression on her much more than he cared to admit, even to himself.

Elsie came through from her room. 'You look flustered, Phil.'

'I'm fine, just hot from the cooking. You sit yourself down and I'll get you some wine.' He'd already opened a bottle of red wine for Elsie, something she always drank with a roast. He poured her a glass and put the bottle within Elsie's reach on the table. 'Juliet, are you coming through?'

'She's just putting Allan back.'

Juliet came in.

'Make yourself comfortable,' he said. 'Do you want another tonic? I've some non alcoholic fizz if you'd like to try some.'

'I'll just have water, thanks. Sorry about that, Elsie, making the wrong assumption about the picture. None of my business.'

Elsie waved her hand in a dismissive gesture. 'It's fine. I'll tell anyone who'll listen about Allan. It's all too late now, both him and George are gone, so it does no harm.'

'Juliet, do you want to come and help yourself?' Phil asked.

'Shouldn't Elsie go first?'

'I'll put something on a plate for her,' he said.

'He knows what I like and how much I can eat,' Elsie said.

Phil watched Juliet take a little bit of everything before she sat down. 'Apple sauce and gravy are on the table,' he told her.

'Thanks, Phil. It looks delicious.' She put her plate down but didn't start to eat.

'Don't let it get cold and let his hard work go to waste, love,' Elsie said.

Juliet nodded and put a spoonful of the homemade apple sauce onto her plate before pouring a little gravy over the pork.

Phil put Elsie's plate, with a tiny portion of food, in front of her and passed her the gravy jug.

'Thanks, lovey. Looks up to your usual standard.'

He was anxious to steer the conversation onto Juliet, to try and get her talking a bit more about herself. He felt she'd divulged little about herself when they'd met at the restaurant. As he piled his plate with meat, potatoes and vegetables, he tried to think of a safe question to ask her. 'Juliet, tell me about your friends.'

Juliet put her knife and fork down and looked at him. 'Tell you what?'

He shrugged as he sat down at the table. 'Just tell me about them. Who do you hang out with? Where did you meet them – school or work or were they neighbours? What do you like to get up to with them?'

'Nothing to tell,' she said. She picked up her fork and played with a piece of parsnip.

He was confused. She looked uncomfortable, but it wasn't an intrusive question. He wasn't asking her about her old lovers or anything. 'No anecdotes about what you and your friends got up to on a hen party or anything?'

'I don't really have any,' she said, colouring slightly.

'Any anecdotes?' he asked.

'Any friends.' She looked ashamed as she said it.

'Phil, you're embarrassing the poor girl. Leave her be. Lovey, let me tell you about George.' Elsie began the story of how she met her husband.

Phil zoned out. He looked at his lunch without enthusiasm. He wasn't sure what had happened. He'd made Juliet feel bad and Elsie'd had to intervene to make him stop. He still couldn't understand Juliet's response to his innocent question. How could she have no friends? Everyone has friends.

'Don't let your meal get cold, Phil,' Elsie said, her voice sharp.

He took a forkful of roast potato.

'The food's lovely, Phil. Thank you for cooking.' Juliet looked at him and he could see sadness in her expression.

'Sorry if I spoke out of turn. I didn't mean to upset you,' he said.

'It's fine. I know it probably seems odd to you, but I've never really surrounded myself with people. I'm quite happy ploughing my solitary furrow, I guess.'

'And that's your choice, lovey.' Elsie spoke before Phil had the chance.

He wondered how Juliet could live her life without people around her for support. 'Yes, of course. It's your choice.' He felt the need to explain himself. 'Sorry, I was just trying to get to know you. I like asking questions. Must be because of my job.'

'Tell me about your friends, Phil.'

He felt a knot of annoyance in his stomach. He didn't want to talk about himself. He wanted to know about her, break through more of that outer layer. But it would have been rude not to respond. 'I'm lucky. I have a friend from school who I've known since I was thirteen. I have a couple of good friends from my military days, guys who started basic training on the same day as me. And some close colleagues in the police. I'm also close to my ex's brother. We really got on when I first met Sal and we've stayed in touch.'

'That's great. And what sort of things do you get up to with them?' Juliet looked genuinely interested but then she spent her working life being attentive to complete strangers. She must be well practised at feigning interest.

'Go out for a drink, watch rugby, game of golf, do a bike trip somewhere.'

'Bicycle or motorbike?' Juliet asked.

'Motorbike. Though I'm between bikes at the moment.'

'Sorry, I've just realised I'm stopping you eating,' Juliet said. 'And it's so lovely.'

Phil looked down at his barely touched plate. 'I'll just heat it up a bit.' He got up and put the plate in the microwave.

While he waited for his food to warm through, he looked at Juliet. She'd asked Elsie for more information about George and was listening intently to the response. She looked beautiful and he couldn't help but stare at her.

The beep of the microwave woke him from his daydream. He used a tea-towel to pick up his now volcanically-hot plate and took it back to the table. His appetite came back a little and he began to enjoy his meal, as he listened to Elsie telling Juliet about her husband.

'If he was an antiques dealer, how did he manage not to keep all the nice pieces for himself?' Juliet asked.

'He struggled, which is why upstairs is chock-a-block with furniture,' Elsie said.

'It is lovely to be surrounded by nice things, though. Makes you feel special when you have beautiful items around you. And you have the added bonus they remind you of George,' Juliet said.

'I can't get up there much to enjoy them. Bloody arthritis plays havoc. Phil's a godsend. Helps me up there every so often and he took a video of it all for me, so I can take a…what was it you called it?'

'A virtual tour,' he said.

'What a clever idea,' Juliet said and smiled at him.

'You'll have to take her up there to have a look,' Elsie said to Phil.

'I will, after I've shown her the allotment. Don't want to run out of daylight. Assuming you don't have to cut and run after lunch?'

'I'm free all day. Happy to fit in with whatever you want to do. Just chuck me out when you're fed up with me,' Juliet said.

'Then you'll be here for ever,' he said.

Elsie laughed. 'Oh, he's smitten already, lovey. You can get away with murder.'

'Well, maybe not murder, given my job,' he said. 'Have you had enough?' he asked Juliet, whose plate was empty.

'I have, thank you, particularly as I think I spotted pudding over there. I want to make sure I've got space for that.'

'Declare yourself,' he said. 'Custard, cream or ice-cream?'

'Hmmm, depends on the pudding,' Juliet said.

'Apple crumble.'

'Got to be custard, then,' said Juliet.

'I'm with you, deary,' Elsie said. 'He loves his ice-cream.'

'It's a close second,' Juliet said. 'The hot and cold vibe is great but I think comfort food like crumble demands good old-fashioned custard.'

'You finished, Else?' Phil asked.

'Yes, thanks.'

Phil abandoned his half-eaten dinner and cleared away the plates.

He noticed Elsie nudging Juliet. She spoke quietly but he could still hear. 'You're putting him off his food. Told you he was smitten.'

Juliet looked over towards him and winked.

He felt boosted by the gesture and took the crumble out of the oven. He made custard the way his Mum had, with powder from a tin, sugar and hot milk. He took the ice-cream from the freezer and ferried it, the crumble, bowls and spoons over to the table with the custard. He began serving.

'How far is the allotment from here?' Juliet asked. 'Just a small piece for me, please. As long as I'm allowed to come back for seconds.'

'You may,' he said. 'The allotment's not far, fifteen minutes' walk. I can drive us there if you'd rather.'

'I love to walk. That's one of the great things about where I live in London, Elsie. I can walk easily to anywhere in central London from my flat.'

'Is that what keeps you so fit?' Elsie asked.

'I run in the early morning before I start work.'

'Juliet spends a lot of her time at work,' Phil said to Elsie. 'I'm amazed we've got her for the whole day.'

'A girl's head can be turned with comfort food,' Juliet said.

'What do you do for a living, deary?' Elsie asked.

'I'm PA to the Chairman of Cross International, Daniel Cross.'

'I've seen him on the business programmes. He's quite a dish, isn't he?'

Juliet laughed at Elsie's description. 'I suppose he is, but I've never thought of him like that. He's more of a father figure to me.'

'And what does a PA do?' Elsie asked.

'All sorts. I sort out his diary, his travel, his correspondence. Organise meetings, events. I have a company flat so I'm close to the office at all times and can look after visiting businessmen.'

'Do they stay over at your place?' Elsie asked.

'Only once so far, when a hotel messed up our booking. It's more about having somewhere to entertain them between meetings and events, filling in the gaps in their schedule with a city tour or a shopping trip. Sometimes I'll take them out for a drink or a meal. I'm very lucky. I go along to most of the events we take visitors to, so I get to see lots of theatre and exhibitions, and I get to eat in some very nice restaurants.'

'You don't get much downtime, though, do you,' Phil said, knowing he was pressing buttons he shouldn't.

'I don't want much downtime. I enjoy the things I get to do.'

'But when do you get to be you?' he asked.

Juliet frowned. 'I'm me all the time.'

'I mean, relaxed you. Chilling on the sofa in your PJs, eating popcorn with no make-up on, binge watching *Succession* or *Shetland* or whatever. Doing all this corporate stuff, you must have to put on a front, a facade.'

'No, I think it's just me all the time, Phil.'

He didn't believe her and wondered if she could see that in his expression.

'I like doing that stuff. I'm not having to pretend.' She pushed her empty plate towards the middle of the table and sighed. 'Don't think I can manage a second portion. Probably need to walk it off.'

'Did you like it?' he asked.

'I did, thank you. Ages since I had a proper pudding,' Juliet said.

'Would you like a cup of tea, Elsie?' Phil asked.

'Yes please, love.' Elsie finished the last mouthful of wine in her glass.

'Juliet, would you take Elsie back to her room?' he asked.

'Sure.'

'I'll make Elsie's tea and we'll get off to the allotment. Or would you like some tea now?' he asked.

'No, allotment sounds good,' Juliet said.

'The loo's the door opposite, if you need it,' he said. He began to tidy up the kitchen, packing the dishwasher with as much as he could. When the kettle boiled, he made a small pot of tea and put it on a tray with some milk. He carried it towards Elsie's room. As he neared the door, he could hear Elsie's voice.

'He doesn't mean to come across like that. He seems worried about you.'

He stopped outside the door so he could hear Juliet's response.

'I'm sure you're right, but he's no need to be.'

'Tea,' he said loudly and walked in.

'Thanks, Phil. You two get off now. I'll see you when you get back.' Elsie picked up her remote control and turned on the television.

Phil followed Juliet out of the room.

'Can I help tidy up?' she asked.

'No, you're fine. Let's go.'

They went out into the weak sunshine of the afternoon and walked quickly and silently along the road. Phil was trying to think of something to say but feared saying the wrong thing more than he disliked the silence.

'How long have you lived here?' she asked.

'A couple of years, now.'

'It's nice, the set-up you have with Elsie. Mutually beneficial.'

'I landed on my feet, certainly,' he said. 'Listen.' He put out his arm to stop her walking and turned to face her. 'I'm sorry if I'm making you feel bad. I'm not trying to criticise.'

She shook her head. 'Don't worry. I'm hardened to criticism.'

'But it's not criticism,' he said.

'I'm sure you don't mean it to be. But your incredulity at my answers to your questions makes it feel like that.'

'Sorry,' he said.

They walked on in silence.

'It's in here.' He turned into the allotment entrance and opened the gate. He walked to Elsie's plot and opened up the shed so he could get his tools. 'Let me tell you what we're growing.' He talked her through the different plants, sharing the successes and failures of the season.

'What's your favourite crop to grow?' she asked.

'Peas and beans are always good value and pretty reliable. Sprouts are great if you can protect them from the cabbage whites.'

'The what?' she asked.

'Butterflies. The fine netting has worked well so far this year. Courgettes are productive, so there are always way more of them than you need. But probably strawberries are my favourite. There's nothing quite like picking and eating a strawberry that's just ripe and has still got the warmth of the sun on it.'

'Sounds lovely. What can I help with?' she asked.

'I need a second pair of hands to help me tie up these plants. It's always fiddly, trying to hold the plant against the cane while you tie a knot in the string. Let me get the string out.'

'Ooh, can I look in your shed?' she asked.

He was surprised by her request. 'Sure.'

She went in and he followed her. She sat down on one of the stools, closed her eyes and breathed in the scent. 'Smells like my dad's shed. It's amazing how scent can evoke such strong emotions and memories.' She looked very young to him, even though she was only four years his junior.

'What comes to mind?' he asked.

'Dad mowing the grass, the smell of that. He'd make bird boxes for blue tits in his shed, with me watching. We'd see the adult birds taking food in and I'd make a wish that they'd fledge at a weekend so I could see them leave.'

'It sounds like you do have some happy memories of childhood.'

'Yes, but I can't think of the nice things without the sad ones coming to mind. Sometimes it's better not to remember anything,' she said.

'I wish I could give you some of the great memories I have from my youth.' He was taken by surprise when she stood up and kissed him, hard, as though she was in desperate need of human connection. He pulled away. 'Easy, Tiger.'

'Sorry,' she said.

'Don't be.' He put his arms around her and she rested her head on his chest. He held her in silence and felt her relax against him.

After a couple of minutes, she pulled away. 'Thank you.'

'Are you OK?' he asked.

'Never better. Where's this string then?'

He opened the cupboard behind her and took out the ball of gardeners' twine.

'Gosh, that's all very neat. Do you have OCD?' she asked.

He detected a hint of mockery. 'Not quite, but I do like things tidy. Mess makes my brain feel cluttered.'

'I'm like that at work.'

'What about outside work?' he asked.

'I don't have a life outside work, so you keep telling me.' Her tone was playful.

'True,' he said. 'Come on.'

They went back outside and spent fifteen minutes tying up the brassica plants more firmly. Jools kept stopping when she heard a blackbird singing. 'I really miss birdsong. Sometimes I hear it in one of the London parks, if it's quiet enough, but not often. It's such a peaceful sound.'

'I take it for granted,' he said. 'Would you like some veg to take home with you?' he asked.

'You're very kind, but I don't really cook. I'm always out.'

'Let's get back to the house then, shall we? Did you have a particular train in mind?'

'Last train goes just after midnight, but I can get an earlier one.'

'You really did give me your whole day.' He locked up the shed and they began walking back to the house. 'Tell me, what would you have done if you hadn't been here?'

'I'd have gone to Heathrow to pick up a package this morning, after a run. Then maybe taken a walk to one of the Sunday markets, Petticoat Lane or Camden. I love the green spaces, so I might have gone to St. James's Park or Kensington Gardens, where I'd have bought a coffee and maybe treated myself to a cake after a walk around. Headed back to the flat and done some yoga, listened to some music or read a book.'

'The package. Is that work?'

'Yes. It's a gift for Daniel's wife, but I said I was busy so he got someone else to pick it up.'

'Is no part of your home life off limits to the company?' he asked.

'It is if I say it is. Like today. If I can help though, I will, no matter what time.'

'As long as you're OK to say no,' he said.

She stopped walking. 'Yes.'

He turned around so he was facing her.

'Phil, is your desire to make me out to be a victim purely based on your dislike of Daniel? Or is it your under-estimation of the control I have over my life? Or, perhaps even a wish to make me feel like a victim so you can be my knight in shining armour?'

Her words shocked him. 'I hope it's none of those things. A clumsy attempt to make sure you're OK, I guess. I don't under-estimate you, nor think you're a victim. Maybe I do have a bit of a downer on your boss. But it's just concern, looking out for your fellow man. Or in this case, woman.' God, you're really messing this up, he said to himself. Everything he said seemed to strike the wrong note, to annoy her, or in her eyes belittle her. Why did he care? He wasn't desperate to be in a relationship. He wasn't lonely or missing having someone in his life. He found her attractive but he found plenty of women attractive.

They arrived back at the gate of Elsie's house.

'Phil, I know I keep sounding a bit abrasive. You seem to bring out the fighter in me.'

'Is it because I dare to challenge the premise that your life is great? And you've no-one who's close enough to you to say it? To point out that your lack of support from friends and family might have skewed your view on what's acceptable for your employer to demand from you?'

'No, it's because you seem to be coming from a position that your view, your way of thinking, is the right way, the only way. It's the certainty in your voice that pisses me off. The arrogance.'

Well. That put the tin hat on her wanting to see him again. He opened the front door. 'Do you want me to get your bag?'

'Do you want me to go?' She sounded surprised.

'I assumed you were so pissed off with me that you wouldn't want to hang around.'

'Quite the opposite. It's so odd for me to have to justify my situation, that I find it fascinating to hear your viewpoint. How can any of us learn about ourselves if we're not prepared to be challenged on our choices? Shall we have a cup of tea? I'm parched.' She went into the house.

He wasn't expecting that. As he walked into the house, he heard Juliet tap on Elsie's door and offer her a fresh pot of tea, before joining him in the kitchen, carrying Elsie's tea tray. 'Come on, Inspector, get the kettle on.'

As he waited for the water to boil, he admitted to himself that her "bring it on" attitude to his challenges made her even more interesting. Was she for real? Or was she just playing with him? 'I'll take you around upstairs if you want to see George's furniture. It is stunning.'

'Great,' she said. 'Is that where you sleep?'

'No, my room's next door.' He gestured with his head towards the hallway.

'Can I see that too?' she asked.

'Why?' he asked.

'Curiosity.' Their eyes danced a flirtatious jig.

'Be my guest,' he said. 'I'll just finish up here.'

He tidied up the rest of the lunch detritus and put on the dishwasher. He walked to his room with two mugs of tea and found her bent over in front of the bookcase in the corner. Her top had ridden up and he could see a birthmark on her back, vaguely in the shape of a butterfly. He felt an urge to crouch down and kiss it. 'Curiosity satisfied?' he asked.

She stood up. 'I'm certainly intrigued that there is a well-thumbed copy of *Fifty Shades* within your very eclectic book selection,' she said and a smile played on her lips. 'I shall resist the urge to ask you which part you enjoyed most. Come on, take me to Elsie's treasures.'

He left their tea on the hall table and the two of them walked up the curved staircase. Phil opened the door to the first room. The furniture was covered in dust sheets but he peeled off the nearest one to reveal an ornate Chinese cabinet with mother of pearl inlay.

'Wow! Is everything this beautiful?' she asked.

'It's certainly of this quality.'

Juliet turned to face him and put a hand on his arm. 'Do you think it might be time for our next practice?' She ran a finger over her lips.

He felt a wave of lust come over him and nodded. As their lips touched, he pulled her into him, running his hands up and down her back. He could feel his arousal building.

She continued her very thorough exploration of his lips and mouth.

His phone buzzed in his pocket.

'Ignore it,' she said and kissed him harder.

'I can't.' He took his phone from his back pocket and was disappointed to see it was Boyd, who would only be calling if there was something urgent. 'Sorry,' he said to her. 'Tom?'

'Sorry, Guv. We've got another victim.'

'Oh, shit.'

'Only this one didn't make it.'

'I'll be there as soon as I can.' He ended the call. 'It's work. Serious. I'm really sorry.'

The disappointment in her face was clear. 'Don't be. You have to do your job.'

'Do you want me to drop you at the train station?' he asked.

'Don't worry about me. Do you want me to do anything for Elsie before I go? Or would you like me to stay with her?' she asked.

'She should be fine,' he said.

'I'll go and say goodbye to her, then.' She gave him a brief but passionate kiss. 'Thanks for today.'

They went downstairs and he picked up his car keys from his room, allowing himself a private smile as his eyes flicked towards the bookcase. He heard Juliet's voice.

'Bye then, Elsie. See you soon.' Juliet came out and met him in the hallway.

He poked his head around Elsie's door. 'I'm afraid he's struck again, Else. I'll see you when I see you. Could be a while.'

'You go get the bastard, Phil.'

'I'll do my best.' He waved Juliet towards the door and they walked out into the dark of the early evening together. 'I'm going to drive past the station so it's no trouble to drop you.'

'OK, thanks.' She got into the car and they set off.

'I'm likely to be a bit busy with all this, but maybe when it settles down, we can get together again?' he asked.

'Sure.' She didn't sound as enthusiastic as he felt about the idea but maybe it was disappointment at the turn of events.

He pulled up at the back entrance to the station after a short drive. 'You look after yourself,' he said. 'Don't work too hard.'

'You too. Thank you for a lovely day. And for your honesty,' she said and smiled at him as she got out.

He watched her disappear from view into the station building as he waited for the vehicle in front to do a complicated manoeuvre into a tight space. He drove as quickly as he dared to the police station where he was based, trying to focus on the road instead of thinking about Juliet.

He walked into the incident room. The team was all there.

Tom was standing up, sharing details of the latest discovery. 'Boss,' Tom said.

'Carry on, I'll catch up,' Phil said. He sat down with the rest of his team. Memories of Juliet evaporated as he gave his full focus to the case.

Chapter 11 - Juliet

Juliet got on the next London-bound train, disappointed that her day with Phil had been cut short. Their kisses had made her ache to get closer with him. Her mind drifted and she was surprised by the announcement of the train's arrival into Waterloo station, twenty minutes later.

She was glad to have met Elsie and had agreed to visit her on her next free weekend to help clean her room. Juliet wasn't particularly good at cleaning. She was lucky her flat had a cleaner who came in once a week and did a thorough job of keeping the place pristine. Even luckier that the cleaner's responsibilities extended to changing the bedding and washing it too. All Juliet had to do was wash her own clothes and towels.

She wasn't sure of her motivation for helping Elsie. It was, if she was honest, partly a way of being able to spend time with Phil, but it was also because she realised how little of her life involved helping others. Elsie had been an interesting conversationalist and Juliet was keen to find out more about the infamous Allan as well as Elsie's husband, George.

She felt a little jealous of Phil and tried to imagine what her life would have been like, had her adoptive parents been like his. But that wasn't his fault. She wondered for the umpteenth time where her adoptive mother might be. Maybe she had a second family by now and lived with a good man. Someone like Phil, protective and supportive.

She stopped off on the way to the flat to pick up some popcorn. Once home, she switched her phone to silent and changed into an old t-shirt and leggings before laying out on the sofa under a blanket. She found one of the television shows Phil had mentioned and began to watch the first episode.

Three episodes in, she noticed her phone was flashing with an incoming call. It was Daniel. She ignored the call and carried on watching to the end of the programme. She pressed hold at the start of the next instalment and rang her boss. 'Daniel, what can I do for you?'

'Where are you?' Not so much as a hello.

'At the flat.'

'You said you were going out.' He sounded irked.

'I was out but now I'm back. What do you want?'

'Just to talk about the latest on Travis.'

'OK.' She went to sit at the table and switched on her laptop.

'You think he's playing away?' he asked.

'Well, the text messages are certainly pointing to that,' she said.

'And who is this woman?'

'His PA.'

'No imagination, these guys,' he said.

She sighed. She didn't want to be having this conversation. She wanted to carry on watching TV and eating popcorn. 'Anything else?'

'No, I'll catch up with you in the morning. You sound distracted.'

'I'm just not in work mode.'

He snorted. 'You go back to your popcorn and telly.' He hung up.

'Bastard,' she said to the empty room. He'd already checked up on her, could see from the security cameras that she was in front of the TV, even knew what she was eating. She got up and went to the cupboard in the hallway that held the fuse box. She'd asked an electrician who'd come to do some PAT testing to label the different fuses. She turned the camera fuses off and went back to the sofa. Curling up under the blanket, she pressed play on the remote control and ignored the flashing phone, knowing it would be Daniel moaning about the camera switch-off. Screw him, for once.

She woke up on the sofa just after 10pm. She grinned to herself, feeling like a naughty schoolgirl for playing hooky. But it was the weekend and she was entitled to time off and to her own privacy. Phil's comments had reminded her of that, though she wouldn't admit it to him.

She picked up her phone and looked to see how many calls she'd missed from Daniel. She was disappointed to see the last missed call was from Phil. She rang him back but there was no response. She sent him a picture of the abandoned blanket and empty popcorn packet with the message "Good advice x".

She was surprised to get an immediate answer.

"I am useful for some things".

"I can think of at least 3", she replied.

"Only 3? Wounded".

"OK. I can think of more than 3 but I only have proof of 3. So far".

"So far? Which 3?", he asked.

This was fun. "Cooking, gardening, flower arranging. Oh, make that 4. Forgot kissing. Looking forward to more research so I can add to the list x".

She stared at her phone, willing a further response from him, but she guessed, as the seconds turned to minutes, that he'd had to turn his attention back to his job. The news was full of the case he was working on. Gruesome details of the serial rapist's latest victim, whose death now made him a murderer, were on the BBC news website. Juliet shivered at the thought of it, imagining what it must have been like to be left to die, feeling the life seep out of you. Maybe the victim hadn't been aware, maybe she'd passed out from the shock of the initial assault. The news reports said the police hadn't entirely worked out where she'd met her killer. The girl was no saint, from the way the internet was describing her, though the press would only share the most lurid of details. There was no interest from their readers if she'd led a blameless life, it seemed. She'd been drunk from a night in the pub with friends then walked home. She had a standard route but could take a shortcut along the canal, but who'd do that in the dark on a moonless night? Perhaps the killer had offered her a lift.

Juliet tried to imagine herself in the same situation. Would she have taken a lift if a stranger offered? Maybe if it was late and she'd had a few drinks, she might have done. Though she'd not had a drink in a long time, she still had painful memories of poor judgement in the grip of alcohol. One experience of a man thinking her saying No was coquettish foreplay instead of her refusing sex. It had been easier to let him get on with it at the time, but the self-loathing she felt from not having stopped him had haunted her for a long while, till she decided to put it behind her. With so many painful childhood memories buried, she'd become adept at pushing thoughts of what had happened to her into the background, till they faded to almost nothing. Almost.

Chapter 12 - Daniel

Daniel sat back on the chair in his home office, reviewing the company's latest sales figures.

Patrick came in through the open door. 'The cameras in Jools's place have gone off.'

'What? I was just talking to her.' He chose the number from his recently called list but she didn't pick up. 'Bloody woman.'

'What is it?' asked Patrick.

'She's switched them off, I bet. She was in a funny mood.'

'I can check the footage.' Patrick disappeared and came back ten minutes later. 'Yes, she went and opened the cupboard in the hall just before they stopped transmitting, so chances are she's flicked the fuse.'

Daniel shook his head. 'She's no right.'

Patrick looked at him.

'What?' Daniel asked.

Patrick had been working for Daniel for nearly 20 years. They'd known each other since school and Daniel trusted Patrick more than anyone else, including Giselle. Coming from the same background and having a shared history meant Patrick understood Daniel's drive to succeed and his need for an iron grip on every aspect of his business empire. 'She's every right, Dan. It's not fair we can watch her every move.'

If anyone else had challenged him so openly, Daniel would have sacked them on the spot.

'You're lucky you've got away with it up to now,' Patrick said.

'I guess,' said Daniel. 'But she's changed. And that's starting to worry me.'

'You think PC Plod is affecting her judgement?'

Daniel gave the question serious thought. 'She's guarding her private life for the first time. She never did that when she was with that scrawny little runt. He never gave a shit what she was up to.'

'Our friend Cameron?'

Daniel nodded and they shared a smile. Cameron had been with Juliet for eighteen months when he'd let her down badly. Daniel had arranged for some swift justice to be meted out, though Cameron had no idea the violence towards him was anything to do with his dumping Juliet. Neither had Juliet.

'What are you going to do about Jools?' Patrick asked.

'Do you think I should do something?'

Patrick shrugged. 'It's not up to me.'

'Maybe some surveillance at weekends, just so we know where she's going.' He thought about how Juliet would react if she found out she was being followed. 'Actually, no. Not for the moment.'

'Anything else?'

'Yeah. That bastard Harvey. He refused to step down from the board on Friday, so I need something to make him think again.'

Patrick nodded. 'We've got plenty. He's been very foolish over the last couple of years with some young women and some even younger men. Don't imagine his church-going wife will take kindly to the photos.'

'Perfect. I don't mind writing him a fair reference but I want him out. I've lost faith in his business acumen.' Daniel was still angry that Harvey, with an arrogant sneer on his upper-class face, had refused to resign, looking at Daniel like he was dirt.

'You should never trust these posh fuckers,' Patrick said.

'I never bloody learn, do I? Still too easily impressed by the silver spoon. Think they're gonna have the integrity of Morse, just 'cos they went to Oxford.'

'You need to remember - Morse was just the Sweeney in disguise.'

They laughed.

'Make sure the next time I try and take one of them on, you remind me of that,' said Daniel.

'You got it. Any chance I can get off for a couple of hours? Got Jackie giving me an earful about one of the girls.'

'You don't have to ask, Pat. You need time for the family, you take it.'

'Cheers.' Pat left the room.

Daniel drifted off in thought. It was the one thing he envied Pat, having children. Giselle couldn't have kids and it had broken their hearts when they'd found out. She'd wanted to foster or adopt but he couldn't tolerate the idea. He realised his reaction was primeval but he couldn't bear the thought of the spawn of another man being brought into their home to be passed off as his own. Giselle had suggested surrogacy with an egg donor but he knew she struggled with the concept of a baby that was his but not hers. They'd taken a pact to enjoy life as a couple to its fullest. But it still ate away at him, all these years later, the niggling disappointment that his bloodline would end.

He wasn't sure if Giselle felt the same. They'd stopped talking to each other about it years ago. He had a feeling it must still loom large in her regular psychotherapy sessions. Maybe he should try and speak to her, broach the subject. Ask how she was doing when so many of her friends were becoming grandparents.

As if on cue, Giselle appeared at his office door. 'You look so sad, love. What is it?'

'Oh, nothing. What can I do for you?'

'Patrick told me he was going home and Mrs Jackson's away at her sister's, so I wondered if you fancied an early night.'

He smiled at her. 'You don't have to ask twice, you know that. I've never craved another woman like I crave you, Gizzy.' He took her hand and kissed it gently. 'You're my life.'

Chapter 13 - Elsie

Elsie felt she could only truly relax once she had the house to herself. She could shout at the telly, fart loudly and rant at the neighbour's dog barking without fear of being judged. She still found it hard to share her home, though Phil was about as nice as a companion could be. He managed to make her feel like she wasn't a burden.

Her friend Hilda had warned against letting a stranger live with her, fearing they would take advantage. Elsie felt she'd figured Phil out from the first day she'd met him. He was a family man who desperately missed his children. Elsie had met his boys when they'd last visited the UK. Of course, they weren't the slightest bit interested in her, which was as it should be. It was clear to her they were dotty about their dad and he was the same about them. They'd been polite, taking off their shoes in the hallway without being asked and shaking her hand solemnly when they were introduced. The ex-wife was bringing them up right, to Elsie's way of thinking, though Elsie was convinced Sal wanted Phil back, even though she'd had her new partner in tow. But nothing had come of it so far.

Elsie picked up the TV remote and began searching for something to watch. She caught sight of her hands, wrinkled with the beginnings of liver spots, and with nails that refused to grow without splitting. Getting older was miserable. Just when you'd sussed out how life worked, who you were and what you wanted from your time on earth, your body started to fail. She'd tried to ignore the arthritis, the same disease that had crippled her mother. Elsie had kept gardening for as long as she could, but she'd had to admit defeat a couple of years back. At least she could still wash and dress herself. She shuddered at the thought of losing the ability to look after her personal hygiene. Phil certainly couldn't be asked for that type of assistance. And she knew, if she needed to, she could sell the furniture upstairs to pay for home help, but she didn't want to. Having those pieces in the house made George's presence real. She could imagine him touching the pieces, running his fingers over the fine wood or silky veneer with as gentle a touch as he'd used on her. She lost herself in the moment.

She came back into the room when her mobile bleeped a reminder to take her medication. It was just out of reach, just as she liked it to be, so she was forced to get up and retrieve it. She knew it would be too easy to sit in her chair all day. Even if she couldn't garden, she could still get out to see her friends, make herself a cuppa or cook a boiled egg.

As she picked up her pill bottle, she noticed Juliet's business card. She was becoming a frequent feature in Phil's life, from what he'd said the last time he'd come back to the house. Since Juliet's first visit, when she'd come to church and then for Sunday lunch, Phil had been completely focused on his latest case, and had only come back to the house twice, but he seemed to have managed to make time for Juliet. Stolen moments, he'd called them, mentioning a late night catch-up over a takeaway coffee and an early morning rendezvous when Juliet was out running. It pleased Elsie to see Phil excited at the prospect of spending time with Juliet, who'd seemed a good match for him, to Elsie's way of thinking. She was feisty and not afraid to speak her mind. Juliet had texted to say she'd try and come over the following weekend, but Elsie only half-expected her to turn up, thinking Juliet might have only offered so Phil would think well of her. Phil was clearly keen but Elsie didn't think he was foolish enough to have his head turned by a pretty face. At least seeing Juliet might stop him running back to his ex.

Early on the following Saturday morning, Elsie's mobile gave a sharp beep.

"Hi Elsie, just on my way over to you. Let me know if you want me to pick up any shopping. Juliet x".

Elsie was pleasantly surprised. "No thanks, lovey. See you soon."

Twenty minutes later, the doorbell rang and Elsie slowly made her way to open it.

Juliet was smiling on the doorstep. 'Hi, hope I'm not too early.'

'Not at all. Can't stop myself waking up at 5am after a lifetime of getting up for work.'

Juliet was holding a bunch of flowers. 'I bought these for you. Thought they'd look pretty in the hallway.'

'That's kind of you.' They looked as though they were from a florist, rather than a garage forecourt.

'Something about the smell of fresh flowers, isn't there? Makes you feel good,' said Juliet.

'I suppose you're right. Though George once had a fling with a florist, so maybe my view's a bit tainted.'

'Did he? You'll have to tell me all about it. I'm such a nosey parker. I love to hear tales of life.'

They walked into Elsie's room. Juliet was carrying a large plastic bag from which she produced dusters, furniture polish and rubber gloves. 'I said I'd dust around a bit, make sure your ornaments weren't getting too grimy. Shall I make a start or do you want me to make a cup of tea?'

'You go ahead, love. I'll put the kettle on for us.'

'Great. I must warn you though, I'm not very good. But I'll do my best.'

Elsie left Juliet opening a new packet of rubber gloves and went to put the kettle on. It was nice she'd not questioned Elsie's ability to carry out the task alone. Some of the well-meaning types from the council spoke to her as though she was a deaf idiot. She made the tea and carried a mug for Juliet into her room before going back for her own. Using a stick meant she had to do everything one-handed.

She sat down and watched Juliet rearranging the dust. 'If you want a bit of advice, love, either dampen that cloth or use some furniture polish on it. That way you'll catch the dust, not just move it around.'

'Sorry. I said I was rubbish. But I can learn.'

'How come you don't know? Did your mother never teach you?' Elsie asked.

Juliet explained about her upbringing.

'Have I put my foot in it?'

'Course not. It is what it is.' Juliet sprayed her cloth with Mr Sheen and starting wiping down the mantelpiece again.

'And how do you keep your own place tidy?'

'There's a cleaner,' said Juliet.

'You landed on your feet,' said Elsie.

'I did, though the benefits are cancelled out by the negatives. It's not my place. I have to entertain in it and the bloody cameras drive me up the wall.'

Elsie frowned. 'Cameras? What, inside?'

Juliet blushed. 'Sorry. I shouldn't have said that. Please don't mention it to Phil.' She locked eyes with Elsie to emphasise the plea.

'I won't. Us ladies have to stick together. Talking of which, I gather you've seen him since you were last here.'

Juliet smiled. 'Yes, quite a few times. It's been lovely. He gets in touch if he has a few spare moments. Mostly later in the evening, so we've met up for a quick coffee in the local McDonald's. We can't always get together but even when it's just a phone call, it's been nice. He mentioned a few days back that he doesn't start work till 7am but wakes up much earlier, so I changed my morning running route to go past his station. Did that a couple of times this week and we had five minutes to chat.'

'Just a chat?' Elsie asked.

'Maybe the odd kiss, too.'

'It's not just him that's smitten, then?' Elsie asked.

'No comment.'

Elsie frowned. 'Why d'you say that?'

'I don't want to jinx it, I guess. If I think about it, think about him, I feel all bubbly inside. That's not me at all. It's a bit scary.'

'Just enjoy it, lovey. Nothing like that first flush of love, is there?' Elsie asked.

'I'm not sure I really know. It's all a bit alien to me. But he's obviously mentioned to you that he's seen me. How does he sound about it all?'

'He sounds happy, probably happier than I've heard him in a long time, so I'm glad you're feeling the same. He doesn't deserve to be messed about. As for it all being odd for you, I'd say don't think about it too much. I've always thought early love makes you feel like you're standing in sunshine. Why don't you just close your eyes and bask in it?'

Juliet smiled. 'Thanks. I will.'

'Now, I'm wondering if I can ask you to help me with some purchases? Phil's very good, but I don't want to embarrass him by asking him to order some underwear for me.'

'I'm sure he wouldn't mind but I'd be glad to. Are you happy shopping online? Or would you rather go shopping?'

'I used to love shopping up West. Walking along Oxford Street, going in all the department stores. But that's a thing of the past.'

'Why? We could go up there now. Car's outside. We could be there in an hour.'

Elsie opened her mouth to object but could think of no reason why not. Her world had shrunk in the last three years and here was an opportunity to go into town, to her favourite shops. 'But, are you sure? Don't you have plans later?'

'I'm busy tomorrow afternoon but free till then. In fact, why don't you pack an overnight bag? Come and stay at the flat. The view of the river at night is stunning. We can go out for a meal somewhere.'

Elsie felt a smile breaking out. 'Could we go to Luigi's? It's just off the Strand. That's where George proposed.'

'Luigi's it is. Come on, girl, let's get you packed and ready for a capital adventure.'

Elsie felt like a giddy schoolgirl. Juliet pulled a small overnight bag from under the bed and put it on a chair so Elsie could pack her clothes and toiletries. Juliet focused on her phone. 'OK, I've booked us into Luigi's for 7:15pm. They should be free of the pre-theatre diners by then.'

'Smashing,' Elsie said.

FAKING IT

They walked out into the unseasonably cool morning and Juliet helped Elsie into the car. Elsie sat back as Juliet navigated the route, enjoying the views as they got closer to her beloved London. Juliet drove more quickly than Phil but with a confidence that put Elsie at ease. Soft music played in the background, she suspected chosen with her in mind, as Frank Sinatra, Dean Martin and Connie Francis crooned a soundtrack to their journey. Elsie asked Juliet about her childhood and was struck by the bleakness of her adolescence. 'So, you're all alone in the world?'

'I prefer to think of it as being by myself,' she answered, as she reached out of the window to take a ticket from the car park machine.

As they walked out of the car park, Elsie realised how close they were to Oxford Street. They walked the short distance to John Lewis, where Elsie was keen to look in the lingerie department. Not finding what she wanted, Elsie worked her way slowly down the street, chatting to Juliet as though they'd known each other for years. They reached Selfridges and Elsie felt herself taking an anticipatory deep breath. As she walked in through the revolving doors, she felt a tingle of excitement, the same feeling she'd had when she'd first visited the shop as a teenager. The heady scents of the perfume counter assailed her, along with the warmth and wonder of it all. There was nowhere like London for making you feel alive.

After a successful purchase of Elsie's preferred underwear, Juliet took her into Dolly's, one of the in-store cafés. They had tea for two with a selection of cakes to keep them going till dinner.

As Elsie took a forkful from a mini-Victoria sponge that was the perfect combination of light sponge, densely delicious buttercream and sweet raspberry jam, she felt a wave of affection for the stranger sitting opposite her. 'This is so kind of you.'

'My pleasure. I'm used to showing people around London, but it's lovely to do it for someone who loves this city as much as I do,' said Juliet.

'It gets in your blood, doesn't it? Oh, balls, that's my phone.' She took the call. 'Hello, lovey.' She put her hand over the phone. 'It's Phil,' she mouthed at Juliet.

'Hey, Else, I've just come back to the house to pick up some stuff. Just checking you're OK, seeing as you're not about.'

'I'm fine,' she said.

'Where are you?' he asked.

'Oxford Street, shopping.'

'Oh, right. Who are you with?' he asked.

'Juliet.' Elsie smiled.

'What, my Juliet?' he asked.

'Ooh, is she *your* Juliet now?' Elsie winked at Juliet.

'Figure of speech. OK. Well, that's nice,' he said.

'It's bloody marvellous. We're in a café in Selfridges and we're off to Luigi's later. And I'm staying at her place on the river tonight.'

'Well, you enjoy yourself on your ladies' day out.' He sounded bemused.

'Bye, lovey.' She ended the call. 'Well, that surprised him,' she said.

Juliet grinned. 'It's good to keep men on their toes. I'll send him a message. "Am I *your* Juliet??" Oh, he's typing, Else. He's said "In your dreams, Missy. At least I hope so" and put a winking face. I'll send him back a kiss emoji.'

As they sat in the café finishing their tea, Elsie wondered again if Juliet was only paying her attention to get closer to Phil, but it didn't ring true. It sounded as though Juliet was managing to get close to Phil without any assistance required. And Juliet did seem to be having a nice time today. Or maybe she was just good at pretending.

They left the café with a doggy box of leftover cakes and walked back to the car, visiting more shops en route. Juliet drove them speedily across the river and into the underground car park of her apartment complex. She had the same patience as Phil, getting Elsie out of the car and into the lift, like there was all the time in the world. The lift went silently to the top floor and Elsie could see there was only one other flat on that level.

Juliet ushered her in. 'Make yourself comfortable.'

Elsie took off her coat and walked towards the windows. 'What a view.'

'It's great, isn't it? I look at it every morning and remind myself how lucky I am. Too easy to forget. Shall I put the kettle on? Or would you like something stronger?'

Elsie smiled to herself. 'I'd love a whisky and soda.'

Juliet opened a wooden inlaid cabinet, that was in pride of place on the main wall, to reveal a full array of spirits, liqueurs and mixers. 'Here you go.' Juliet poured herself a tonic. 'Cheers.'

They touched their glasses against each other. Elsie took a sip.' Ooh, that's just right. You don't drink at all, do you?'

'No. Life's easier that way.' Juliet didn't seem to want to elucidate.

Elsie's phone pinged in her handbag. 'Who's that?' She pulled it out of the Mulberry knock-off she'd bought many years ago in Petticoat Lane. 'Oh, bloody hell.'

'What is it?'

'Phil's reminded me about taking my tablets. But I've left 'em behind, on the bloomin' bedside table.'

'When do you need them?' asked Juliet.

'Should take 'em tonight, before bed.'

'No problem. I can either drop you back after dinner or I can go and pick them up now so you can stay overnight. Don't mind which.'

'You're very...what's the word? Accommodating? Flexible?' Elsie said.

'You make that sound like a bad thing,' said Juliet.

'It must be wearying for you.'

Juliet's eyes narrowed as though she was thinking. 'It's habit. Constantly looking for the best options or solutions for the people I'm with. I suppose it's hard to switch it off.'

'As long as you don't focus too much on everyone else's pleasure and ignore your own.'

Juliet didn't respond and her gaze dropped to the floor.

Elsie wondered if she'd hit a nerve. 'I don't mind which you do. You're the one with commitments. I'm free as a bird.'

'Let me find out what Phil's doing.' Juliet tapped her phone and turned to look out of the window. 'Hi, are you at the house? OK, I'll go there to pick up Elsie's tablets. Do you? Yes, that'll help. Thanks.' She turned back to face Elsie. 'He's got some tablets in his car, apparently, for emergencies, so he's going to leave them at the front desk of the police station. It'll be quicker for me to get there than the house. I'll go after dinner.'

'He's a good lad. You too. Well, not a lad. You're a kind girl.'

Elsie wondered, not for the first time, if she'd had a daughter, whether she'd have been like Juliet. Now she was getting older, Elsie realised that having a child would have been nice. But there was no point in living in What If Land.

Chapter 14 - Juliet

Juliet arrived at the car park of the police station and pulled into the nearest vacant space. It was the designated slot for DCS Pidgeon, according to the sign. She walked quickly to the front entrance.

A woman was berating the man behind the desk. 'But Sergeant, you know Del, he's a good lad, really. Can't you let him out?'

The Sergeant looked weary. 'I know he's not a bad lad but it's out of my hands. He's being charged this time. No more cautions.'

The woman let off a series of expletives and pushed past Juliet as she left. The Sergeant shook his head then looked at Juliet warily, as though trying to weigh up whether she was going to be trouble. 'Can I help you?'

She smiled. 'Hi, I'm hoping something's been left for me to pick up.'

He frowned. 'Are you a solicitor?'

'No. Phil Haywood, DI Haywood, said he'd leave something for me.'

The policeman's eyes lit up in recognition. 'Wait there, Miss.' He picked up the phone next to him and dialled a number. 'It's Dougie. Yes. Now.' He replaced the receiver. 'He'll be here shortly.'

'Thank you.' Juliet felt a wave of pleasure at the thought of Phil coming to see her. When he'd said he'd leave the tablets at the front desk, she'd assumed he'd be too busy to see her.

The side door opened and he appeared. 'Hi Jools.'

'Hey. Hope I'm not dragging you away.'

He ushered her onto the visitors' bench. 'It's good to have a break. How's your day been?' he asked.

She smiled. 'It's been lovely. We've just had a meal at Luigi's. Apparently, George proposed to Elsie there, so she was telling me all about him.'

'It's very kind of you, taking her out.'

'She's an interesting person. Have you got the tablets?'

'Yeah.' He fished out a pill bottle from his pocket and handed it over to her.

'What are these for?' she asked.

'Her heart condition.'

'She's not going to keel over on me, is she?' Juliet asked.

'Not as long as she takes these.' He looked at his watch. 'As long as she has one before midnight, she'll be fine.'

'I better get back, then.' She stood up and looked at the Sergeant. 'Thank you.'

The Sergeant nodded and smiled.

'I'll see you to your car,' Phil said.

A man was coming in as they reached the door.

'Alright, Tom?' Phil seemed thrown by his colleague not moving out of their way. 'Tom, this is Jools, Juliet. Jools, this is Tom, DS Boyd.'

'Nice to meet you, Tom,' she said and smiled as she shook his proffered hand.

He grinned back and moved out of the way. 'Likewise.'

Phil gestured with his head for Juliet to go through the door.

She walked out into the chill of the night to her car.

'Interesting choice of parking space,' he said.

'I figured DCS Pidgeon will be anywhere but here at this time of night,' she said.

'No comment,' he said.

'Well, I'll see you sometime,' she said. 'Hopefully for longer than our usual fifteen minutes.'

'Yeah, fingers crossed we'll have a real breakthrough soon in this case. We've had a few false dawns.'

'Good luck with it.' She moved towards him in the hope he'd show her some intimacy and was rewarded with a long, slow kiss. 'Thank you.' She noticed his gaze move to a window a few floors up and could see a number of people looking out of the window. 'Was the kiss for my benefit or theirs?' she asked.

'It was entirely for mine, I confess and slightly against my better judgement, given the audience,' he said.

'Well, let's make it worth their while.' She pulled him back towards her and kissed him with a passion she'd not felt for a long time. 'You look after yourself, DI Haywood.'

'Sorry I can't spend more time with you.'

'No problem. Don't work too hard.' She opened the driver's door and slid into her seat. She put the window down to hear what he was saying.

'Drive carefully, Jools.'

She pulled away, waving at him then up towards the window at his colleagues. It was always so nice to see him. She admitted to herself she was falling for this man, feeling like an insect caught in a pitcher plant. Wanting more nectar, even though she knew she was close to being too far down to turn back. A part of her didn't want to escape. The rest was scared. What if Elsie was wrong and Phil didn't feel the same way about her?

She arrived back in her apartment to find Elsie relaxed in front of the television, where she'd left her watching one of her favourite movies,

Miracle on 34th Street, which Juliet had managed to find for her online. As Juliet walked into the main room, the little girl was shouting "Stop, Uncle Fred, stop!" and Juliet watched in silence as the romantic leads embraced. As the end credits rolled, Juliet could see Elsie was wiping away a tear.

'Hallo, lovey. Gets me every time, that one,' Elsie said.

Juliet passed her the tablet bottle.

'Thank you. Did you see Phil?' She struggled to open the bottle.

'Yes, but only for a few minutes. Let me.' Juliet twisted the top with ease and handed both the lid and bottle back. 'Do you want some water?'

Elsie shook her head. 'Whisky will be fine.' She swallowed the tablet with the last of her drink. 'Oh, there was a visitor.'

Juliet felt a shiver of discomfort. 'A visitor?'

'Somebody called Patrick. Said he worked for Daniel.'

'What did he want?'

'I'm not really sure. Said he wanted to speak to you but didn't seem fussed that you weren't here. Left a box on your bed.'

'Pat works for Daniel as a chauffeur, gopher, whatever,' Juliet explained. 'They were at school together.'

'What's in the box, then?' Elsie asked.

'No idea. Might be something to do with the guy I'm picking up tomorrow. Did Pat ask who you were?'

'He did. I said I was a distant relative.'

'OK.' Juliet wondered why Pat hadn't called her, either before his trip or after he'd discovered Elsie in the flat. She was curious about the box but didn't want to open it in front of Elsie.

'When you entertain these people, what do you have to do?' Elsie asked, catching Juliet by surprise.

'Just make them feel special, spoiled. You know what guys are like. Want to feel important, like to be flattered.'

'Do you have to…you know?' Elsie raised her eyebrows.

'No, I don't.' Juliet felt herself blushing.

'Then what makes you uncomfortable when I ask about it?'

Was it that obvious? Juliet weighed up the level of honesty to share. 'I suppose it's what you'd call industrial espionage.'

'Do you slip 'em a Mickey Finn and rifle through their pockets?'

'What's a Mickey Finn?' Juliet put the name into Google on her phone. A Mickey Finn was exactly what she slipped them, but was it wise to admit it? 'Something like that, but please don't tell Phil. Don't think he'd approve, officially or unofficially.'

'I'm sure he wouldn't but he doesn't understand what women have to do to get on in this world,' Elsie said.

Juliet smiled. 'Thanks. I appreciate the solidarity.'

'So does it bother you, what you do then?'

Juliet shrugged. 'It never used to but I'm not sure I ever really thought about it. Now I have, I'm wishing I could skip that part of my job. In reality, I think I'd have to leave if I didn't want to be a part of it.'

'Would that be so bad?' Elsie asked.

Juliet shrugged. 'It'd be hard to give up this place. And Daniel's been really good to me. But the actual job, I could do that anywhere, for anyone. I don't know how Daniel would feel about me leaving.'

'Does that matter?' Elsie asked.

'Like I said, Daniel's been good to me, so I wouldn't want to let him down.'

'Might he turn nasty?' Elsie asked.

'I don't think so.' Juliet wasn't absolutely sure. Daniel was very passionate about loyalty in his team, so he might see her leaving as a betrayal of sorts. 'Do you want another drink, Else?'

'No thanks, love. Should probably get to bed now. You've a busy day tomorrow.'

Juliet made sure Elsie was settled in the guest room before she went to her own room. She hoped her next visitor was going to behave. As far as she knew, it was just a babysitting job, with no need of Mickey Finns, as Elsie called them. Daniel now had other people to call on for that, although Juliet knew she hadn't entirely escaped from being a part of it. Daniel's latest suggestion of her hiding in the guest room until the drugs took effect hadn't been tested yet and she hoped he'd forget about it.

She opened the box Pat had delivered and found a fresh batch of the tablets used to drug the clients. She put them in the safe that was hidden in the corner of the bedroom with the rest of the supplies.

Juliet looked at the clock for what felt like the hundredth time. It was 4:23am. She would not be on good form in the morning. She had to take Elsie home before picking up her latest guest from the airport. He was coming in on a short-haul flight so wouldn't be tired. He would want a full London tour, knowing her luck, rather than a snooze in his hotel. She pushed herself to go to sleep but by 6:30am, gave up trying. She showered, dried her hair and put on make-up that she hoped would hide the weariness she felt.

Elsie was already in the sitting room when Juliet came through. 'Morning, lovey. You alright? You look a bit flat.'

'I'm really tired. Didn't have a good night.'

'Why's that?'

She shrugged. 'Not sure.'

'I've managed to strip the bed, given you said you had a visitor.'

'That's kind of you, but he's not staying. I entertain here but I won't have them sleeping here.'

Elsie nodded. 'Good decision.'

'Can I get you some breakfast? A cup of tea and some cereal or toast? I have some frozen Danish pastries I can bake.'

'Would you mind if we went back now? I'd just like to, well, I can't easily use your shower. I need grab rails.'

'Oh, Else, I'm sorry. I should have thought.'

'Why should you? I'm not your normal type of visitor.'

'I'd much rather have you here than anyone else. But if that's what you want, that's fine. I'll just get my bag.' She went to her room and picked up her handbag. It would be good to drop Elsie off this early, as she might get time for a sleep before the airport run. Assuming she could sleep, with this hard-to-pinpoint cloud of gloom hanging over her.

As they pulled out of the apartment car park, Juliet asked Elsie about her career and what it entailed. 'You said you worked for the Government, but you didn't elaborate.' She took a sideways glance at Elsie.

Elsie looked directly at her. 'I suppose you could say it was similar to what you do, so I have sympathy for your position, though I was working for the country, not a private firm.'

'How did you get the job?' Juliet asked.

'I was approached. I'd done well at school, had a knack of problem-solving, cryptic crosswords and the like, that got noticed by my English teacher. Her husband worked for the Government and she mentioned me to him. Even then, ten years after the end of the war, there was so much to do they recruited a lot of people to keep an eye on potential enemies of the state. I was just one of many.'

Juliet was fascinated to hear more of the detail. She negotiated a busy roundabout before continuing the conversation. 'But what you were doing, that's a whole different ballgame. I mean, that's serious stuff, serious people you were dealing with. Guns and real danger, I'm guessing.'

In her peripheral vision, she could see Elsie shaking her head.

'I'd say you're living a far more dangerous life than me, lovey. You're alone with strangers, male strangers who are bigger and stronger than you. Who might not want to play along with the game you've planned. Might not react to the drugs in a predictable way. Might realise what's being done to them and take against it. Even if they don't suss it out at the time, what if they work it out afterwards? It's not your boss they'll take it out on, is it?'

And there it was. A description of the black cloud hanging over Juliet that had kept her awake last night. She'd never articulated her working activities to anyone before and knew she'd never acknowledged to herself the reality of her situation.

'And of course, lovey, there's a small matter of the illegality of it all. I was working for the Government, who sanctioned my actions. You don't have that luxury.'

Juliet pulled up at a pedestrian crossing. She looked across at Elsie as an elderly man dragged an overweight pug over the crossing. 'How much do you think Phil knows about what I do?'

'Hardly anything at the moment. But he's smart, so it won't take him forever to work it out. You'll have to do one of two things. Stop doing it or stop seeing him.'

Juliet thought about Elsie's words as she drove the rest of the way back. As she pulled up at the house, she turned to Elsie. 'It's not that simple, is it? Even if I stop seeing Phil, he could still investigate me. In fact, me saying I don't want to see him might make him all the more determined to go after Daniel and me. Though he might not be bothered either way.'

'Come on, lovey, no false modesty. All this effort he's putting in to getting time with you. You know he likes you. How much do you like him? Truthfully?'

'I like him a lot. It makes me smile to think of him. I guess what's hard is separating the personal and the professional. However much he might like me, my proximity to Daniel and…the other stuff, what I do, well, he won't like that at all, will he?'

She switched off the engine and got out of the car so she could help Elsie to the door. She needed to get home and think. And sleep. She realised she wasn't up to entertaining a guest today and would ring Pat to see if she could negotiate a break from duty, once she'd got Elsie settled.

Phil opened the door as they walked up the path. His car wasn't in its usual spot, so Juliet was taken by surprise.

'Hey,' Juliet said and smiled.

He nodded at Juliet. 'Hallo Else,' he said. 'Just came to pick something up. You got a minute?' He helped Elsie to her room, barely acknowledging Juliet's presence.

Juliet hovered in the hall. Something was up. Perhaps there'd been another murder victim. She could hear talking but couldn't make out the conversation. When Phil came out, he didn't make eye contact with her. 'I'll just say goodbye to Elsie then I must go,' she said.

He nodded at her but said nothing. His face had an odd expression she couldn't read.

She knocked on Elsic's open door. 'Else, I need to go.'

Elsie beckoned her in. 'Thanks for a wonderful day, lovey. It was very good of you to give up your time for me.'

'Glad to do it, I had fun. Is he alright?'

Elsie shrugged.

'OK, well, might see you next weekend.'

Elsie took her hand and squeezed it. 'Maybe. You take care of yourself, alright?'

Her expression of concern made Juliet shiver. She walked out of the room and saw Phil's outline through the front door.

She went outside and he looked up.

'Jools.' He didn't quite meet her gaze. 'I need to speak to you.'

'What's up?'

'I don't want you to think I've not enjoyed spending time with you, but I don't think we should see each other anymore.'

She felt like she'd been punched in the stomach. 'What?' She tried to mask the look of horror that she knew had crossed her face. 'Right. OK.' She heard herself gulp as a way of fighting the emotion and forced herself to smile. 'Well, it's not like it was serious, is it?' She heard her voice crack. 'I mean, it's hardly been any time at all. No problem.' She stepped backwards and her legs wobbled.

'Are you OK?' he asked.

'Fine.' She turned and half-ran to her car and started it up, dragging on her seatbelt so she could pull away as quickly as possible. She drove around the corner and stopped in the first parking space she could find. Tears were running down her cheeks. She felt winded by the sucker punch of his rejection. He'd seemed so flirtatious, so attentive, so interested. All the effort he'd put in to capturing those stolen moments and kisses, and now this. What had happened? It made no sense. She cried for a few minutes, blinded by tears and by the shock of his announcement.

It took her a few minutes to stop sobbing and be able to drive. She wasn't sure where to go. She drove aimlessly, heading towards London, eventually deciding to go to Richmond Park. She needed time to think, to marshal her thoughts so she could work out if she was upset by the rejection itself or by the thought of not dating Phil. But first, she had to get out of her work duties for the day. She was in no fit state to entertain anyone.

Chapter 15 – Daniel

'She said what?' Daniel shouted down the phone at Pat.

'Said could I pick up Michel from the airport. Something about having had a rough night. She sounded upset.'

'I'll talk to her.' Daniel stabbed at the screen of his mobile to call her. 'What's going on, Jools?'

'Morning, Daniel. I hardly got any sleep and I'm struggling a bit now. I know cultivating the relationship with Michel is important to you, so I was seeing if I could get someone else to look after him.'

Daniel felt a knot of annoyance in his stomach. 'Jools, if you're not up to doing your job, I'll get someone else to do it. Can you get out of the flat? Can't have you there if you're poorly. Leave the keys at the front desk.'

'OK. I'll find somewhere else to sleep and recover.'

He didn't care that she sounded pissed off with him. 'Be out of there by 12. I'll see if that girl Megan can do it. She's been reliable in the past. I'll ring her now.' He didn't give her a chance to respond before he ended the call. He rang Pat back. 'Don't worry about doing the airport pick-up. Gonna get someone else to stand in for Jools. Do you have the number of that Welsh girl who helped us out a few months back?'

'Megan? Let me call her and sort it.'

'Jools'll get the flat ready and be out by 12.'

'Is she OK with that?' Pat asked.

'I couldn't give a flying fuck. She can go sleep off her hangover or shagover or whatever it is somewhere else.'

'Understood. Let me check with Meg. There are some other people I can try if not.'

'They need to be classy. This one's a pretentious prick.'

'Leave it with me, Dan. I'll call you back.'

Pat rang him back after ten minutes. 'Meg'll be at the airport to meet him. She was delighted to hear from us. Keen to do more work for you, she said.'

Daniel allowed himself a smile, thinking how much he'd like to let Megan do more for him. But he knew he had to curb himself. Giselle wouldn't let him shit on his own doorstep. His wife had, in the past, found him some high-end companions to act out his fantasies but it was very much on the basis of her granting him a free pass with a woman of her choice. Giselle took pleasure from the idea of controlling his access to women, she'd said, and he was happy with the arrangement. It stopped things getting messy if Giselle was procuring them. There was no needy voice at the end of the phone that way, someone begging him to leave his wife and have a relationship with them instead. He needed Giselle more than he would ever let on, even to her. She was the bedrock of his life, the constant factor through it all, the star in the dark sky that led him to calmer seas.

He sought her out to talk about Juliet. He found her in the warmest part of the house, where the morning sunshine was streaming in. She was sitting at the table, the light catching her hair, revealing coppery tones amongst the mainly chestnut locks. Her hair was thick and lustrous, just like in one of their own TV ads. She was peering at the newspaper, in a manner that told him she should be wearing her reading glasses. She didn't like to admit she needed them. He'd had to nag her to go to the opticians and had offered to pay for laser surgery but she was even less keen on that than the thought of wearing glasses. He thought she looked very sexy in glasses. The dark frames played into his fantasy of the strait-laced secretary who would let her hair down and become a sexual animal, just for him.

'You got a minute, Gizzy?' he asked.

She looked up and smiled. 'Of course, my love.'

He explained about Juliet and his annoyance at her request. 'Am I being unreasonable?'

'No. I mean, it depends on why she had a rough night. If she's genuinely ill, you asking her to get out of her flat…'

'My flat,' he corrected.

'It is her home, Dan, whatever the ownership status. Where will she go if she's ill? You said she didn't have any friends.'

He gave the question some serious thought but said nothing.

'Like I said, depends on what's wrong with her. If she just got pissed, that's her own bloody look out,' she said.

'She never drinks. And she was entertaining an old woman last night. Pat saw her, reckons she's late 70s, early 80s maybe?'

'Means nothing. My mum could drink anyone under the table. Who is this woman? Family?'

'Jools has always said she doesn't have family. Pat said a family friend, distant relative. Something like that.'

'How does he know?' Giselle asked.

'He dropped a package off at the flat last night. The old biddy was there on her own. Jools had gone on a mercy dash to pick up her heart pills or something.'

'Talk to Jools tomorrow. Find out what the situation really is. You'll know what to do. You always do.'

Daniel was due to meet Michel early on Monday about a distribution deal and spent most of Sunday preparing for the negotiations. Pat texted to confirm Megan had done the airport pick-up and Michel was safely in his hotel, where Megan would pick him up later for a tour around London.

Pat texted him a second time. "Forgot to confirm. That package was delivered as requested yesterday. The special photos."

Daniel smiled to himself. That should have the desired effect.

He was glad to sit down that evening with Giselle for a proper roast dinner. It was a rarity that they were both around and free on a Sunday evening. Their housekeeper, Mrs Jackson, had cooked roast beef, roast potatoes, Yorkshire pudding and roasted vegetables with a thick, tasty gravy. Giselle said no to dessert but Daniel treated himself, knowing he would have raging indigestion that would keep him awake but deciding it was worth it at the sight of the steaming sponge pudding, gleaming with a crown of sticky golden syrup. As he poured a puddle of hot custard around the edge of a generous slice of the fluffy sponge, he was taken back to his childhood. There was never a lot of money, but puddings were cheap to make and his mum had been adept at producing them, week in, week out, much to Daniel's and his father's pleasure. Daniel closed his eyes for a moment and breathed in the scent of artificial vanilla in the custard and the honeycomb-like aroma from the hot golden syrup. For a moment, he was transported back to the small dining table tucked against the kitchen wall where he and his parents had eaten every meal. The anticipation of the pleasure from the first mouthful was fulfilled by the light sponge, the syrup that was sweet but not cloying and the custard that was creamy and thick.

Giselle smiled, seemingly pleased he was enjoying the treat.

'You sure you don't want some, Gizzy?'

'No. Too much sugar does my insides no good.'

'It is glorious.' He took another spoonful then another and suddenly the plate was empty and he was scraping at the tiny morsels left clinging to the bowl. He could hear his mum telling him to leave the pattern on the plate as he put down the spoon. He had a rare moment of feeling both physically and mentally replete.

He sat back and smiled as he balled up his napkin and put it on the table. In that moment of peace, Juliet's face came to mind. It was both pleasurable and frustrating as he began to think about how he would tackle this latest issue with her. He grimaced as he felt the first sign of indigestion coming on.

Chapter 16 – Phil

Phil arrived home from work a few days after Elsie's trip to London, having spent three nights sleeping at his desk while the case was at its height. He went to check in on Elsie.

'You didn't say whether you went through with it.' Elsie looked directly at him and he felt uncomfortable.

'With what?' he asked, despite knowing what she was talking about.

'Giving Juliet the elbow. When she dropped me off.'

He sat down opposite her. 'Yeah, I told her I didn't think we should see each other anymore.'

'You never said exactly why. Not that you owe me an explanation, but I'm curious.'

'Sorry. I know you get on with her,' he said.

'That's hardly the point,' she said. 'What made you do that? You seemed to be getting on so well. All those little trysts you were telling me about. You seemed to be enjoying yourself.'

'I just realised she was probably only seeing me to feed me lies about Cross. I felt like she was playing the part of "girlfriend". Rarely showed any emotion towards me, at least, none that I believed. Kisses, but no vulnerability. She wouldn't let me in, didn't trust me. I felt like I was getting a curated version of her.'

Elsie cocked her head to one side. 'You'd barely starting courting. Did you let her in? Show her the un-curated you?'

He thought for a while, aware of the clock on the mantelpiece, ticking to mark the time he was taking to answer. 'I've shared personal stuff with her, about my adoption, my marriage, my kids.' He nodded to himself. 'I've shared a lot more than she has.'

'So, what *do* you know about her?'

'I know what she does for a living, how she spends her spare time. I know things. Not feelings.'

Elsie raised her eyebrows. 'Is that because of her background?'

He shrugged and stared at the floor. 'Possibly. She told me about her adoption, but still...'

'Have you spoken to her about this?'

'I kept trying to ask her questions about herself but she'd always change the subject. You remember how she was when she was here that Sunday. The barest of answers to any queries then following up with a question, so she never had to give away anything about herself.'

'Perhaps she thinks you won't like her answers.'

He looked up. 'Hmmm. Doesn't trust me with the truth. That just backs up my decision, doesn't it? If she doesn't trust me, where is there to go?'

'Well, of course, it's up to you. Seems a bit of a swift decision based on not much evidence but it's your life, lovey. I just have this feeling, for all her confidence and bravado, she needs rescuing.'

He shook his head. 'She's way too self-sufficient for that.'

'I'm not so sure. Anyway, it's done now.' She sighed.

Elsie was disappointed in him, he knew, but he couldn't tell her the real reason.

'Any chance of a cuppa?' Elsie's voice cut across his train of thought.

'Sure,' he said, glad of the change of subject. He went into the kitchen and made tea for them both. There was a tin of Elsie's favourite Chocolate Oliver biscuits on the dining table. She rarely bought them because they were expensive. He could see the seal was unbroken so he put the tin on the tray with the tea mugs. He walked slowly back to Elsie's room to avoid spillage.

Elsie was staring out the window.

'You been treating yourself?' He waved the tin of biscuits.

'Not me. Juliet bought them for me when we were in town.'

He shook his head. 'Of course.'

'We'll see, shall we, if she keeps in touch with me after your decision,' Elsie said. 'Go on then. Open 'em up.'

Phil left Elsie to enjoy her tea and biscuits and went back to his room. He took out the envelope that had been left for him at work the previous Saturday. He'd put it in the car and had only opened it ten minutes before Juliet and Elsie had come back from London.

He pulled out the contents. Four 10"x8" photos, dated earlier in the month, showing Juliet sitting on top of a man in her bedroom. Both she and the man were naked and in the throes of sexual activity. Phil's first thought was that the date stamp had been doctored, that it couldn't have been taken since he'd started dating Juliet, but the vase with the flowers he'd bought and arranged for her were there on the bedside table. And it was definitely Juliet. The butterfly-shaped birthmark on her back, just above the waistline, was visible. Phil had seen it when she'd bent over to look at the bookcase in his bedroom.

The idea that she was having sex with someone else, be it casual or as part of a relationship, had hurt his pride. It wasn't as though they'd declared exclusivity; it was too early for anything like that. But he remembered her saying at the end of their first date that she hadn't been intimate with anyone for a while. The woman in these pictures didn't look like someone who was reticent about intimacy.

To him, the only logical conclusion was that she was playing him, probably to milk him for information about Daniel Cross. And Phil knew that meant she'd hurt him, sooner or later. Dump him when he'd served whatever purpose she had in mind. He'd decided it was best to get out, before he got in too deep.

Chapter 17 - Elsie

Elsie was surprised to hear from Juliet the next day.

'You said you wanted a hand with sorting some of your clothes. I can come over on Sunday, if you want, after you've been to church,' Juliet said.

'Are you sure, lovey? After what's happened?'

'You mean with Phil? That's nothing to do with me coming to see you,' Juliet said.

'If you're happy to come over.'

'Definitely,' said Juliet.

'Shall I see if Phil's planning to cook a roast? I'm sure he won't mind you eating with us.'

'I'd rather not. No point in making him or me feel awkward,' Juliet said.

'If he's around, I'll send him down the allotment while you're here. He'll probably be working anyway.'

Elsie had hoped she might be able to effect a reconciliation but it was too early for that. She thought Phil and Juliet wanted their heads knocking together. They needed each other more than they realised.

Juliet was waiting at the house when Elsie and Phil returned from church. Juliet showed no sign of being in any way upset at Phil's rejection, Elsie thought. Phil was polite but distant and Juliet didn't show an ounce of emotion as they asked each other about their health.

Elsie closed the door to her room and sat down in her chair, opposite Juliet. 'So, how are you? Not too upset with things?'

Juliet looked at her, pressing her lips together before responding. 'I was. It was a bolt out of the blue. Took me a few days to process it all but I'm fine now. I'm used to rejection. What does that old song say? "Pick yourself up, dust yourself down and start all over again." Something like that.'

'Good for you,' Elsie said.

'It was probably a good thing. He said he stifled his first wife by being over-protective and I'd have found that hard to put up with.'

Elsie nodded. 'It's probably to do with his beginnings in life. He wants to keep everyone safe so they'll always be there for him.'

Juliet nodded. 'Did he give you any idea about why he decided to end it?' she asked.

Ah, thought Elsie, I was right. She is still interested. 'You sure you want to know?'

She watched Juliet's face processing the choice. She looked young and vulnerable all of a sudden, all that confidence and bravado gone.

'Yes.'

Elsie told her what Phil had said.

Juliet nodded and sighed. 'It's similar to what my last boyfriend told me when he dumped me.'

'Tell me about him.'

'Cam. Cameron. I met him through someone in the office and he seemed nice. Friendly but not pushy. Attractive, kept himself fit. Asked me out on a date and he was easy to talk to. Seemed kind, if a bit shallow, but what bloke isn't? Of course, now I say that, I don't think that's how I'd describe Phil. He seems really genuine. Authentic. A decent human being with a big heart.'

Elsie decided not to respond.

'Anyway, Cam and I carried on dating and we became an item. It was lovely waking up in someone's arms. So lovely it got to be a habit. And I slowly started to believe we might have a future together and that being with him could be a safe environment. I don't mean safe as in not in real danger, just safe to let a little bit of me out in the open. Be honest about the dark ugly bit of me I keep hidden. But one day, Cam just said he didn't want to see me anymore. He said there was no-one else involved, just that he never saw the real me and that I bottled up emotion and never shared anything with him. I was in a real state. But Daniel was there for me. And I found out that Cam had started seeing someone else as soon as he'd dumped me. It made the rejection doubly hard, somehow. And then Cam got mugged. Beaten up really badly. He was left disabled from the waist down. And I wanted so much to comfort him and look after him, but of course, he had someone else to do that.' She took a deep breath and let it out quickly.

'Is there something in what Cam and Phil said then, do you think?' Elsie watched Juliet's face close down.

'Probably. I suppose what shocked me most about Phil was that it was quite early on in our relationship. Too early for him to expect me to open up. Felt a bit harsh and so sudden. As though he'd switched from hot to cold in a moment. But it's just another sign that I'm better off on my own.'

'You don't believe that, lovey,' Elsie said.

'I think I do. I'm damaged goods. Not capable of functioning in the emotional way I should, so it's probably better not to inflict it on others.' Juliet's voice sounded over-bright.

'I'm probably speaking out of turn, but I think that's a coward's way out. The only failure is failing to try. Don't lock yourself away, particularly with that job of yours. It's skewing your perspective of what's right and wrong.' She looked across at Juliet. 'I've said too much.'

Juliet shook her head. 'No. Food for thought. I appreciate your honesty.' She smiled. 'Enough of this. Shall we tackle this clothing mountain of yours? And while we're doing that, I want you to tell me all about Allan. How did you meet?'

Elsie smiled. 'I met him when I was seventeen. He was just a year older than me. My aunt lived in rural Suffolk and I went to stay with her that summer. She had a group of friends that used to come to her house. In those days I guess they were still called bohemians, as it was well before the hippy era. They were very arty and not like most other people. They would have tennis parties and picnics, talk about philosophy and art. To me, Aunt Lilla was thoroughly exotic and she became a bit of a role model.' She took a sip of water.

Allan's mother was in Lilla's group of friends and he came along to one of the tennis parties. We hit it off. Neither of us was any good at tennis, so we'd sit and talk, exchanging views on all sorts of things, from world politics to the best dog breeds, films, the magic of numbers, astronomy, poetry. We explored the boundaries of our thinking together, all the time testing our family-imposed ideals. It was wonderful to talk to someone in such an open and honest way. Most boys and men I'd come across were only interested in forcing their views on you, trying to convert you to their way of thinking, all to feed their ego. But Allan was different. And though we talked and talked, and spent so much time together, we never kissed or anything. We were just fascinated by each other.'

'It sounds brilliant,' said Juliet.

'At the end of the summer, my parents came to visit for the last week of my trip and they took a very harsh view of Allan. They asked him all sorts of questions but he had no prospects in their eyes, nothing to commend him. And it turned out his parents wanted him to have an altogether different life.'

'So, what happened next?' Juliet asked.

'With both families against us, we knew our relationship was doomed. We clung to each other that last week. I told him how I felt about him, how I wished I was with him when we were apart. And on the last day, he kissed me, and said that he would always love me. We agreed that when we were older, we would fix our own destiny so we could be together. But I think by the end of that week, he'd decided I'd be better off without him. He kept in touch afterwards but I could feel him withdrawing from me, from us. And then I met George. My parents liked him. And he took me out to a dance and to the pictures and I slowly started to believe that my fate was to be with him. But I never forgot Allan. And after George and I had been courting for a few months, he popped the question at Luigi's, one Saturday night, and I spent days agonising. George seemed to understand. He somehow knew there was someone else. And he said to me that though he might not be the best, he hoped he'd prove good enough. And, well, I thought that was good of him. To recognise that someone else might mean more to me. The day before we got married, I received a letter.' She picked up her handbag and pulled out her purse. She handed a battered piece of paper to Juliet.

"My own little one

You know why I write but I must say it again. I love you and only you. I know just how you feel, those nights of yearning, but somehow not lonely.

Little one, I want to say so much but I cannot. Everything was against me, even my job is not sure now from one day to another. I want to give you some of the fine things of life, you were made for nice things and I must have been made for nasty things, but there is always God and He knows all things and will take care of you and that will be my happiness if nothing more. Whatever happens and wherever life takes us and however far apart, just remember that your own Allan is ever the same and cannot forget.

With fondest love and best wishes

Your Allan."

'Oh, Elsie, that's heart-breaking.'

'Of course, it was too late then. I couldn't let George down. So, I married him. And the next thing I knew, Allan had left for New Zealand. He still wrote to me, sent postcards and letters. But it was the correspondence of a friend, protecting me so if George ever read them, he wouldn't think anything was amiss.'

'But he still loved you, obviously. Did you ever see him again?'

Elsie nodded. 'Allan came back to England for a visit, just after George and I celebrated our fifth wedding anniversary. When I hadn't fallen pregnant, we'd had the doctor check us out and we'd found out it was George that was the problem. George was heartbroken, saying he wasn't a proper man and that I should find myself a real fella who could give me a family. So, I was feeling sad and a bit angry and everything, when I met up with Allan. In secret. I told George I was going up West to meet a friend for afternoon tea, but I met Allan in a hotel near Marble Arch. And he made love to me. I still feel bad about it, even now. It wasn't like today with people just swanning in and out of bed with each other. It was a big deal. But I knew it would be my only chance to be close to him, so I took it. It was the sweetest and saddest moment of my life. Realising in those few stolen hours that Allan was the love of my life. Knowing he was going back to New Zealand, to his wife and child. After he'd gone, I found out I was expecting. But I couldn't keep it. It would have killed George. And he was a sweet person who didn't deserve to be treated that badly.'

'Did you have the baby?'

Elsie shook her head. 'No, a friend knew someone who could make it go away. I suffered for weeks afterwards. But the pain was nothing in comparison to the guilt.'

Juliet could feel tears forming. 'What an awfully sad story. So did you and Allan still keep in touch?'

'We exchanged Christmas cards and birthday cards and the odd letter. All above board, of course. But even with the bland words, I could still hear Allan's heart calling me.'

'Did you ever tell him? Allan? About the pregnancy?' Juliet asked.

'No. It wouldn't have been fair.'

'Is Allan still alive?'

Elsie shook her head. 'He moved back to England when he turned sixty. Died aged seventy-one, quite suddenly, according to his widow. She wrote to everyone in his address book with the news. I couldn't bear to go to his funeral. Not sure I could have held it together. And George was still alive then. I think he knew though, when I mentioned my friend

Allan had died. He said "So that's that, then." As though he realised it really meant something.'

'And you and George didn't ever talk about it?'

'No. Our generation was brought up to keep it all buried, hidden. But once George died, I put Allan's picture up on the mantelpiece next to George's and would think about all those conversations we used to share. And I wonder what it would have been like if we'd been together and had a family.' Elsie took a tissue from the box on the table and dabbed her eyes.

'I really appreciate you telling me the story. Have you ever visited Allan's grave?' Juliet asked.

Elsie shook her head. 'I don't know where it is.'

'You can find anything on the internet if you know where to look. If you ever want to visit, put a flower on his place of rest, I'll gladly search it out and drive you down there. We could get a place to stay, spend a bit of time enjoying the scenery, so it's not all graves and gloom.'

'You're big-hearted, lovey. Maybe one day.'

Juliet looked across at the wardrobe in the corner. 'We should make a start,' Juliet said.

'Yep. Enough talking. Let's get on with this clear out.'

Chapter 18 – Juliet

Juliet left Elsie's house a few hours later with half-a-dozen bin bags full of old clothing. She hoped she could find a vintage shop in town that would appreciate their quality. Elsie had suggested she keep a couple of vintage handbags and a 1920s-style choker that had made Juliet feel very chic when she'd tried it on.

It was one of those days when Daniel had told her to stay away from her flat, because a young woman called Tiffany was hosting a new contact of Daniel's. Guy Winterton worked for a rival organisation but was giving the impression he could be an ally, willing to share intelligence at a price. Daniel wanted to make sure he had some dirt on Guy to fall back on, in case their relationship went sour. Tiffany had been tasked with getting some pictures of Guy in a compromising position.

Juliet decided to drive out to Windsor, where she knew there was a sister hotel to the one Cross International used in central London. She hoped her corporate loyalty card would get her a cheaper room. She rang her contact in London who agreed to help and a few minutes later, got a text to say a room had been booked for her.

She drove into the car park and took her overnight bag from under the bags of clothing. The room she was given was lovely, but even at a heavily-discounted price, was still more than she could afford on a regular basis. She'd have to rethink her position on entertaining clients if she couldn't come up with somewhere cheaper to stay. There was plenty of space at Elsie's, but she didn't feel she could stay there after Phil had rejected her. The idea of coming across as emotionally needy made her shudder.

She took a walk around Windsor and went down the Long Walk, stopping at the statue of King George III to look back at the castle. It did look beautiful in the milky half-light of the early evening.

Back in her room, she ate the complimentary chocolate bar and apple in an attempt to avoid the cost of room service. A cup of instant coffee finished off her meal and she drifted off to sleep in front of an uninspiring documentary about penguins.

She was woken by her phone. It was 01:31. She didn't recognise the number but answered anyway. She could hear a girl crying, trying to speak.

'It's…Tiffany.' There was a gulp and a sob.

'What's the matter?' Juliet asked.

'I need help. There's blood everywhere. Please.'

'I'll be there as soon as I can.' Juliet dressed hurriedly and packed her bag, an icy fear inside her. Something really bad must have happened.

The roads were eerily quiet and Juliet arrived an hour and a quarter after the call.

The night porter saw her walking up the stairs from the underground car park and beckoned her over. 'Is everything OK, Jools?'

'Not sure. Just here to check.'

'Some bloke left here covered in blood, raving,' he said.

Juliet felt sick. 'Shit. You haven't called anyone, have you?'

He shook his head. 'We're told to be discreet about whatever goes on, but if you want me to call the police or anyone else, let me know.'

She gave him a half-smile of gratitude before getting into the lift. She let herself in to the apartment, nervous at what she'd find.

Tiffany was sitting on the sofa, shivering. She looked around in fear. 'Oh, Jools. I'm so glad it's you.' She looked as though she'd been in a boxing ring, with a cut over her right eye, and dark, purple patches around the eye socket. Her hands were bloodied and Juliet saw one of her kitchen knives on the coffee table, still wet with blood. It made her feel nauseous.

She sat down next to Tiffany and took her hands. 'Are you OK? Tell me what happened.'

Tiffany's storytelling was all over the place, but Juliet managed to ascertain that Guy had been keen to have sex with her. They'd been drinking in a bar for a couple of hours and when they got back to the flat, Guy refused to have more champagne. Tiffany hadn't known what to do, so had gone along with the idea of sex. She'd foolishly switched on the bedroom cameras without putting on some music in the background. Anyone with keen hearing could hear the cameras whirring as they started to record and Guy had twigged. He'd made Tiffany switch them off then hit her in the face a number of times before trying to have sex with her. As a precaution, she'd put a kitchen knife under a pillow and had used it to slash his arm when he was on top of her. He'd staggered out of the flat, ranting as he left that he'd kill her.

Tiffany was still in shock and Juliet debated what to do. She knew she should call the police to report Guy for the assault but that had implications for Daniel and Cross International, as well as Tiffany and even herself. And Tiff needed to see a doctor.

Juliet sent a text to Pat with scant information but it was enough for him to ring her back immediately. She told him as quickly as she could what had happened.

'I'll get a doctor for Tiffany,' he said. 'And I'll get there as soon as I can.'

Juliet felt a wave of relief.

By 6am, Tiffany's injuries had been cleaned up, Daniel had been briefed and between them, Pat and Juliet had cleaned and tidied away the evidence of what had taken place. Normally, Juliet would have been in work at 6:30am but decided to get ready in her own time. She was tired from the disturbed night.

She arrived in the office and was switching on her laptop when her mobile rang. It was Phil. Intrigued, she answered it. 'Hi, Phil. Is something wrong?'

'Are you OK, Jools?' His voice was wavering with emotion.

'I'm fine. Why do you ask?'

'We've had a report of an assault that took place at your flat,' he said.

Juliet felt as though an ice-cube had been dropped down her back. 'A report? From who?'

'Some guy reckons he was stabbed there. I got wind of it because he's accused...well, it doesn't matter. I recognised the address.'

'I didn't sleep in the flat last night.' That was true.

'So, you're alright? Great. Where were you?'

She debated what to say. 'Out with a friend.'

'Right. OK.' He didn't sound as though he believed her.

'Was there anything else?' she asked. She needed to speak to Daniel.

'No. One of my colleagues will be in touch with you formally. I just wanted to check on you.'

'Thanks for the heads-up, Phil and for your concern. Bye.' She let out a sigh. Given the events of the past twenty-four hours, given police were aware of something happening in her flat, it was lucky she wasn't dating Phil. How would she have been able to take Tiffany's call if he'd been around?

She went through to Daniel's office where he was on the phone. She scribbled "Need 2 talk now" on his notepad.

'Two minutes, Jools. Yeah, yeah. Sorry, gotta go. I will, Geordie. Bye.' He looked up at her. 'What's so urgent?' he snapped.

'Just been tipped off. The police know about the assault at the flat.'

'How the fuck do they know that?' he asked.

'Guy must have reported it,' she said.

'Then he's a fucking idiot. He's on camera hitting her and trying to have it off with her before she stabs him.'

'But he's not. He made her switch off the cameras.'

'She switched the bedroom cameras off. But there's a little camera in the hall that runs off the main circuit. It points into that main bedroom and the door was open.'

Juliet let that sink in. She hadn't known her movements were being filmed from the hall if she left her bedroom door open. She parked that thought, so she could deal with the here and now. 'You'd think someone like him would be wise to secondary systems.'

'I think he's too arrogant to worry whether he's being filmed from fifty angles. Reckons his hotshot lawyer wife can get him out of trouble.' He frowned. 'Are you OK?'

His change of subject took her by surprise. 'I think so. Not sure how I feel about the flat, sleeping there.'

'Where were you last night?' he asked.

144

'I had to be out of the flat, so I booked into a hotel.'

His face registered a succession of emotions – surprise, confusion and sadness. 'Do you want to come and stay at mine for a couple of days? Put a bit of distance between you and all this?'

'Yes, please.'

'Good. Feel like we could do with a proper chat away from here. And Giselle would love to see you,' he said.

'Thanks.' She was worried about Daniel wanting to talk to her and not entirely sure Giselle would be glad to see her, but was pleased to have somewhere else to stay. 'Will you ring Giselle to let her know?'

'Yes. Now, let's see if we can get that lawyer wife in here to see the footage of her hubby. I'm sure she can make him drop any charges.'

'Do you want me to contact her?' she asked.

'Yeah. Get her in.'

Juliet went back to her desk and looked up Guy's wife on Wikipedia. A stern-looking woman, Caroline Hartley-Winterton had steely grey eyes that could wither a man at thirty paces, if her photo was anything to go by. Juliet tracked down contact details for her organisation. The number went to voicemail, so Juliet put a reminder in her calendar to try again later, as well as a reminder in Daniel's calendar that she was coming to stay at Cross Hall that night. He was prone to get side-tracked with business issues and Juliet did not want Giselle taken by surprise.

After a very difficult call with Ms Hartley-Winterton's PA, Juliet managed to get a meeting set up between Caroline and Daniel at 3pm. She hoped the exchange between Daniel and Caroline would make all the mess go away, but there was always a chance the police could press charges without Guy's input.

She put her head around the door to let Daniel know about the meeting. 'Is there anything else we need to do about Tiffany?'

'I've got Pat sorting it. Of course, depends on the meeting with the lawyer as to what else she might need, but he's arranged a trip for her so she can recover away from prying eyes.'

'Was she happy with that?' she asked.

'Apparently. He's sorted out some time away at a spa. Her family think she's gone on an urgent business trip abroad. She'll get some compensation, enough to buy the car she wants or something, so it's worked out all right.'

'What if the police want to speak to her?'

'Don't worry about it.' He frowned. 'Didn't you say you were tipped off? Are you still with that DI?'

She shook her head. 'No, we're not seeing each other anymore, but he heard it all kicked off at my place, so he thought I might have been hurt.'

He smiled. 'How touching.'

She found his mocking tone irritating.

'Makes you wonder, though,' he said. 'How does a DI in Serious Crime hear about something like this?'

Juliet suspected Phil's mission to nail Daniel was well known and that any mention of Daniel was relayed to Phil as a matter of course. She decided not to share her thoughts. 'Yes, that does seem odd.'

He gave her a look that made her shiver before nodding his head in the direction of the door to dismiss her.

She went back to her desk, concerned that Daniel would want to talk about Phil later. She wasn't sure she had any answers.

'Jools. It's lovely to see you.' Giselle's hug was warm. 'I know I see you out and about but it'll be so good to catch up properly, away from all that business talk. Can I get you a drink?'

'Tonic would be great, thanks.' Juliet sat on the end of a huge cream leather settee that could have accommodated a football team. She watched Giselle fix their drinks. Daniel had gone upstairs to change and hadn't yet revealed the outcome of the 3pm meeting to her, though her gut told her it must have gone well, otherwise he'd have been ranting about Guy on the journey home.

Giselle handed over a drink. 'Sorry, Jools, I should have asked. Do you want to freshen up? I can show you to your room if you'd prefer.'

Juliet wasn't sure she had the energy for anything, after losing so much sleep the night before. 'I'm fine, thanks.' She took a long sip of her tonic and felt herself relax a little.

'How are you, Jools?' Giselle sounded like a psychiatrist addressing a needy patient.

Juliet gave the question some thought. 'It's been an odd twenty-four hours,' she said. She acknowledged in her own mind how hard it had been to have to vacate her flat. To have no-one she could go and stay with. To be alone in a hotel room, knowing what was happening in her home. And to have to dash back, in the middle of the night, to comfort a girl, a teenager, who'd been seriously assaulted. It could so easily have been Juliet who'd been on the wrong side of Guy. She couldn't stop herself and burst into tears.

'Oh, you poor love.' Giselle got up from her seat to give Juliet a hug. 'Do you want to talk about it?'

Chapter 19 – Daniel

Daniel undressed in the bedroom as he prepared to shower before bed.

Giselle sat on the end of their bed and watched him. 'You know I still find you attractive, Dan, even now you've got those little white bits in your beard.'

'I should hope you do, my love. Can't think about life without you.'

'Hmm, I reckon if I wasn't around, you'd move Jools into this bed pretty quickly. I'm not blind, Dan. I see the way you look at her. And I can see how she worships you, the way she'd do anything for you.'

He looked at his wife, trying not to feel guilty. He'd no reason to be, not based on his actions. Thoughts didn't count. 'Don't be daft, love. Why would she be interested in an old geezer like me?'

Giselle pursed her lips. 'Oh, I can think of at least a few hundred-million reasons.'

'Rubbish.' He watched her smooth the edge of the duvet repeatedly. 'What's bothering you?'

'Juliet. I think you might have to get rid of her,' she said.

'What? Because you think I fancy her?'

'Dan, I *know* you fancy her. But it's not that. It's because she's vulnerable. All the stuff that's been going on. She's spooked by it all, which makes her dangerous. She could be open to blackmail or she could give something away in that state, either to the police or to one of our competitors. She's lost her judgment.'

'And when you say, get rid of her?' Daniel looked across at her.

'Professionally, I mean. Get yourself a new PA.'

'If I sack Jools, it doesn't stop her being vulnerable to others. It stops her learning anything new, but she's got five years of inside knowledge. If I do get rid of her, she's more likely to dish the dirt.'

'I guess that's true,' she said.

'It'll be hard, finding someone else to do what she does. She knows me so well. Half the time I don't have to tell her what I want. It just happens. I'll talk to her myself. She's just a bit shaken up at the sight of Tiffany's face and all that blood. She'll bounce back. Don't forget, I've got just as much dirt on her as she's got on me. I think I'd prefer to keep her inside the tent.'

'Just be careful, Dan.'

'I will, love.' He went to the ensuite to shower, locking the door to give himself some privacy. As he lathered shower gel over his body, he remembered what Giselle had said. The idea of Juliet moving into his bed gave him an immediate hard-on. He often thought about Juliet. On the one hand, he hated that she spent time with other men at his behest, but it didn't compare to the wild jealousy he'd felt when Phil had come on the scene. Her previous boyfriend, Cam, had been just a boy, not real competition. But Phil was an ex-soldier who'd seen active duty in the Gulf. Daniel was sure Phil and Juliet's relationship wouldn't have lasted anyway but he'd taken steps to give it a nudge over the edge, just to make certain. He closed his eyes, imagining Juliet was showering with him and brought himself quickly to orgasm.

He felt light-headed with pleasure and turned the water to its coldest setting to snap himself out of his reverie. He swore under his breath at the iciness before climbing out of the shower and drying himself with a large white bath sheet. He put on a black towelling robe and went back into the bedroom. Giselle had undressed and was wearing a short, sheer nightie. He'd learned that a short nightie meant she was in the mood. He'd need some time to recover.

'I have to tell you, I was relieved when that lawyer made the right decision,' he said, trying to buy some time.

Giselle smiled at him. 'I looked her up online. Did you fancy her? She's your type. Well, your type for secondary sex. A bit bossy-looking. Someone you'd need to tame.'

He grinned and sat down on the bed. 'You know me so well. But I was too worried about getting her to see sense to think about her like that.'

'And did she see sense?'

'Very quickly. Once the footage was shown to her, she realised hubby couldn't argue provocation or reasonable force. We've got to hope she has as much influence as she claims.'

'Over what?' she asked.

'The police. Technically, they could still try and charge Tiffany, or Jools, or me.'

'You? You weren't even bloody there.'

He could see the anger bubbling up inside her. 'I think Guy's already mentioned my name. You know what the police are like, twisting everything. Even if they don't have Guy as a witness, they could still try and make something stick.'

'Bastards. But she has influence, this lawyer?'

'Considerable influence, from what I gather.'

'Fuckin' Jools. This is all her fault.'

He watched Giselle squeeze her hands into fists. 'Why? Because it should have been her entertaining him?'

She nodded. 'She'd have known how to handle someone like Guy.'

'She's lost the taste for it and I can't see this changing her mind. Quite the opposite.'

Giselle shrugged and patted the edge of the bed. 'Like I said. You should get rid of her, before it's too late. But let's not talk about that now.' She leant over, loosening his dressing gown before kissing him. 'Let's focus on you, not Juliet.'

He wasn't sure if it was the kiss or the mention of Juliet that caused his erection, but he was grateful for it.

Chapter 20 – Juliet

Juliet was at her desk by 6:30am the next morning, courtesy of an early wake-up call from Daniel, who'd tapped on her bedroom door at 5am. She was glad to be away from Cross Hall. She sensed Giselle didn't want her around, despite her sympathetic words the night before. She decided she would stay one more night before going back to her flat. She sent Pat a WhatsApp message, asking obliquely about Tiffany, in case the conversation was ever scrutinised.

He rang straight back. 'She's fine, Jools. Enjoying herself at the spa. Looking forward to driving her new car, when she gets it. She seems remarkably unscathed.'

'I'm glad. Tell her I said Hi.'

'Are you OK?' he asked.

'You know me, Pat,' she said.

'That's why I'm asking, hun.'

'I'm alright. Think I'll go back to the flat tomorrow,' she said.

'Probably best. Get back on the horse again, so to speak.'

'Will you be coming in today?' she asked.

'Tomorrow. Just got to sort someone…something out for Daniel.'

'See you then.'

Daniel came out of his office. 'Was that Pat?'

'Yes, I was checking how Tiff was.'

Daniel looked uncomfortable. 'I assume she's fine as I've heard nothing.'

'She is. Did you want to speak to Pat? I can get him back on the phone,' she said.

'No, it'll wait. Let's make a start, shall we?'

Despite having slept relatively well, Juliet found it hard to focus on her work. She tried her best to keep up with Daniel's stream of demands. She was usually in tune with him, but felt as though they were out of kilter.

He began to get annoyed. 'What's wrong with you today? I said the 19th.'

'Sorry, Boss. Are you pissed off with me? About the Guy thing?'

'Of course not.' He looked straight at her. 'Well, maybe a bit. But I've no right to be. I mean, you'd have handled Guy better, dealt with him, like you did Harrison, so we wouldn't have this hanging over us if you'd done your job.'

'But…' She decided against saying what she felt. 'Doesn't matter. Do you want me to resign?'

He paused before responding. 'No. You're the best help I've got in sorting out this mess, you and Pat. But I am struggling to work out your role in the future. The flat and everything.'

'Are you saying if I don't entertain the clients, I can't live in the flat?'

'Well, I need the flat for people to be dealt with in a controlled environment. It's set up for that purpose.'

'I'll move out, then. But you've got to realise, I can't afford anything in central London on my wages, so I'll have to commute, which'll make it tougher working evenings, if I've got to travel home afterwards. I don't have the luxury of a cheap room with Mum and Dad.' She felt irritated by the conversation. Daniel had plenty of places to accommodate her. Cross International had a large property portfolio.

'Maybe I'll move you somewhere less glitzy but still central.' He cocked his head to one side. 'What about the flat here? Hmm, yes. I quite like the idea of having you here, day and night, available if I need anything.' He smiled at her.

Juliet shivered. His sentiment was clear.

'I'll have a think about it,' he said.

She nodded and went back to her office. She'd always wondered if Daniel had feelings for her. When she'd first started working for him, she thought he would assume casual sex with him was part of her job description, but he'd never suggested it. She was glad, knowing it would have changed their working relationship, quite apart from the fact she really didn't think of him in that way. He was a very attractive man for his age, but he was old enough to be her father and she wanted to keep him in her life as a father figure, not a lover. And then there was Giselle. She was as hard as nails, quite ruthless in getting her own way. Just the sort of wife to seek revenge if Daniel strayed. Juliet had enough problems in her life without taking Giselle on as well.

Just after 4pm, while Daniel was chairing the monthly board meeting, Juliet had a text from the ground floor receptionist. "Can you call asap?". Juliet stepped out of the board room and rang back.

'There's a Detective Chief Inspector Matthews in reception with a Detective Sergeant Boyd. They want to talk to you and Daniel.'

'Shit, really? OK, send them up in the lift. I'll keep them busy till Daniel's out of the boardroom.' She recognised the names of Phil's boss and subordinate. She'd not met the DCI before but had met DS Boyd briefly when she'd visited Phil at work. She got up to greet them as they were shown in. 'Gentlemen, good afternoon.' She shook DCI Matthews' hand. 'I'm Juliet.' She smiled at Tom Boyd. 'Detective Sergeant. Can I get either of you a tea or coffee? Or a cold drink?' She watched the glances between the two men as they silently agreed their response.

DS Boyd spoke first. 'No thanks, Juliet. We need to ask you and Mr Cross some questions.'

She ushered them onto the soft seating at the end of Daniel's office space. 'Do you want to speak to us together? Or separately?'

The DCI looked at her. 'We can start with you. Is Mr Cross around?'

'He's chairing a board meeting. Let me just go and tell him you're here and then we can have a chat.' She walked quickly out of the room before the DCI could respond and went along the corridor to the boardroom.

Daniel had recently got into the habit of having his lawyer, David Jones, sit in on the monthly board sessions and she was glad this meeting was no exception. She went back in and saw Daniel look up, annoyed at the interruption.

She walked quickly up to him and whispered in his ear. Even sidewards, she could see his anger at her news.

'Wait here,' he said and cleared his throat to get the attention of the attendees. 'Apologies, it seems I have some visitors who urgently need my attention. We'll reconvene later. Jools will let you know when. David? With me.' He got up and told David what was happening.

David caught up with Juliet as they walked along the corridor. 'Say nothing unless I tell you to.'

She walked back to where the policemen were waiting. Both stood up as she entered and she effected the introductions between the four men before offering refreshments. She was glad everyone declined as she wanted this to be over. She could feel anxiety rising inside her.

The DCI led the conversation. He explained they were interested in the night of the alleged assault on Guy that had taken place at her flat.

'Could you give me that date again?' David asked.

The DCI looked annoyed and repeated himself.

'So, what exactly is it you want to question Mr Cross and Ms Russell about?' David asked. 'I assume this isn't formal questioning otherwise you'd have invited them to the station and would be talking to them separately. And be recording the interviews.'

'Indeed. Ms Russell, I believe you were staying with a friend and not at your usual address, where the assault is alleged to have taken place?'

She was annoyed as she'd told Phil she was staying with a friend, not expecting that to go down as her official statement but said nothing.

'Can you confirm your whereabouts on that night?' The DCI stared at her.

She looked at David, who nodded his assent to her responding.

'I wasn't staying with a friend. I'm not sure where you got that idea from,' she said, feeling mischievous. 'I was staying at a hotel in Windsor.'

'And you were there all night?' DS Boyd cut in.

David asked him to be specific about the timeframe they were interested in.

'Were you at the hotel between midnight and 1:30am?' asked DS Boyd.

'I was at the hotel during that period,' she said.

'What time did you leave the hotel?' DCI Matthews took back the lead role.

David tutted. 'You've asked about the time period you're interested in, so that seems an irrelevance. Let's move on.'

The policemen looked at each other.

David continued. 'Ms Russell wasn't in the flat at the time in question, neither was Mr Cross because he was at home with his wife. The housekeeper at Cross Hall can corroborate. What else do you want to ask?'

'I understand Mr Cross owns the flat at Riverview Terrace.' The DCI stared at Daniel.

'Cross International owns it,' David said.

'And what was Guy Winterton doing there?' DC Boyd asked.

'If Guy Winterton was at a Cross International property, that would be highly confidential, given he works for one of our biggest competitors. And if Guy has alleged something, then he would have furnished you with the details of what he was doing there and why. So, I have to wonder why you're asking?' David sat back.

'Who was at your flat, Ms Russell?' DCI Matthews spoke sharply.

'That would be confidential and we've established it wasn't Mr Cross or Ms Russell. Anything else?' David snapped back. When no question was forthcoming, he stood up. 'Are we done, gentlemen? It appears you don't have much, if any, testimony to ratify. Is that correct?'

'Mr Winterton has withdrawn the allegation,' DS Boyd admitted.

Juliet noticed the DCI briefly close his eyes and shake his head in what looked like frustration at Boyd's admission.

'So, what are you doing here then?' David asked.

'We know a serious assault took place,' DS Boyd said.

'But you have no complainant and no witnesses. Seems as though you're here on a fishing expedition. I think we're done until you decide to make this formal. Daniel?'

Juliet watched David and Daniel leave the room. She stood up and looked at the policemen. 'I'll show you out, gentlemen.'

DS Boyd put his hand on her arm. 'Is there anything you want to tell us, Juliet?'

She shook her head. 'Nothing, thank you, Tom.' A tiny part of her would love to have told them the truth, but how could she do that when Tiffany, Daniel and Pat would all be implicated as well as her? 'I'm sorry you've had a wasted journey.' She led them in silence to the lift and down to the ground floor, escorting them through the security barriers and to the front door. She watched them walking away from the building, wondering if this feeling of nervous anxiety would ever go away.

Chapter 21 – Phil

'How'd you get on?' Phil asked Tom Boyd.

The DS shook his head. 'They'd got a lawyer with them who did all the talking. They've clearly got something to hide.'

'No new insights then, Boss?' Phil asked.

DCI Matthews looked glumly at him. 'Nothing, other than that Cross and your girl are definitely guilty of something. There's no doubt in my mind the assault took place but for whatever reason, Guy Winterton's been persuaded not to press charges.'

'Perhaps he's guilty of something else,' said DS Boyd.

'He's not the nicest of people. And he's married to that bloody lawyer. You know, the stroppy cow the celebs always wheel out,' Phil said.

'Well, if she's been persuaded her husband shouldn't press charges, he must have done something very wrong. Maybe Cross showed her evidence of that to persuade her,' said DCI Matthews.

'Maybe it's Guy we should go after?' DS Boyd said.

'With what?' the DCI snapped. 'We don't know anything about what happened. There must have been another person at the flat with him, but we know it wasn't your girl.'

'I've just had confirmation that she was at the hotel that night,' Tom said.

'And there's no CCTV footage inside the apartment block?' DCI Matthews asked.

'It was malfunctioning that day, apparently,' DS Boyd said.

'How very fucking convenient. What about ANPR for your girl's car? See what time she left and got back. That might give us a timestamp to work back from and check other CCTV in the area,' the DCI said.

Phil was surprised how quickly his boss was getting hooked on the investigation. Like himself, Dave Matthews was known for pursuing cases obsessively and this one had, for whatever reason, got to him. 'I'll do that.' Phil wondered if the DCI was taking it too far.

Phil stepped out of the office and went to his car to make a call. 'Hi Jools.'

'I didn't expect to hear from you, Phil. Is everything OK?'

'Yes, well…yeah, it's fine. But I need to ask you something off the record.'

'Right.' She sounded suspicious.

'It's just…why did you go back to your flat at a quarter to three on the night that assault took place?'

There was a silence.

'You've met my boss. He's got me checking ANPR and CCTV, trying to get a handle on what happened to Guy and when. He asked me to find your car. I thought it'd be fine, that it wouldn't show up till later in the morning, but there it was. Why'd you go back so early? Did you have to go and help?'

She gave a long sigh. 'Phil, if I'm going to be questioned about this, it'll have to be formal and the company lawyer will have to be there.'

'I'm not asking you formally. I'm asking you as a friend. If the DCI gets the bit between his teeth, he won't let go. Despite Guy not wanting to take it further, it's obvious something happened and Guy's been leant on to stop it coming out. You're implicated, with your car turning up in the middle of the night. I'm worried for you. I can't bury this, Jools. I can't pretend I haven't found it.'

'I understand, Phil, and I'd never ask you to compromise your professional integrity. You must do whatever you have to do, but I'm not going to say anything about it now. Better anything you find out is done officially, then you're not left to decide what to pass on.'

She had a point. 'OK Jools, but be warned. Dave Matthews doesn't give up easily.'

'Thanks. I don't mean to sound ungrateful. I appreciate your concern.'

'I better go. Take care of yourself, Jools.'

'You too, Phil.'

He ended the call and stared at the phone. He'd been foolish to think she'd divulge anything. He wondered if she was in danger from Cross if she gave anything away. She'd never seemed fearful of Daniel, quite the opposite. She'd always described Cross's behaviour towards her as very protective. But Juliet was an expert at giving an air of assurance and calm. Maybe it was all a façade and she was vulnerable. Elsie reckoned she needed rescuing. Perhaps she was right.

He got back to his desk, as the DCI was calling the team together.

'So, what have we got? Phil, any luck with that ANPR?' Dave Matthews said.

'Yes, Guv. Her car passed the camera near the entrance to the apartment block at 2:46am.'

'Excellent. That gives us a timeline then. Any other CCTV footage yet?'

'Not from me. Still working on it,' said Phil.

'Have we got any footage of Winterton?' the DCI asked.

'Seen on foot on a nearby camera at 1:23am,' said DS Boyd, 'looking in a bit of a state.'

'So, something happens, he leaves, whoever was there with him calls your girl. She's in Windsor, hot-foots it back and gets there at a quarter to three. Now we're starting to get somewhere,' DCI Matthews said.

'On a hunch, I checked the registration of the car that Cross's main driver, Pat Malcolm, uses,' said DS Boyd. 'That turned up just after 3:50am. Left forty-eight minutes later and, though it's not the clearest footage, looks like he has an extra passenger on board.'

The DCI rubbed his hands with apparent delight. 'Let's see if we can follow his car and work out where he took this mystery passenger.'

Forty-eight hours later, the DCI and his team had worked out that Pat had driven his passenger to a country house hotel, that the passenger was called Tiffany Maddern and that Tiffany had been sporting facial injuries when using the hotel's spa facilities.

The team was in the briefing room, sharing the latest information and Phil was feeling nervous on Juliet's behalf. As the DCI finished getting updates from each team member, Detective Chief Superintendent Pidgeon walked in.

'Carry on,' the DCS nodded at DCI Matthews.

Phil could see his boss looking decidedly uncomfortable at the DCS's unexpected appearance.

'So, Guv, what's the next step? Are we going to pull Guy Winterton in for questioning? Given the anecdotal evidence of the state of Tiffany's face, are we going charge him with assaulting her? Even though we've not tracked her down yet? She's probably been paid not to say anything, of course.' Lewis Deacon, the youngest member of the team, was trying to impress the DCS with his grasp of the case, not realising the mistake he was making.

DCS Pidgeon looked across at his DCI with a face as ominous as a thundercloud. 'Are you…? Why aren't you fully focused on the Johnstone case?' He stared at the DCI without saying anything for a long time, while the rest of the room stared at the floor in collective embarrassment. 'Let's talk in my office, Dave. Now.'

Phil watched his boss follow DCS Pidgeon out of the room like a guilty schoolboy. Now he was the most senior person at the briefing, the others were looking to him for guidance. 'OK, let's put this on hold and review progress on the Johnstone case. We'll reconvene in an hour.'

DCI Matthews came back to the incident room twenty minutes later and beckoned Phil into his office.

'Have we been closed down?' Phil asked.

The DCI nodded. 'Don't quote me but it wouldn't surprise me if Pidgeon's a mate of Guy and his wife.'

'Did you just get a telling off?' Phil asked.

'He said I came close to a formal warning. But I don't think he'd want attention drawn to his keenness to ignore such an obvious crime.'

'I've asked the team to re-focus entirely on Johnstone,' Phil said. He went to leave when the DCI put his hand on Phil's arm.

'Keep pushing with that girl of yours, though. See if you can get her to tell you what really happened.'

Phil shook his head. 'She's not my girl anymore.'

'Did she blow you out?'

'Other way around,' said Phil.

'Pity,' the DCI said. 'Would've been good to have her on our side.'

It went through Phil's mind that he should resume his relationship with Juliet but he dismissed the idea immediately. He'd only be using her and even though he reckoned she'd been doing the same to him, he knew he was better than that.

Phil could feel his eyes starting to ache as he kept staring at hour after hour of CCTV footage. He rubbed his temples to try and reduce the strain. He'd wanted to do his fair share of the tedious effort it would take the team to review everything they'd gathered. He was sure though, if they examined it all, they'd find that one useful piece of data that would lead them to the perpetrator.

He refocused his gaze onto his mobile when it started to vibrate. 'Hey, Olly. Long time, no speak. How're you doing?'

'Good. You fancy a quick session up the driving range? I'm finishing early and we're overdue a catch up.'

Phil looked at his watch. 'Yeah. I'm getting nowhere fast, here. Feel like I'm walking up Everest in concrete boots. I could get there for 4:30pm?'

'I'll book us in. See you down there.'

Phil called over to Tom Boyd. 'Going out for a bit. Need some thinking time.'

'OK, Guv.'

'Make sure everyone takes a break,' Phil said.

Tom nodded and went back to staring at his screen.

Phil drove to the house. The traffic was busier than he'd expected with school pick-ups slowing him down. He dashed into the house and retrieved his golf clubs from the cupboard under the stairs. He put his head around Elsie's door. 'Hey, Else.'

'Hi, lovey.' She got up from her chair.

'Just off down the driving range. Meeting Olly.'

She looked none the wiser.

'Sal's brother,' he said.

'Oh, yeah. Not too busy at work then?' she asked.

'Overly busy, but I need some head space.'

'There's a bulb gone in the kitchen,' she said.

He looked at his watch. 'I'll change it tonight when I get back, OK?'

'Alright,' she said. 'Enjoy yourself.' She went back to her chair.

He felt a twinge of guilt but pushed it away. He'd always hated being late for anything. He drove to the golf club and found Olly in one of the bays, already practising.

'You're in there,' Olly said, pointing to the adjacent space. He hit the ball and it flew a couple of hundred yards.

'Nice shot.' Phil sat on the bench by the back wall and changed his shoes.

Olly was a left-hander, which meant he and Phil were facing each other. It was a double-edged sword, Phil thought. Good because they could talk while they practised. Bad because Phil hadn't played for a while and knew Olly would be scathing if Phil's shots weren't up to scratch. As if to prove the point, Phil hooked his first drive to the left under Olly's critical gaze.

'How long since you played?' Olly asked.

'Last time you and I did, when we played that double round,' Phil said.

'It shows.' Olly lined up his next shot and Phil watched him effortlessly swing, hitting the ball in the sweet spot that all golfers practise to achieve. It sailed off, straight and true, into the far distance.

'Good one.' Phil took his own shot and sliced it to the left.

Olly shook his head but said nothing. He hit another great drive.

Phil's play got worse. He'd hoped the golf would be a distraction from life but it seemed life was messing up his golf.

Olly rested his driver against the divider between their bays. 'What's putting you off your stroke? Work or a woman?'

'A bit of both,' Phil said.

'So, there is a woman in your life?'

'Yes and no.'

'She's in your life and you don't want her to be? Or she's not in your life and you wish she was?'

Phil tried another shot and watched as it flew at a forty-five-degree angle to the right. 'Sod it.' He rested his weight on his club. 'She was in my life, now she isn't and I'm torn about whether to ask her out again.'

Olly stared at him for a while.

'What?'

'Sal was curious to know if you were seeing anyone.'

Phil felt a jolt of surprise. 'Why?'

'I think she's started to realise being a copper's wife wasn't that bad after all.' He picked up his club and lined up his next shot.

'You're kidding?' said Phil.

'Nope. So, this woman. Did she do the dumping or did you?' Olly's ball sailed off down the centre line.

'God, you're on fire today,' Phil said. 'It was my decision.'

'Why?' Olly watched as Phil managed his first straight shot of the session. 'At last.'

'Long story.'

'But you want her back?' asked Olly.

'Maybe.'

'How do you feel about Sal?'

'How do I feel about her? Or how do I feel about the fact she might be regretting her decision to leave me?' asked Phil.

'Either. Both.' Olly sighed. 'Mate, I promised her I'd ask. Well, I promised Mum and her, and you know what a scary duo they are.'

'Do I ever. I'm sad Sal's having regrets but I don't want to go back to that life. Too much has happened.'

'What's this woman like?'

Phil gave it some thought. 'Bright, ballsy, intriguing. And beautiful. But dangerous.'

'Dangerous? What is she, a bloody terrorist?'

'I think I'm being played,' said Phil.

'Why would she do that?'

'Her boss is someone I've been investigating.'

'Is she dodgy too?' Olly asked.

'That's the million-dollar question. Elsie reckons she's a good girl caught up in bad things but I'm not so sure. I think she's pretending to be interested in me, just to get an inside track on the investigation.'

'You got a picture?' Olly asked.

Phil pulled his phone from his back pocket and searched for the photo he'd taken surreptitiously at the church, when he'd spotted Juliet reading one of the plaques. 'Here,' he said and showed it to Olly.

'She is way out of your league,' Olly said and laughed.

'Exactly.'

'I'm joking, mate. Why shouldn't you have a girl like that?' Olly asked.

Phil thought back to the pictures he'd been sent of Juliet naked and wondered about telling Olly. 'As you say, out of my league.' He put another ball on the tee and hit it hard, channelling his frustration about the anonymous sender of the photos. He connected with the ball perfectly and it flew towards the 250-yard marker. He felt a wave of satisfaction from the improvement.

'That's more like it,' Olly said.

After they'd worked their way through their remaining supply of golf balls, Olly asked if Phil had time for a drink.

'Yeah, a quick one,' Phil said. They went to the clubhouse and he ordered two pints of lager, taking them over to the table where Olly had sat down.

'Cheers,' they said in unison and took a long sip.

'What shall I tell Mum and Sal?' Olly asked.

Phil put down his glass. 'That I'm seeing someone.'

'And that it's serious?'

'Yeah. Say you got the impression I was serious about her. I don't want to tell your sister I'm not interested. But I'm not going back to her.'

'I don't blame you,' said Olly. 'I remember how shitty it was for you when she left with the kids. That's hard to forgive.'

Phil took another sip of his drink. Sal had been harsh in her criticism of him and it had felt like each argument rubbed lemon juice into the open wound of his guilt about neglecting his family because of his devotion to his job.

'So, what you gonna do about this girl?' Olly asked.

'Still trying to work that out.'

Olly's phone rang. 'Hey, love. What? When? Shit. Sorry, on me way.' Olly grimaced. 'I'm supposed to be at the school for some meeting about Zack. He locked a kid in a cupboard. Sorry, mate.'

'No worries. It's been good to catch up.'

'Let's not leave it so long next time.' Olly dashed out after draining his glass.

Phil stayed to finish his pint. He was surprised about Sal even thinking she wanted a reconciliation. He replayed in his mind the events that had led to the end of their marriage. Her complaints about his working patterns and her description of how lonely she felt, had made him realise how stressful it was for her trying to bring up their boys almost single-handedly. It had hit him hard, when she'd said that even when Phil was at home, he was distracted with whatever case he was working on and didn't give her and the boys any quality time. The shock, when he'd heard about the affair she was having, had been followed by the slow realisation that her complaints about his behaviour had only started after the beginning of her new relationship. She'd been playing him, trying to make him feel he was a bad husband to justify her sleeping with someone else. She, their sons and her new man, had all moved to Malta to live with her parents, who owned a hotel. Phil had been heartbroken that his boys were suddenly a flight away, instead of in the next room. He lost himself in the moment.

'You finished with that?' The barman's voice brought him back to the present.

'Yeah. Thanks.' He handed over the empty glass he'd been clutching and the barman moved to the next table to carry on collecting empties.

Phil went out to his car. He wasn't ready to go back to work but didn't want to go home. An urge for female company made him ring

Anna, an old friend, who worked as a high-end escort. He'd met her years ago when he was a young DC in Vice. They'd developed an affection for each other over the years and, though Phil would often pay for her time, it wasn't just about sex. It was mostly just a chat, a hug and a few lingering kisses.

She answered straight away. 'Darling, it's been an age. How are you?' Her voice was as smooth as melted chocolate.

'Lonely,' he said.

'Come over after 8pm. I'll make myself available, as it's you.'

He sent a text to Elsie, saying he'd be late back and went in search of a decent bottle of already chilled white wine. He sat in the car park at Anna's place, thinking about Sal and Juliet. It was hard to think of two more different people, yet he'd fallen for them both. For all the good it had done him.

He knocked on Anna's door just after 8pm. He handed over the wine as she let him in.

'Thank you but you didn't need to do that, my love. There's always a drink for you here. Come in.' She was a beautiful woman, slightly older than him with long, dark, lustrous hair and the most perfect cheekbones. She was always groomed, self-assured and meticulously made-up.

They sat down after she'd poured them both a large glass of wine.

'If I drink all that, I'll have to stay over,' he said.

She shrugged. 'You're more than welcome to share my bed. I've had my last caller today.'

'You're always so good to me, Anna.'

She took a delicate sip from her glass. 'That's because you are one of the few decent men in this world. A genuinely nice human being. What's bothering you?'

He began to tell her about Juliet. 'I don't regret ending the relationship with her. I think I just miss having someone around.'

She took the glass out of his hand. 'Well, you can have someone around tonight.' She began to kiss him, her soft lips moulding themselves over his.

He felt himself getting aroused but was distracted when his mobile started ringing.

'Ignore it,' she said.

But he couldn't, despite his frustration that his phone seemed determined to stop him kissing beautiful women. He pulled himself away and looked at the screen. No name came up and he didn't recognise the number. He pressed the green phone symbol. 'DI Haywood.' He listened to the voice on the other end of the line.

It was the son of one of Elsie's neighbours. 'Elsie's had a fall. They're taking her to hospital. I'm locking up the house so it's safe, but Dad thought you should know.'

Phil struggled for a moment to take in what the man was saying. 'Right, OK. Thanks. Are they taking her to the General?'

'That's what they said,' the son responded.

'I'll get over there. Thanks for the call.'

Phil looked at Anna. 'Sorry, my landlady's had an accident. I need to go.'

Anna sat back, putting her hands up to show he was free to leave. 'Sure. You're close to her, I think.'

He nodded.

'You go. I understand.'

He reached into his pocket for his wallet.

'There's no need. I hope she's OK.' She gave him one last kiss. 'You take care of yourself. And come and see me again soon.'

Phil drove as quickly as he dared to the hospital. When he got there, he discovered from the nurse on duty that Elsie hadn't regained consciousness and it seemed as though the doctors were concerned, from the carefully chosen phrases she was using.

From what he could gather, Elsie had been trying to reach into a kitchen cupboard and had used a step stool to get to the top shelf. When he remembered she'd asked him to change the bulb in the kitchen, he felt guilty and sick. The bulbs were in a cupboard above the microwave. She must have tried to get a new one and lost her footing. The paramedics believed she'd hit her head on the corner of the cooker unit. By luck, one of the neighbours had popped in for a chat and had seen Elsie on the floor through the window.

If only Phil had gone home. If only he'd changed that bulb when she'd mentioned it. His mind started wandering. If only he'd still been with Juliet, he'd have been at home or maybe Juliet would have changed the bulb. Juliet. He should probably tell her about Elsie. He rang her number.

'Phil?' She sounded wary.

'Sorry to bother you,' he said.

'You're not ringing about Guy, are you?'

'No. It's Elsie. She's had a fall,' he said.

'What? How is she?' Her voice wavered.

'She's unconscious, in hospital,' he said.

'Is that where you're calling from?' she asked.

'Yeah.'

'I'll come over, shall I? I'm still in the office but it shouldn't take me long to get there. Can you text me the details?'

'Why are you at work at this time of night?' He shook his head. 'Doesn't matter. I'll send a text.'

'Thanks.' She hung up.

He stared at the phone, wishing things were different.

Chapter 22 - Juliet

Juliet went into Daniel's office, where he was working on one of his secret projects. She hadn't wanted to go back to the flat and Daniel had kept working, so she'd taken the opportunity to tidy her office space, in the hope he might let something slip about his latest obsession. She'd got used to him being secretive over the years. Half his ideas never lasted beyond a day. Most were consigned to the bin within forty-eight hours. But this one had taken his attention for nearly a week. Juliet waited for him to acknowledge her. He looked up, saying nothing but raised his eyebrows as if to ask what she wanted.

'I need to go. Sorry,' she said.

He frowned. 'What's up?'

'You know the old lady that came to stay?'

'The copper's landlady?'

She nodded. 'She's been injured in a fall. She's in hospital.'

'And you want to go see her?' he asked.

'Yes. Go sit with her for a bit.'

'Off you go, then. I'll see you Monday,' he said.

Now it was her turn to frown. 'But it's only Wednesday.'

He stood up and reached across his desk to put his hand on her shoulder, giving her a friendly smile that unnerved her. 'Have some time off on me. Focus on your old dear.'

'Thanks. I appreciate that. Ring me if you need anything.'

He sat back down and his attention was lost, so Juliet went back to her desk, closed down her laptop and dashed to the car park.

The traffic was quiet and she was walking into the hospital within an hour of Phil's call. She found the ward and asked the solitary healthcare assistant at the nursing station for Elsie's bed number. She found the cubicle and gingerly pulled back the curtain.

Phil was sitting next to the bed, looking concerned as he watched Elsie. 'Jools.' He stood up.

She embraced him stiffly, not wanting him to feel uncomfortable but longing for the sort of hug he used to give her.

'Nice of you to come,' he said.

'Do you want me to get you a coffee or something?' she asked.

'Can you sit with her while I go and stretch my legs?'

'Sure. I can stay as long as you like,' she said.

He nodded a thank you, picked up his jacket from the back of the chair and disappeared through the cubicle curtain.

She sat down. 'Hey Elsie, what happened?' She knew there'd be no response but had seem too many news stories where talking to people had brought them back to consciousness. She started to chat about what was happening at work and how Daniel was being secretive but soon ran out of things to say. She found a website on her phone that had the latest details and gossip on *Eastenders*, Elsie's favourite soap, and read through the plot highlights. It didn't feel odd having a one-way conversation. It was no different to the inner monologue that constantly streamed through her brain when she was home alone.

Phil came back after half an hour. He'd bought a bottle of water for her and offered to get her a coffee from a machine. 'It tastes pretty grim but it's marginally better than nothing,' he said.

'No thanks. Water's fine.' She felt another overwhelming urge to hug him but didn't think he'd be too happy if she did, so they sat in uneasy silence for a while. She felt they ought to be interacting with Elsie, so she found a quiz website and began firing questions at Elsie, hoping Phil would join in. It wasn't long before he started to respond, offering suggestions to the answers. It made the time slip by relatively painlessly, removing emotion from the situation. After several sets of questions, she'd discovered Phil was strong on history, geography and science, but less good on art, literature and entertainment. They'd have made a good quiz team between them.

As the clock ticked over to 1am, they both showed signs of weariness.

'Do you want to go, Phil? Get some rest? I've got the next few days off so it doesn't matter if my sleep's disturbed.'

'Are you sure? Why are you off?' he asked.

'I'm sure. Daniel said I could take some time away to focus on Elsie.'

'That was kind of him,' he said.

'He's always been good to me,' she said, expecting Phil to try and counter the statement.

'I might go back to the house, then. Get some rest and pick up some of Elsie's things for when she wakes up.'

'Yes, let's think positive. I'll wait here till you're back,' she said.

He stood up and didn't say anything for a minute.

Without concern for the reaction, she got up and gave him a brief hug and a peck on the cheek. 'I'll see you later, then.' She sat down and put her hand over Elsie's.

Phil left the cubicle and Juliet looked at Elsie. 'Oh, Else. I wish things were different. Yes, I know. I need to open up to him. Be more honest. But that's scary when he's in the police. I'm not sure what I was even thinking, given what I get up to at work. But I liked him. Still like him. Maybe I should have stuck with Cameron. At least he didn't care what I did for Daniel. Not that I had much choice when Cameron dumped me, but I could have fought harder to make him stay. Still, maybe whatever Cam was caught up in is what caused his accident. Not that it was an accident. Someone beating him up that badly, to the point where he couldn't walk, he must have really pissed someone off for that kind of punishment. I think I showed you a picture of him, didn't I, Elsie?' She took out her phone and looked at a photo of her and Cameron attending his friend's wedding. He was good looking, with a muscular torso and thin hips. He'd been a tiger in the sack. 'Maybe I should get in touch with him, try and be a bit more honest with him about myself and how I feel. It could work better, second time around, if I open up to him.' She sat back, staring into space.

She woke with a start when a nurse came in to check on Elsie just after 5am, but drifted off again. By 6am, she realised she probably wouldn't sleep anymore, so went to the loo and refreshed her make-up. She sat back in the chair next to Elsie and started telling her what was happening in the world, working her way down the articles on the BBC news website. It was just after 8am when Phil re-appeared.

He looked as though he'd managed to get some sleep and have a shower, his hair still damp at the back of his neck and his shirt freshly ironed. He handed her a cup from Starbucks. 'There you go.'

'Thanks.' She stretched and rubbed her neck.

'No change, I assume?' he asked.

She shook her head.

'Did you sleep?'

'A bit,' she said.

'Why don't you go back to the house now and get some rest? Use my bed. No point in you going all the way back to London. I can sit with her.'

'Don't you need to be at work?' she asked.

'I've told them I'll be in this afternoon. I mean, there's nothing to say either of us has to be here,' he said, 'but…'

'I agree,' she said. 'We need to make sure someone's here when she wakes up.'

He nodded.

She took a sip of her coffee and felt more awake. 'I'll be back by midday.'

He handed her his house keys. 'Thanks, Jools.' It was his turn to initiate the hug.

She felt the warmth of his body envelop her and hung on to him for as long as she dared. Hug over, she walked across to the car park, paid the exit fee on her way out and drove the short distance to the house.

The front garden looked as though it needed attention. The weeds were encroaching on Elsie's beloved flowers. Juliet let herself into the house and the smell of the place struck her. Every home had its own smell and the only one you never really knew was your own place. Elsie's house had an overwhelming scent of antique wood, like one of those old-fashioned hotels where the furniture isn't repro. She opened the door to Phil's room, immediately smelling his musky aftershave. It was reassuring and she stripped off after drawing the curtains. She set an alarm on her phone for 11am.

She was surprised to be woken by the alarm. She never slept during the day. It took her a few minutes to wake up, checking the news and social media apps to bring herself back to the present.

She had brought her overnight bag in from the car. It had everything she needed in case she ever found herself away from home. She took a shower and began to feel ready to face the day. She arrived back at the hospital just before midday.

Phil was talking on the phone when she got to the ward. He lifted his head to acknowledge her presence while he finished his call. 'Hi,' he said. 'I'm really sorry, but I need to get back to work.'

She felt disappointed and relieved at the same time. She tried to make her smile look sympathetic. 'No problem. I'm happy to stay around.'

Juliet decided to drop Cameron a WhatsApp message, to see if she could start a conversation with him. Trying afresh with him had to be part of the answer to leading a better life, given she couldn't make it work with Phil. She still had to fathom out how to untangle herself from her job and from Daniel but felt that was going to be harder still.

A nurse came in, had a look at Elsie to see if everything was OK then left again with barely a nod to Juliet.

'Service with a smile, eh, Else? I wish I'd done something like nursing. A vocation. I thought what I did for work was exciting, daring. But it's just wrong, isn't it? You made me realise that. And why am I doing it? What do I get out of it apart from a nice view? I take all the risks and get none of the benefit. All for Daniel. I've been a bit of a fool, really.' She looked up, sensing movement. Elsie's head moved from right to left, just slightly, so her face was pointing more towards Juliet. Her eyes stayed shut. Juliet took Elsie's hand, willing her to wake up but there was nothing.

Cameron's response to her message made her phone beep. "Happy 2 meet 4 a coffee. R U OK?"

She sent back a message, explaining she was with a friend who was unconscious in hospital.

"Did ur friend incur DC's rage 2?"

Juliet frowned at the screen and sent back a "?".

"Doesn't matter. Which hosp?"

She sent him the details but was distracted by his puzzling message. As she stared into the middle distance, a terrible thought crossed her mind.

She rang Pat.

'Hi Jools. You any idea what's got Daniel distracted?' he asked. Pat rarely wasted time on small talk.

'No, he's keeping this project close to his chest. Maybe he's set his sights on another company to take over.'

'What did you want?' he asked.

'I really need you to tell me the truth about something, Pat. Did Daniel have anything to do with Cameron's assault?'

There was a long pause.

Juliet let out a gasp. It was true? 'But why?'

'Because of you,' he said.

'I never asked for him to be hurt.'

'No, but Daniel saw how upset you were when Cameron left you. When you found out he was seeing someone else.'

She struggled to process the revelation. 'But to do someone permanent damage, put them in a wheelchair. Because I was upset he'd left me?'

'That wasn't the plan. The guy who did it went too far.'

Juliet couldn't think of anything to say.

'Of course, I'll deny any knowledge of it, and so will Daniel, if you ask again,' he said.

'I won't be asking again. Thank you for being honest.' She ended the call. She felt numb and sick.

Elsie's head moved again.

A couple of hours later, Juliet had another message from Cam. "In Reception. Which ward R U in?"

She was surprised and nervous at the thought of seeing him, now that she knew she'd been the cause of his injuries, albeit indirectly and unwittingly. She got up to pull back the curtain surrounding the bed. Cam appeared at the entrance to the ward, being pushed by Billie.

'Hey, Jools. Are you OK? You remember Billie, don't you?' he said.

Juliet forced a smile in Billie's direction. 'Hi. Yes, I'm OK. How come you're here?'

'We've been in the area, looking at hotels,' he said cryptically. 'What's the prognosis for your friend?'

'Not sure. Just hoping she'll wake up.'

'We'll pray for her,' Billie said and touched Juliet's arm.

As Juliet tried not to flinch at the intimate gesture, she noticed Billie was wearing an engagement ring.

Cameron followed her gaze. 'We got engaged last week. Hoping to get married early next year.' He beamed. 'That's why we're checking out venues, for the wedding reception.'

Juliet felt his happiness bore into her like a laser. She'd never seem him look this happy before. 'Congratulations.' She gave them both a peck on the cheek. 'Could you wait here for a couple of minutes, just while I use the loo?' She dashed off to the sanctuary of the bathroom to process Cam's news. She'd been kidding herself that she could get back with him, selfishly assuming he'd be available and willing to try again with her. With that possibility off the table, what else could she do? She felt she had to take positive action. Maybe it would be enough to leave her job, to separate herself from Daniel and the work she did. Elsie had said she mustn't lock herself away but perhaps a change of work scene would be enough to sort out her life. It was definitely the right start.

Chapter 23 – Elsie

Elsie came to. Her eyes felt sticky and didn't want to open. She blinked a few times and focused on her surroundings. The place smelled of disinfectant and cheap hand wash. There was a plastic curtain up around the bed and a young man in a wheelchair beside her bed, with an even younger girl. He seemed vaguely familiar. Elsie tried to speak but her throat was dry.

The girl looked at her and realised what Elsie was after, pouring some water from a jug into a beaker. She offered the beaker up to Elsie's mouth.

Elsie took a sip, licked her lips and said 'Who are you?' Her voice was croaky.

The man spoke. 'I'm an old friend of Jools,' he said. 'She's just gone to the loo.' He looked away from Elsie towards the end of the ward. 'Here she is now '

'Elsie. Oh, thank goodness you're awake.' Juliet bent over and gave Elsie a gentle kiss on the forehead.

Elsie was glad to see Juliet. 'Hallo, lovey.' She sat back and watched as Juliet ushered the boy and girl away before sitting on the chair by the bed.

'Oh, Else, it's so good to see you. I should get a doctor.'

'No rush, lovey. I'm not going anywhere.'

A nurse came by and noticed Elsie was awake. She called over a colleague and they began fussing, checking the monitor and asking questions. Elsie tried to listen in to Juliet, who was talking on her mobile.

'Hi, Phil. Yes, she's woken up. And she seems fine. Yes, I understand. Elsie will, too. I'll see you then.' Juliet hovered at the end of the bed while the nurses finished their activities.

'Don't tire her out,' the eldest of the nurses said to Juliet. 'She needs to rest.'

'Bugger that,' Elsie said, when the nurses had moved away. 'How long have I been here, lovey?'

'Since last night,' said Juliet. 'We've been worried.' She squeezed Elsie's hand.

'How's Phil?'

'Oh, you know. Busy at work. I just rang him, told him you're back with us. He's chuffed to bits. He said they'd made a breakthrough in the case but he'll try and get here as soon as he can. I said you'd understand.'

'I don't suppose, by some miracle, that you and him have got back together?'

Juliet shook her head. 'If I'm honest, Else, I don't think that's ever going to happen.'

'Something's changed though, hasn't it? You seem different.'

There was a silence.

'What is it?' Elsie asked.

'Our last couple of conversations made me realise I need a career change. You've woken me up to the risks I'm taking. Not sure if you remember?'

'I do. And Hallelujah to that. What are you going to do?'

Juliet shrugged. 'I've got to figure that out, what I want to do next. As well as working out how to extricate myself from Cross International.'

Elsie frowned. 'Is that going to be a problem?'

'There's only one way to find out.'

Elsie squeezed Juliet's hand. 'You need to realise you have power in all this.'

'Do I?'

'You have information. That's your power,' Elsie said.

'Daniel holds all the aces though. He'll have plenty of evidence of me doing things I shouldn't. And he's my landlord.'

'You can stay at my house. We can make some space upstairs for you. Don't let that be the reason you keep doing what you're doing. Take my house key out of my purse, go on. You can move in today if you want.'

The bossy nurse came back. 'Let's get some rest now, Elsie, please.' She turned to Juliet. 'It would be better if you left, so Elsie can focus on recuperating. Now she's awake, you should really only be here during visiting hours.'

'Why don't you go and see your boss, right now?' Elsie said to Juliet, ignoring the nurse. 'Tell him your decision. We can make it work.'

Juliet nodded and took Elsie's handbag from the small cupboard in the bedside table. Fishing out the key, she smiled. 'Thank you. I'll come back later, OK?'

Elsie smiled. 'Thanks, lovey. You know, I've often wondered what it would have been like to have a daughter. I'd have loved her to be like you.'

'You're very kind. I'm not sure I'm a role model for anything.' Juliet gave her a final hug and left the ward.

Elsie drifted in and out of wakefulness, plans for the future bubbling inside her head. This scare had made her realise she needed to make the most of every moment. At her age, she didn't dare hope for too many more years, but she still had enough time to put everything in order, as well as enjoy the rest of her life as much as she could.

She woke to see Phil sitting by the bed, staring at his mobile phone. 'Hallo, lovey. You managed to drag yourself away from work then?'

He reached over and held her hand. 'I have.'

'Have you caught the bastard?' she asked.

He nodded and smiled. 'Yep. I've left him talking to his lawyer but I've got to go back soon so we can start the formal questioning. But we've some really strong evidence, so I'm hopeful we'll be charging him in the next day or so.'

'It's good of you to come with all that going on,' she said.

'How are you feeling?'

'A bit light-headed. A bit sore in places. But OK. Glad to be alive. Have you seen Juliet?' she asked.

'No. She texted to say she was leaving you to sleep on nurse's orders. But I've not heard from her since,' he said.

'I do hope she's alright.'

'Why?' Phil's face was full of concern.

'Oh, nothing.'

'Should I be worried, Else?' he asked.

Elsie wondered about telling him anything. But what good would that do? She shook her head. 'She's a big girl. She can sort her life out.'

The concern stayed etched on his face.

'You get off and make that bugger confess. I'm hoping they'll let me out soon and we can celebrate you putting him away. Maybe I can take you and Juliet to Luigi's.'

He stood up and bent over her, kissing her forehead, just like Juliet had. 'You take it slow, Else. No breaking out of here till they're sure you're well enough.'

'Yes, officer.' She touched her forehcad where he'd kissed it, moved by the gesture. If Juliet was the daughter she'd like to have had, Phil was definitely the son. Such a fine, upstanding man.

'I'll get back to see you as soon as I can,' he said. 'But get them to call me if there's anything you need.'

Chapter 24 – Juliet

Juliet went straight up to her office and found the CIO's secretary was using her desk.

'Hallo, Jools. Didn't think we were seeing you this week. Daniel told me to sit here while you were away. Is everything OK?'

'Yes thanks, Paige. Where's Daniel?'

'I think he's in the boardroom. He's been there most of the day. No idea why. There's been all sorts of comings and goings in the last couple of days. Lots of people around who I don't recognise. It's all been a bit weird.'

Juliet had been hoping to get some quiet time with Daniel but it didn't sound as though that was going to be possible. 'OK, thanks.'

'Do you want me to go?' Paige asked.

'No, you stay there. I'm going to try and find Daniel. See if I can talk to him.'

She walked to the end of the corridor and past the directors' offices to the boardroom door. The blinds were down so she couldn't see who was in there. She decided to text Daniel rather than barging in. His response to her message that she was back in the office was a terse "OK". The response to her second text that read "Do you need me in the boardroom?" was "No".

She felt deflated, having worked out what she wanted to say to him as well as finding the courage to say it.

She decided to go back to the flat and pack up her belongings. It wouldn't be ideal, having to live in the same place as Phil but Elsie was right, it was better than staying in her job for the sake of a roof over her head. She went back to her desk and told Paige she was going to her flat.

'I thought Megan had moved in there.'

'Not yet,' Juliet said. At least she hoped not.

The flat was messier than she would have left it. Her clothes were still in the main bedroom wardrobe, but Megan had left clothes, shoes and underwear strewn all over the guest bedroom floor. Juliet took some pictures of the mess before taking a pair of suitcases out of the hallway cupboard and packing up her clothes and shoes. She looked around the apartment to see what else she could rightfully call hers. There were toiletries and a few books but that was all. She remembered her passport and share certificates were in the safe, so she got those out before taking her luggage down to the underground car park.

Elsie's house was quiet when Juliet arrived. She let herself in and took the cases up the stairs, one by one. There was no obvious bed for her to use, with all of George's furniture crammed into the rooms. Maybe she'd buy a camp bed as a temporary measure. She'd need some bedding, too, though she could get a sleeping bag and use Elsie's bed till Elsie came out of hospital.

She didn't want to spend very much till she had a new job. It was quite a scary prospect, walking away from everything she'd known for the last five years but it was scarier still to think of carrying on. To think of putting herself at the mercy of people like Guy Winterton, with the risk of ending up injured like Tiffany, or worse. To continue breaking the law by drugging people and stealing information from them. To be vulnerable to her victims' anger at what she'd done to them. She knew she couldn't do it anymore. How had she sleepwalked through life to end up on the wrong side of the law?

She drove back to the office with a sinking feeling about talking to Daniel. She wasn't sure what she feared more, his anger at her leaving or his efforts to persuade her to stay. The nearer she got to London, the more anxious she felt.

By the time she got back to her desk, Paige had gone home. Juliet walked along the corridor to the boardroom and the door was now ajar. She took a look inside to see Daniel talking to Pat, too quietly for her to hear what they were discussing.

Daniel spotted her first. 'How's the old biddy?'

'She's awake now, thanks.' Juliet felt a bit sick. 'Can I have a chat?'

Pat got up. 'I'll leave you to it.'

'No, you stay,' Daniel said.

Juliet wasn't sure if it was better or worse having Pat there.

'What is it, Jools?' Daniel's stare was hard and without warmth.

She took a deep breath. 'I've decided it's time to move on.'

'Move on? From what?' Daniel's voice was steely.

'From Cross International.'

Daniel shook his head. 'No. You can't leave. I need you to stay here.'

She took in another breath then let it out slowly. 'I'm not asking, Daniel. I'm telling you.'

'Have you been poached? What bastard's done that? I'll break their fuckin' neck.' He looked at Pat who shrugged his shoulders.

'No. I haven't got another job yet. I've just made the decision that I can't do this one anymore,' she said.

'Don't be stupid.' He stood up. 'You're not leaving. I'm not wasting my time on this pointless conversation.'

'I'll leave my resignation letter on your desk,' she said, refusing to be side-lined by him.

'Why would you want to leave me? I've always looked after you. Treated you well,' he said.

'I can't be the paid escort and spy anymore. With what happened to Tiffany and everything, I just can't do it anymore.' She took a deep breath. 'And when you say looked after me, crippling my ex-boyfriend does not count as looking after someone.'

His eyes blazed. 'Is that some kind of threat?'

'No. I'd never threaten you. I've no intention of betraying you or anyone else. That's not what this is about, Daniel. I just want out.'

'You know I've got plenty of evidence of you breaking the law on camera, don't you? If you try and bring me down, I'll bring you down right back. Don't think that copper of yours can protect you.' He was towering over her now and she was grateful Pat was still in the room.

Her legs felt wobbly but she stood her ground. 'You're not hearing me, Daniel. I don't want to bring anyone down, least of all you. I just can't do this job anymore. I'm too scared.'

'Scared? Why? Because your beloved boyfriend doesn't approve? I knew he was fuckin' trouble the moment he turned up here.'

'He's not my boyfriend. And if he knew what I do for you, he'd have arrested me by now. He's all black and white, no grey at all.'

Daniel stopped and looked at her. 'Jools, I need you to stay because of what's about to happen.'

'What?' She looked at him warily.

'The company's being taken over.'

'By who? Why would you let that happen? You always said you'd rather die than give up your business,' she said.

'I want out, too. I've had enough. Gonna take the money and retire somewhere warm. But I need you to support the new chairman, make sure he's got everything he needs. You'll do that for me, won't you?'

'How long for?' she asked, hating herself for even contemplating staying.

'Six months, max but maybe only three. As a reward, I want you to join me out in the sunshine. Come and enjoy the high life. I'll buy you your own villa.'

She stopped to think. 'What do I have to do for the new chairman? I'm not entertaining people like Guy or Harrison, putting myself at risk.'

Daniel looked sideways at Pat. 'That's fine.'

'Just being his PA?'

'That's all you'll have to do,' he said.

'And what do I get if I agree to stay? If it's that important to you and him that I hang around for a while?'

'What do you want? Apart from an all-expenses-paid life in the sunshine,' he said.

She thought for a while. 'I'd like a bonus for staying around. An extra six months' pay seems reasonable, if I stay for six months.' It would be handy to have some cash as a buffer till she found her next job. Daniel's talk of a life in the sunshine didn't seem realistic. Giselle wouldn't put up with Juliet being around, she was sure. And was a lazy life in the sun really what she wanted? She was much too young for retirement, but the thought of starting afresh did appeal. Maybe she could reset her life somewhere new. She'd always liked Edinburgh when she'd visited. Or Manchester. Just somewhere far enough away from Woking. And Phil.

'Done,' he said. 'I'll make sure you're paid a generous bonus. Let's round it up to a year's salary.' He smiled. 'Who knows? You might even find you enjoy working for my successor.'

'Who is it? Anyone I know?' she asked.

'My lips are sealed till the takeover's gone through,' Daniel said.

'OK.' She felt a bit defeated by what had happened, but if Daniel was moving on, perhaps it would be alright to stay if she could go back to being a PA. But where would she live? 'What about my flat?'

'Stay there. We're going to put Megan up in another place, so she's available if needed.'

'OK. Thanks,' she said.

'Off you go, then.' He dismissed her like a headmaster speaking to a naughty pupil.

'When will the takeover be announced?' she asked.

'Sometime next week. And listen. Don't worry about coming back till it's all official. Go and spend some more time with your old biddy.' He turned towards Pat to continue his conversation.

Juliet left the boardroom and went back to her desk. It crossed her mind as odd that Daniel didn't want her there but it was probably just because all the takeover activity would be focused around legal, commercial and financial considerations, as well as sorting out all the communications for the staff and press. It would no doubt involve long hours so she should be thankful she didn't have to be around.

The more she thought about it, the more she realised it was a better outcome than she could have hoped for. A safe job for six more months, the flat all to herself again and no need to do anything other than help the new chairman settle in. And at the end of it, a year's pay-out and a fresh start. Of course, it was possible the new guy might want her around longer. The future didn't seem so scary anymore.

She decided to drive back to the hospital via the house, so she could pick up her belongings to bring them back to the flat. As she turned into Elsie's road, she saw Phil's car parked in the street and changed her mind. It would be too hard to explain to him why she'd left her belongings and was now picking them up again.

At the hospital, she found Elsie sitting up in bed, looking a lot more like her old self.

'Hallo, lovey.'

'You're looking brighter, Else. How are you feeling?'

'Raring to go. Well?' asked Elsie.

'What?'

'Don't be coy. Did you see your boss?'

'I did,' Juliet said.

'And you told him you were leaving?'

'I did, but he persuaded me not to,' Juliet said.

The disappointment on Elsie's face was tangible. 'Oh, lovey.'

'It's fine. There's a really good reason.' She told her about the takeover and how her role would be different, safer.

Elsie shook her head. 'You've got to do what you think is right but...' She sighed.

'But what?' Juliet asked.

'I really don't think it's a good decision for you to stay. I hope you don't regret it.'

'It'll be fine, Else. It couldn't have worked out better. All the benefits without any of the negatives. And it's only for six months. I'll be able to find myself a new job in slow time,' she said. 'Trust me.'

Chapter 25 – Phil

Phil helped Elsie out of the car and into the house. It had been five days since she'd woken up and she'd been discharged on the basis she would have some support at home while she recuperated. Phil's suspect had been charged with murder and rape, and the case was winding down. He'd agreed with his boss he would take some time off to make sure Elsie was OK.

He was almost sorry Juliet was taking time off to help out. He still felt awkward and suspicious in her presence. He'd heard from Elsie that Daniel Cross was retiring and was going to live somewhere warm - the cliché of the villain's choice for an escape - but Phil had resigned himself to the fact there was little point in pursuing Cross anymore. He hadn't heard who Juliet would be working for, but he could tell Elsie had reservations about the situation from the way she described it. Or rather, not described it, as it was obvious there were some aspects she was keeping to herself.

He'd moved Elsie's television nearer her bed so she could watch it from there. He got her settled into her room and went to make them both a cup of tea. He knew he'd have to spend some time tidying the garden as the weeds, particularly the nettles, were starting to take hold. He hated nettles. However carefully he treated them, he always seemed to get stung.

He took two mugs of strong tea into Elsie's room and sat on the edge of her bed.

'Oh, that's lovely, Phil. Gnat's pee, the tea in that hospital.' She smacked her lips as she took another sip. 'Is Juliet coming over later?'

'Said she'd be here around 7pm-ish.'

'Have you sorted out a space upstairs for her to sleep?' she asked.

'Not yet. She said she'd bring a sleeping bag and use the sofa in the front room for tonight.'

Elsie frowned.

'I know but she did say she'd rather I started the battle with the weeds than bother with furniture moving,' he said.

Elsie chuckled. 'She can be a bit bossy, can't she?'

Phil gave a flat smile. 'She certainly knows her own mind.'

'She really needs to get herself a companion. Someone who'll show her it's OK to be open and honest about herself. I don't suppose you've thought any more about er…' she stopped.

'About what?' His voice sounded sharp, even to his ears and he felt guilty for its tone.

'Nothing. None of my business,' she said.

He watched Elsie finish her tea, trying to think of something to say, but his mind stayed blank.

'I think I'm gonna have a bit of a rest, if you don't mind,' she said, as she put down her empty mug.

'Not at all, Else.' He picked up the mug and tapped the bedside table. 'Your phone's here. If you need anything, just call me. I'll only be out in the garden.'

He was glad to get outside, away from Elsie's gaze and into the fresh air. It was disappointing to see just how much the weeds had taken over. There'd been some warmer weather and quite a bit of rain that had made some of the late flowering plants come alive again but the weeds had done even better. He'd put on a sweatshirt so his arms were covered and pulled on his thickest gardening gloves to try and foil the nettles' desire to sting him. As he worked, he got warm very quickly and foolishly pushed up the sleeves of the sweatshirt to his elbows to cool down. It was a move he quickly regretted when he felt a nettle brush his forearm. There was a moment when he thought he'd got away with it but his skin quickly turned red, and white bumps began to spring up. He swore under his breath and pulled his sleeves back down. He continued for another half-hour, feeling as though he was taking revenge for his pain by cutting the nettles down and pulling at their roots. He tried to ignore the itchy discomfort on his arm but knew it would be best to wash the stings with soap to counteract the acid.

He took the nettle cuttings to the garden bin then took off his gardening gloves and went inside to wash. He stuck his head around Elsie's door and was glad to see she was asleep. He took off his sweatshirt and ran some warm water. He rubbed a wet bar of soap over the area where the stings were showing and felt some relief from the tingling sensations. He was startled by the front door opening. He hadn't closed the bathroom door so had full view into the hallway. It was Juliet. She was dressed casually but looked chic.

'You're early,' he said.

She turned towards him. 'Hi. Yes, traffic wasn't too bad for once.' She walked up to the threshold of the bathroom. 'Are you alright?'

He held up his arm. 'The nettles got me.'

'Looks like you got them back, from the amount you've pulled out.'

'Are you OK? You look like you've been crying,' he said.

'I have. Got something in my eye on the way over here and it was streaming by the time I got the eyelash out.'

He said nothing. Both her eyes looked red. It was obvious to him she'd been crying. It seemed she couldn't help herself, redefining the truth to suit her own ends as usual.

'I'll just go and get my things out of the car,' she said.

'Did you remember to bring a sleeping bag?'

'I did,' she said and went outside.

When Juliet came back with a suitcase, Phil asked if she'd stay around while he went up to the allotment.

'Sure,' she said. 'That's what I'm here for.'

'Thanks. I don't think we need to be here absolutely every minute of the day but I think we should be around to help Elsie for the first few days, till she's properly back on her feet.'

'I don't mind at all. I've got time off work so I'm happy to be on full-time duty. You can come and go as you please,' she said.

He nodded but didn't trust himself to say more. He wondered if she found it as uncomfortable being around him as he did around her? Maybe it had been a bad idea getting her to come here, but Elsie had been keen. It was obvious Elsie liked Juliet a lot and Juliet seemed to do all the right things when it came to making Elsie like her. But he still had a niggling feeling that Juliet was playing a game, going through the motions and pretending to like Elsie. What he couldn't fathom out was why she would do that.

Chapter 26 – Juliet

Juliet was glad when Phil went to the allotment as she wanted some time to think. She'd spent a couple of days in the flat, tidying up the files on her laptop and archiving her emails. She'd also searched for information about the takeover and had stumbled across a letter Daniel had saved in the wrong folder. She felt sick when she saw that Jeremy Harrison was listed as Daniel's successor. She'd left the flat immediately, sent an empty email with the title "How could you?" to Daniel and driven over to Elsie's, crying for half the journey.

Daniel called her while she was driving. 'Jools. What the fuck is this email about? How could I what?'

'Jeremy fuckin' Harrison. You bastard.'

She heard him curse under his breath.

'How do you know that?' he asked.

'It doesn't matter how I know. How could you think I'd work for that scumbag when you know what he did to me?' she asked.

'Come on, it wasn't that bad, was it? Anyway, he likes you. Wants you with him, by his side while he's settling in. Realises what an asset you are to the organisation.'

'He's a bully who treats people like shit.'

'Only when he thinks he's being played. He's alright. Very sharp. He'll do well for the business with that lawyer's brain of his,' he said.

'Huh. And I'm just collateral damage?'

'Jools, you don't have anything to fear from Jeremy. If I thought you did, I'd never have suggested you stay on,' he said. 'It's only six months, that's all. Then you can have your bonus and come out to Cyprus, get some sun. We can relax together.'

'I hope you're right, Daniel.' She finished the call and sat around the corner from Elsie's to compose herself, before driving the last 100 metres and going into the house. She'd been startled to see Phil and annoyed with herself that she hadn't hidden her swollen eyes from his forensic gaze. She was sure he hadn't believed her eyelash story. But did it matter whether he believed her or not? Why should she care?

Now Phil had left the house and Elsie was asleep, Juliet needed to work out a strategy for dealing with Jeremy Harrison, to make sure she didn't find herself in a vulnerable position. She decided to call Pat and talk it through with him.

'Hi, Jools, you OK? Daniel said you'd heard the news.'

'Are you going to be alright working for Harrison?' she asked.

'I'm not staying. Jackie and I are going to go to Cyprus with Daniel, for a while at least.'

She felt deflated. 'Nice for you. Bit of warmth for winter.'

'Yes. The girls are all grown up and have their own lives, so no-one will miss me and Jackie for a few months.'

'When are you leaving?' she asked.

'Next week some time.'

'Nice. Have a safe flight.' She ended the call and stared at her phone. That wasn't good. She'd at least hoped Pat would be around to support her after Daniel had gone.

She got up and went to check on Elsie, who looked as though she'd just woken up.

'How are you doing, Else? Cuppa tea?'

'Hallo, lovey. Ooh, yes please. Where's Phil?' Elsie asked.

'At the allotment. Should be back in another hour or so, he reckoned.'

'He's a good lad. Well, you both are. I'm lucky to have you around.'

'Thanks.' It did feel nice to Juliet, being able to help her.

'Have you met your new boss yet?'

Juliet felt herself flinch at the question and hoped Elsie hadn't noticed. 'No, not yet. Sometime next week it'll all be announced, I'm told. Till then, it's a secret.'

'Well, you know my feelings about you staying there. I'm sure there'd be an office job around here you could do. I'd only charge you minimal rent. Whatever you could afford, really. We can sort you out a nice area upstairs. Private, so you can have people over.'

'You're so kind. I don't deserve it,' Juliet said.

'Course you do, lovey. You give so much to others. You're allowed to receive their kindness back. Life isn't a one-way street.'

'It's too risky if you rely on other people,' Juliet said.

'Only if they're the wrong people. Decent people won't hold it against you, if you need help and support.' Elsie was looking straight at Juliet and Juliet couldn't hold her gaze.

'I know you're right, but it's hard to stop trying to be self-sufficient. Too many people have given me nothing in return, so I've stopped asking.'

'Oh, lovey. You need to keep asking. And start hanging around with the right type of people.'

After five days of looking after Elsie and avoiding Phil at every opportunity, Juliet began to look forward to going back to work. Every time she tried to start a conversation with Phil, he seemed embarrassed or awkward in her presence, so she stayed out of his way as much as she could. Elsie was getting stronger and Juliet expected Phil to tell her she didn't need to stay any more. But she was enjoying spending time with Elsie. They would tackle cryptic crosswords together, play cards and talk about their favourite movies and TV shows. And slowly, Juliet began to relax around her, revealing snippets about herself, her childhood and her struggle with relationships. And as long as Elsie was around, it was OK being there. If it was the three of them, they would talk about the garden and the plans for what to grow in the allotment next year. But when Elsie was asleep or Juliet and Phil were in the kitchen fixing dinner, the conversation was very functional. There was no small talk, no chatting, just practical questions like "Can you pass that pan?" or "Do you want salad or veg with that?" Juliet found it wearying and sad.

News of the takeover of Cross International broke the next morning. Juliet told Elsie and Phil over breakfast that she would be going into the office the next day.

'That's good.' Phil smiled at her, for the first time since Elsie had come home.

His pleasure at the news felt like a little stab in the heart to Juliet.

'If you're sure, lovey,' Elsie said.

'I'm looking forward to it,' Juliet said. 'And I'm going to go back to my flat as well, if you're both OK with that. You don't really need any more help from me, do you Else?'

'I'd like to pretend I do, but no, lovey. It's been kind of you to be here for as long as you have. Have you met this guy who's taking over, your new boss?' Elsie asked. She picked up her phone to check the name on the news website she'd been reading. 'Jeremy Harrison?'

Phil stared at Juliet and his eyes narrowed. 'Jeremy Harrison? Please tell me this is a joke.'

Juliet said nothing.

'A joke? What do you mean?' Elsie asked.

'The same Jeremy Harrison who made you perform a sex act on him against your will?' Phil asked.

Elsie let out a gasp.

'You showed me the bruises on your wrist from your last encounter with him. Remember?' he asked.

Juliet blushed, feeling like a kid having been caught writing on the wall by the head teacher. She said nothing.

Phil raised his eyebrows.

'Yes. It's the same guy. But this…this is going to be different. We'll be working together. A professional relationship. He's asked for me specifically to help with the transition,' Juliet told him.

'I bet he has.' Phil shook his head and sighed.

'What?' Juliet asked him. 'I'm going to be his PA, nothing else. I can provide continuity once Daniel's gone.'

'Jesus, Juliet. Are you that naïve? This guy's not going to respect boundaries. He's not the type. If he's treated you badly once, he'll do it again. And the fact that you're there will make him think it's OK to treat you like that, that it's what you want from him.' He put his hands on Juliet's shoulders and looked at her till she held her gaze. 'Don't do this.'

Juliet felt annoyed at being backed into a corner. She was concerned about working with Harrison but had managed to convince herself it would be OK. She didn't need Phil scaremongering like this. And she certainly didn't want him telling her what to do. However politely he was doing it, that's what he was doing. She jerked herself away from him and stood up. 'I need you to back off, Phil and leave me to get on with my life.'

'I can't let you do this,' he said. 'It's madness.'

'Excuse me? Did you say you can't let me? Who the hell do you think you are? You don't have any say in my life. Even if we were still dating, which we're not because you dumped me, remember, it would still be none of your fucking business.' She shook her head and laughed in mock disbelief. 'It's almost funny. You want to protect me from Harrison, but you hurt me more than he ever did.'

Phil took a step back as though she'd hit him, before recovering his angered stance. 'Fine,' he said, putting up his hands in mock surrender. 'Your decision. Good luck with it.' He spat out the words and walked out of the room.

Juliet let out a slow breath before she turned to Elsie. 'I'm sorry, Else. You shouldn't have been subjected to that, not in your own home. Please don't worry about me. This guy will behave himself in the office and that's the only place he's going to see me. Now, I'm going to get packed and drive to the flat. Get moved in and ready for tomorrow. I'll come and say goodbye.' She walked out of the room before Elsie could say anything to make her change her mind. She could feel her cheeks flushing with a mixture of embarrassment and anger.

She packed all her belongings and took them out to her car. She went to Elsie's room and found her checking the latest share prices on her phone.

'I'm going now, Else. If you're sure you don't mind.'

Elsie shook her head. 'I don't mind, lovey. And don't be angry with Phil. It's only 'cos he cares about you, worries about you.'

'I don't want you or him worrying about me. I can take care of myself.'

'It's not because we think you can't. It's because we don't want you getting hurt.'

'You're kind to care about me. Don't think I'm not grateful.' Juliet fought back the mix of emotions bubbling inside her. 'But I have to make my own decisions.'

'I know that and so does Phil. But you can't expect us to stand back and say nothing when we think you're doing the wrong thing. I hope you wouldn't do that to us, if the roles were reversed.'

'No, I'd have told you not to stand on that stool to reach that lightbulb if I'd been around,' she said, giving her the tiniest of smiles.

'Touché.'

Juliet gave her a hug.

'You take care, alright?' Elsie said.

'I will, Else, I promise. And I'll come over next weekend to see how you are.'

She went into the hallway and wondered whether to say goodbye to Phil. Deciding she would feel too guilty if she didn't, she tapped on his bedroom door. She heard movement and the door opened a little.

'You off then?' He looked at her but didn't keep eye contact.

'Yes, I want to get organised for the morning. Make sure I'm ready to deal with whatever happens.'

He nodded.

'And I'll come over at the weekend to see how Elsie's doing. But if she needs me for anything in the meantime, just let me know.'

He nodded again.

'OK. Bye, Phil.'

'Bye.' He closed his door.

She felt a knot of disappointment in her stomach. She put up her hand to knock on his door again and hesitated. It was a lost cause, their friendship. She had to let it go.

She spent the drive to London with her teeth clenched in a mixture of frustration and anger. She got back to the flat and took her suitcases to the bedroom but struggled to summon up the enthusiasm to unpack. She'd hated parting on bad terms with Phil and was annoyed that they'd had their row in front of Elsie.

She decided to go for a run and dug her running gear out of her suitcase. She went out into the late afternoon drizzle, the weather matching her mood. She took a route to get her as far away from tourists and people as possible. Her legs didn't want to run and felt leaden as she pounded the quieter streets around Waterloo and Southwark. She stayed out for an hour, frustrated that the buzz she usually got from exercise had failed to materialise. It still made her angry that all the fears she'd managed to pack away at the back of her mind were now front and centre. Phil had no right to do that to her.

As she walked up the stairs to her flat, she thought about what she might do to minimise the chance that Jeremy could try something. She'd make sure she didn't stay late in the office. She and Daniel had often worked into the evening and would be the only ones there. She'd speak to Bernie and ask him to make sure whoever was on duty in the Security team kept a watchful eye on Mr Harrison while she was in the building.

She went into her bedroom and got a trouser suit out for the morning, deciding a skirt was too risky. She glanced at the camera in the top corner of the room. Much as she had hated the fact there were cameras in her home, Jeremy would know that too, which would be likely to curb his behaviour, should he dare to be there. Given his experience on the previous visit, she thought that was unlikely.

Phil's facial expression from earlier came into her mind. His level of anger had surprised her. It seemed odd that he got so worked up, as if he cared about her, yet had dumped her after such a short time. Did he care about her or not? Perhaps he was just a control freak. She chewed the inside of her lip. Or maybe he had a point. Maybe she should be ultra-cautious when it came to Jeremy. She went to the cupboard in the hallway and switched around the labels on the fuses. Just in case anyone but her wanted to turn them off.

After showering, she put on a little make-up and went to the local shop to buy some milk and bread. She made herself a cup of tea and some toast and settled down in front of the television to carry on binge-watching the show that Phil had recommended.

Chapter 27 – Phil

Phil went down to the allotment after Juliet left and began to dig over the soil in the beds where the vegetables had finished for the season. With a spade and fork, he pierced and sliced the soil as though it was his arch enemy. After half-an-hour, he took a break.

Al came out from his shed and offered him a cup of tea. 'What's pissed you off?' he asked.

'Just life, Al. Just life.'

Al disappeared and came back a couple of minutes later with two mugs of tea. He handed one to Phil. The tea was the colour of rich caramel.

'Cheers,' said Phil.

'How's Else doing? Heard she had an accident.'

'She's doing very well. It's always bad when people her age fall but she's made a good recovery. She's a tough old bird,' said Phil.

'Lucky she is. Talking of birds, how's that girl you brought down here? She was a looker,' Al said.

'We're just friends.' That was pushing it, after their last conversation. 'She's been helping out with Else, actually.'

'You and she not…?'

'No. I'm too dull for her. She likes to live dangerously,' said Phil.

'My Bella was like that. Always liked a bad boy, took risks, flashed her knickers at passing coppers for a laugh. People like her keep you alive. You wanna throw your hat into the ring with that one. Be a bit more dangerous,' Al said, giving him a wink.

'Maybe I will. We're doing well on purple sprouting broccoli this year. You need any?'

'No, I'm good with that too. It's me onions that have let me down, so I won't say no if you've any to spare later on.'

'I'll see how ours go. Thanks for the tea. Better get on.' Phil resumed his digging activities, feeling slightly less angry than before. But only slightly. Juliet was making a big mistake, he was certain. He wanted to shake her for being pig-headed and for not listening to him and not…not what, Phil? he asked himself. She was a grown woman with her own life to lead. When he'd first met her, he'd been suspicious, assuming her affection for him wasn't real. That she was only friendly with him and Elsie as a means to an end. She'd seemed too bloody perfect. And then he'd been sent those pictures and realised she was too caught up in whatever she did for Daniel Cross. Too busy getting up to all sorts with other men, be it for work or pleasure. And now she'd get caught up in whatever Jeremy Harrison had planned for her, either at his hands or God knows who else's. The anger he'd first felt when he'd heard Harrison was going to be her boss reignited in him. She was crazy to stay on. If only he could stop her from doing it. But she saw him in the same light as Harrison, someone who'd hurt her, hurt her more than Harrison had, she'd said. He had no power to stop her, no way to change her decision and he couldn't keep her safe. He sat down on the edge of a raised bed, staring into space, wondering what to do.

He got back to the house an hour later and went to check on Elsie. She was dozing in her chair so he pulled the door closed as quietly as he could and went for a shower. He would make her a sandwich later but needed a snack himself now. On a whim, he sent a WhatsApp message to Juliet. "Settled back in OK?" He watched the progress of his message, one tick then two. He willed the ticks to turn blue but they stayed grey.

She was probably busy, out for a run, at an art gallery or walking along the river. He shook his head. Any of those things were more exciting than working on an allotment with him. He cut two thick slices of bread from a loaf he'd bought the day before and toasted them before treating himself to a generous smattering of butter and some homemade raspberry jam that Al's wife Bella, had made. It made him smile that little old Bella, the top jam maker in the local WI, had been a wild child in her youth.

He sat down to eat, tearing into the toast with abandon, knowing nobody was watching. He felt a trickle of stray butter run down his chin and rubbed it away. He noticed the ticks on his message to Juliet had turned blue, but there was no response.

He put on the TV and dispiritedly channel-hopped for a while, finding nothing that would take away the niggle in his stomach that signalled his unhappiness. He put a message on the family WhatsApp group for his sons, suggesting a video chat later, but Sal replied that the boys were out with friends.

He turned off the TV and threw the remote control onto the bed, pulling on a clean t-shirt when he noticed the one he'd been wearing had a buttery jam stain on the front.

He looked in to find Elsie had woken up so he made her a sandwich. She asked if he would take her for a walk around the garden once she'd eaten and he was glad to oblige. He felt a little rudderless, which he often did between cases. He would never wish for a serious crime to occur but he knew he'd be happier once he had a case to occupy his mind.

Elsie talked about the flowers while they walked around the front garden, stopping in front of a shrub rose that still had a few blooms on it. 'Juliet loved this one, not just because it was called Sweet Juliet. She loved the smell. Said it reminded her of her adoptive mother.'

'Her mother left home because the husband was abusive, Juliet told me,' he said.

'Yes,' said Elsie. 'I don't think she's ever got over both her mothers abandoning her. I mean, bad enough to be adopted and feel the rejection of your birth mother, but for that woman to leave her with the abusive husband and never get in touch afterwards, well, no wonder the poor girl struggles with relationships.'

'Can't be easy for her.' Phil knew Elsie was reprimanding him.

'I think the mother wore a tea rose scent.' Elsie bent down to sniff one of the blooms. 'It always reminds me of old ladies. Never particularly wanted to smell like that.' She shrugged. 'Each to their own.'

Phil had a private chuckle. Elsie never seemed to admit being old but perhaps that was the best attitude to have. They walked back into the house and he followed Elsie into her room to make sure she was comfortable.

'Remind me again why you didn't want to go out with Juliet?' she asked.

'I didn't believe she liked me. Not really. Thought she was using me,' he said.

'Do you honestly think that?'

He thought for a while. 'I don't want to lie to you, Else. The reason I ended it was because someone sent me some photos of her.'

'Photos of her doing what?' she asked.

'Having sex with someone.'

'Are you sure it was her?' she asked.

'It was her. And it was while I was seeing her, before you ask.'

'But what were they actually doing, Phil? Can I see?'

'I don't think I should show them to you.'

'I really think you should.' Elsie sounded surprisingly firm.

He went to his room to get the photos. He went back to Elsie's room and took them out, one by one, to show her.

She peered at each one, scrutinising the detail with a magnifying glass she kept by her bed for reading small print. She looked up and shook her head at him. 'Lovey, these are staged. He's out for the count. These are photos to blackmail him. She's not having sex.'

'What?'

'Look at his head. It's not moving from one picture to the next,' she said.

He looked at each one in turn and realised Elsie was right. So much for his detective skills. 'I'm not sure knowing that helps, Else. Maybe she isn't having genuine sex with him but if she isn't, then she's got a side-line in blackmail.'

'Think about it. She's hardly the instigator. She's not the one who's installed cameras in the flat, is she? Who do you think sent these to you?'

'Cross, probably. Or one of his lackeys.' He gathered up the pictures.

'He's got her doing all sorts. Or rather he did have. She's been trying to stop all that, get out from under. Your presence in Juliet's life must have seemed like a real threat to Cross, so he sent you these to frighten you off. And you fell for it.'

'She could have been honest with me,' he said.

'A policeman she barely knows?'

'Whatever the situation, her involvement in something like this is a red flag to me having a relationship with her.'

'So, you're giving up on her?' asked Elsie.

'I'm sure she'll find someone. Someone who's not suspicious of her behaviour,' he said. 'Someone who Daniel Cross or Jeremy Harrison will approve of.'

'If you abandon her, she'll get caught up doing goodness knows what for this fella Harrison and she'll be even more isolated from the rest of the world.'

'That's a pretty bleak outlook,' he said.

'If a good man like you can't see beyond the façade, can't see the decent girl who's caught up in a world she needs to escape from, then no-one will. Given your job, I'm surprised you don't see the danger she's in.'

'Oh, I see it all right. But you saw what she was like when I told her not to work for Harrison. If my instincts to protect drove someone like Sal away, Juliet is even less likely to put up with me interfering in her life.'

'Caring isn't interfering,' she said. 'Caring's being there for someone, offering support. It's not telling them what to do or stopping them doing something, it's being there to help them up when they fall, to listen when they need to talk and offering advice, but only when they ask for it.'

'Did I over-react about Harrison?' he asked.

She shook her head. 'After everything I've just said, I think you were right to react the way you did. Sometimes you have to make people realise just how big a mistake they're making. I'd have been surprised if you hadn't gone a little sparky.'

'For all the good it did,' he said.

'It'll have made her think twice, I'm sure. But you need to follow it up. Tell her how you really feel about her.' She put her arm on his. 'You do like her, don't you?'

He nodded. 'I like her a lot. She's bright and funny and ballsy. But...'

'But what?' Elsie looked at him.

He sat in silence for a while. 'I guess I'm still a bit wary that she's having me on, that she isn't really interested at all.'

'Tell me something. How did she react when you told her you didn't want to see her?'

He remembered the look on Juliet's face. How she'd crumpled before him momentarily, before dashing away. 'She was upset.'

'She was in bits. I saw it. I was watching out of the window.'

He knew she was right. 'Yeah, she was.'

'And that argument of yours, when she said you'd hurt her more than this Harrison fella. That was from the heart, wasn't it? She's not having you on.'

'You're right.' He nodded to himself after thinking for a while. 'I'll go and see her tomorrow. Talk to her.'

Elsie gave a broad smile. 'Tell her how you feel. Open up that big heart of yours.'

'I will. Thanks, Else.' He went back to his room and saw a notification on his phone. Juliet had replied. "Yes thanks; settled in. Sorry to be a disappointment."

He responded with "You're not. And I'm sorry too".

But the ticks against his message still hadn't turned blue by the time he went to bed, just after midnight.

Chapter 28 - Juliet

Juliet woke up when she heard a sound. It took her a second to remember where she was. The TV was on, still paused where she'd got to the end of the episode she'd been watching. It had sounded like the front door opening but perhaps it was in her dream. She sat up and listened. She tensed as she heard footsteps in the hall. They stopped and it went quiet. Maybe it was noise from the flat opposite.

'Jools.'

Oh shit. It was Jeremy.

'What are you doing here?' she asked and stood up to face him.

He smiled. 'Relax. I just wanted to come and say hello, have a little chat before we start working together tomorrow.'

She looked at him, feeling a pit in her stomach. 'How did you get in?'

He waved a set of keys at her. 'This place is a company asset, so I'm entitled,' he said. 'I wasn't sure if you'd be here.'

'Just getting ready for tomorrow.' She switched off the TV. 'Do you want a drink?' she asked.

'I'll get it,' he said. 'Don't want you pulling a stunt like last time.' He opened the fridge and took out a bottle of champagne. He let the cork fly and poured himself a glass. 'Are you sure you won't join me?'

'No, thanks.' She filled a glass with water and waited for him to speak.

'Let's sit.' He put the champagne bottle onto the coffee table and beckoned her to sit next to him by patting the sofa. 'Come on, Jools. We're going to be working together. Talk to me.'

She sat down, as far away as she could at the end of the sofa. 'What do you want to know?'

'Tell me about the board members.'

She gave him a summary of each one, trying to make it sound as though she was giving away confidences but keeping it as bland as she could. The more she spoke and watched him listen, and ask pertinent questions, the more she relaxed. She asked him about the takeover.

He described the venture capitalists, friends from Eton, who had bankrolled the takeover. 'Tell me about you, Jools,' he asked.

'I've been with the company for over five years now.'

'Were you always Daniel's PA?' he asked.

'Not at first. He spotted me in one of the regional offices and asked me to come and work for him.'

'What did he spot about you?' There was a leering tone to his voice.

'My ability to think on my feet and act on my instinct.'

He grinned. 'And your pretty face had nothing to do with it?'

She sighed. 'Jeremy, I've no doubt it helped. But the main reason was how I dealt with Daniel when he visited the office I was working in. The managers were all over Daniel at the start of his visit but by lunchtime, they all assumed someone else was looking after him. Left Daniel in the meeting room on his own. I walked past and saw him looking really pissed off, so I went in, apologised, even though it was nothing to do with me, and asked him questions about the organisation, till finally the regional head reappeared. He told me off for bothering Daniel. Daniel handed me his card and told me to call him the next day, then sent me out so he could reprimand the regional head in private.'

'And he took you on, just like that?' Jeremy asked.

'Well, I had to have an interview. And I'm sure timing had something to do with it. His old PA had retired and he hadn't filled the post. I went up to Head Office to see him and it was the longest and toughest interview I'd ever had. He asked so many questions about different scenarios and how I'd handle them. He asked about my family and friends, trying to work out if I could be discreet. After a couple of hours, he seemed satisfied I was what he was looking for and arranged an immediate transfer.'

'Well, that all sounds very admirable. For my part, I just like your pretty face.' He reached across and stroked her cheek. 'Even now, casual, you look very fuckable. Come on.' He stood up and reached out his hand. 'I want to take you to bed so you can fuck me.'

'No.' She stood up to face him.

'Oh, Jools, you don't get it, do you? I fucking own you now. Daniel's given your leash to me. You're mine to do with whatever I want.' He grabbed her wrist and pulled her towards him till her face was close to his. 'You'll do what I ask, bitch.'

She looked up at the corner of the room toward the security camera.

He laughed. 'I know all the secrets of this place now. I've turned off the cameras. Did it when I came in.'

She could see the camera still had a light on and hoped he wouldn't notice.

'So, you gorgeous little whore, you and I are going to go into the bedroom and you will screw me in any way I choose. Do you get it now, sweet Juliet?' His expression was triumphant.

She smiled at him. 'I'm not having you in my bed, Jeremy. Not with your medical problem, your bedwetting. I don't want you pissing all over my sheets.'

The triumph on his face slid away and rage bubbled to the surface. 'You bitch, fucking whore.' He let go of her wrist and slapped her hard across the face.

She hadn't seen it coming and the pain was unexpectedly fierce.

He pushed her away from him with such force that she went flying over the edge of the sofa onto the floor.

She landed heavily on her back and he came over to where she'd landed and kicked her hard in the side once, twice and then a third time.

She groaned with the pain.

'I am going to make your life the worst kind of hell.' He straightened himself up, smoothed his hair and walked out of the room.

She heard the front door slam and there was a moment of silence before she heard herself start to cry.

She got up slowly once her tears had ceased, testing her movements to see if she was injured, but the only pain she had was from where his kicks had connected with her hip. She went to the front door and put the chain on, to make sure he couldn't come back in. He'd left the hallway cupboard open so she swapped the fuse box labels back. On autopilot, she emptied the champagne from the glass and bottle down the sink and put the empty glass in the dishwasher. She made herself a cup of tea and sat down.

Thinking about what had just happened, she could feel herself beginning to shake inside as the initial shock wore off. She cried for a long time, feeling wave after wave of revulsion, anger and sadness wash over her.

She took some deep breaths to help her calm down and thought of Phil. He'd known exactly what would happen and had said she was being naïve. She wondered if he'd be able to stop himself gloating. He wouldn't say "I told you so" but he'd give her that look of his, the one that made her feel like a toddler on the naughty step. She didn't want to give him the satisfaction of hearing he'd been right.

Her thoughts turned to what she would do about Jeremy. He'd assaulted her, so she should report it to the police. He was a good lawyer though, so he'd probably get himself off, citing provocation. She wondered if he might try and delete the footage of the incident, but then, he didn't think the cameras were on, so why would he?

She decided her top priority would be to make copies of the film. She switched the cameras off before logging into the office security system and copying the data to her laptop. She saved the data onto a USB stick and deleted all the video data from the security system from the time Jeremy had gone into the hallway. She copied it to her personal laptop and decided to watch the footage, now it was safely in her hands.

She felt sick as she relived the event. It showed just how vulnerable she'd been. He was surprisingly strong and she knew he could have inflicted a lot more pain and suffering on her if he'd chosen to.

She could see his face clearly when she taunted him about the bedwetting. His embarrassment became anger in a heartbeat. His violent side had exploded into life, like Jekyll becoming Hyde when he realised she knew his secret. She wanted to make sure he paid for what he'd done to her and maybe learn a lesson. She realised she had the power to show everyone at Cross International his true personality.

She spent the next couple of hours preparing her revenge. She went to a local supermarket and bought a Pay As You Go mobile. As she left the flat, she took a hair off her jacket and shut it in the door. No-one would see it but if it wasn't there when she got back, she'd know someone had been in. She'd seen the technique used in a drama about

WWII spies a few years back and had locked it away in her mental filing cabinet, thinking it might prove useful one day. She decided to drive rather than walk, just in case Jeremy was lurking outside the building.

She prepared a resignation letter and set it up to auto-send to HR at 9am the next morning. Feeling no guilt, she logged into the Cross International Fleet Car System and assigned one of the pool cars to herself for the next three months. She knew no-one would realise she'd done it; their auditing of internal systems was woeful and she would take it back once her notice period was over. Probably.

It took a while to create a video clip of Jeremy's verbal and physical abuse of her and his reaction to her rebuke. It had been hard to watch initially but she felt immune by the time she'd created the final version.

She would move out of the flat in the morning. She wondered where to go. She knew she wasn't ready to go to Elsie's. Maybe she would treat herself to a few days away. She searched Airbnb to find somewhere and ended up looking at the area where she'd grown up. A hot and cold feeling ran through her when she saw her childhood home, Lullaby Cottage, was listed as a rental property. It wasn't available immediately but was free for a couple of days later in the week. She made the booking, wondering how she'd feel crossing the threshold after all this time. She wouldn't stay if she found it upsetting but she was curious to see it again, to try and ignite happier memories of her childhood. She found a nearby hotel and booked to stay there until the cottage was available. That meant she could still see Elsie the following weekend, which she'd said she'd do, before making a decision whether to ask if she could stay. Hopefully by then, Phil would only gloat a little. She was being unfair on him, she admitted to herself. He wouldn't take pleasure from having been right, given what had happened. He was too nice a person for that.

Once she felt ready for the next day, she went to bed. Her hip was painful and she took a picture of the bruises to make sure she had the evidence. She swallowed a strong painkiller, hoping it would help her sleep. She listened to a podcast about London theatre as she drifted off.

The alarm woke her at 6am. She felt buoyed by having been able to sleep at all. It felt odd, getting ready for what would be her last day at Cross International. But she knew it was the right thing to do. It was time to start a new chapter in her life.

Once she was dressed and ready to leave, she put her suitcases in her car before walking to the office.

'Morning, Bernie. How are all your brood?'

He smiled. 'Doing well.' He showed her some pictures from a recent birthday party.

'They're growing up so fast, your grandchildren. You must be so proud.'

He beamed.

'You just going off shift?' she asked.

'Yeah, in about half an hour.'

She wondered whether to say anything.

'Looking forward to your first day with the new bloke?' he asked.

'Not really. In case I don't see you later, take care of yourself.'

He looked at her quizzically. 'You too, kid,' he said. 'Call if you need anything.'

She smiled and walked up to her office. Jeremy wasn't expected till 9am and she didn't think he'd get there early. He'd want people to think being in charge came easily to him, that he didn't need to put the hours in, like Daniel had.

She logged on to her laptop and double-checked the settings on the footage she'd uploaded. The TV screens around the building usually played a continuous loop of good news items about the organisation but today the new chairman would have a starring role. She'd set it to play for an hour. The IT department might work out how to take it down before the hour was up, but they rarely dealt with that particular application, as she'd been responsible for the content for several years, so she reckoned it would take them at least that time to work out which folder held the footage. She'd password-protected it, just to slow them down.

It was 8:55am. She logged off her laptop and waited for Jeremy to appear. He sauntered in, just before 9am. He gave her a venomous look as he walked past her desk but said nothing.

The video began to play in the corridor outside and Juliet watched people's reactions. The general office hubbub began to increase as more people saw the footage. Now she knew her special movie had been seen, she got up and went to the entrance to Jeremy's inner office.

'What?' He spat the word at her.

'I'm resigning, with immediate effect. I'm not working for a man like you.'

'Good. Saves me sacking you.'

'You might want to check your emails.' She walked out as the Finance Director came in. The smile and wink he gave her told her he'd already seen the video.

'Is that your parting gift?' he asked.

She nodded. 'See you around.' She picked up her jacket and handbag and went to the HR department on the first floor.

'Are you OK, Jools?' Sam, the HR director, looked worried.

'Yes, I'm alright. Just a bit bruised.'

She nodded towards the TV screen in the corridor. 'Looked nasty.'

'Nothing that won't heal. I've sent you my resignation letter,' Juliet said.

'I just saw it.'

'I'm leaving now, under the circumstances, but I'm entitled to three months' pay, in lieu of notice. I don't expect the company to quibble about that, given I could sue for what he did.'

Sam shifted uncomfortably. 'Well, you could sue him.'

'I could get the police to prosecute him, but the company, I could sue, I reckon. But that's not my intention, not as long as I get my salary paid. I've put that video out to make sure people know his true colours and now, I just want to leave. Will you make sure he doesn't do anything to stop the payment going through?'

Sam nodded. 'I'll get it sorted today.'

'Thank you. Here's my pass and phone. Laptop is upstairs. Car and flat keys will be left with the concierge.'

'I'm sure you've thought of everything, Jools. I'll miss you. You were so good to me, getting Daniel on side when I needed time off for IVF.' Her gaze went to the photo on the desk of her baby.

'Daniel didn't need a lot of persuading, to be fair. It was always a question of getting him to park his business head for a moment and re-engage his human one,' said Juliet.

'Well, I'll be forever grateful. Oh, look out. We've got company.'

Jeremy burst in. 'You evil bitch. I'm going to fucking kill you.'

Sam stood between him and Jools. 'Jeremy, given the content of the video, I strongly advise you refrain from saying or doing anything.'

'She's humiliated me and she needs to pay for it,' he said.

'You committed a serious assault, to which there are now many witnesses. Don't make it worse. Juliet has resigned and will leave today without taking any further action against the company. Jools, best you go.'

Juliet left the room and walked down to the ground floor. She could see the film clip was still playing in the foyer, much to the surprise of some visitors in the waiting area. There was a ripple of applause from the Sales Team as she walked past their offices on her way out. She tried not to smile as she went out of the main door.

She went around the back of the building and ran into the garage, just as the metal shutters were closing. She knew the combination to the key safe where the spares were held, and found the key for the pool car she'd assigned herself. She drove from the office to the car park of the apartment complex to pick up her suitcases, before exiting and parking up outside. As she walked into the main entrance, she smiled at the concierge.

'Hey, Jools. You OK?'

She handed over the keys to the flat, car and the garage. 'I'm leaving.'

His eyes widened. 'For good?'

'Yes, I'm moving on. Car's in its usual spot.'

'Where are you off to?'

'Wherever the wind takes me. Thanks for all your help while I've been here and pass my thanks on to your colleagues, too. Take care,' she said.

'You too.'

She walked out into the fresh air and felt herself relax. It was done. She was free.

She drove out of the city and headed southward. Stopping for a coffee and some petrol, she thought about Elsie and Phil. They were probably the only people she'd contact about what had happened. Daniel would, no doubt, hear about her departure some way or another. She was disappointed she wouldn't get the bonus he'd offered her but no money in the world could compete with the sense of relief she felt at leaving her job, Jeremy Harrison and Cross International.

She picked up her mobile to ring Elsie but changed her mind. She would have to deal with questions, first from Elsie and then, no doubt, from Phil. She'd send an email. Give herself some time to come up with suitable answers.

Chapter 29 - Phil

Phil walked into the foyer of Juliet's apartment block. It was just after 5pm and he'd managed to get away early from work. He approached the concierge.

'Good afternoon, Sir. How can I help you?'

'I'm here to see Juliet Russell, on the 6th floor. I've tried the entry phone but there's no response. She's probably still at work, so I'll wait, if that's OK.'

'I'm sorry, Sir, but Ms Russell's moved out.'

'What? When? Where she's gone?' asked Phil.

'I'm afraid I can't divulge any information, Sir.'

Phil took out his ID card. 'Sorry, it's a police matter,' he lied.

The concierge checked the ID card before handing it back. 'I'm afraid I don't know, Detective. All I know is the owner of the apartment has given us instructions not to let her back in under any circumstances. He visited her here yesterday but then we had word today she'd been sacked.'

'And you have no idea where she is?' Phil asked.

'I wasn't on duty when she moved out but she left the keys to the apartment about 9:30am, my colleague said. We got the call about her being barred around 11am.'

'She left in her car? The VW?'

'No, that's in the car park and she left the keys to that, too. Belongs to the company, I think,' said the concierge.

'Thanks for your help. I'll try her mobile.'

'If you've the number ending…' he glanced down at a sheet of paper, '…1989, that phone was a company asset too, so it's no longer available, I've been told.'

'Do you have another phone number for her?'

The concierge shook his head.

Phil felt the blood drain from him. What had happened? And where was Juliet? His first thought was to go to Cross International and confront Harrison but on what grounds? But where else could he look? There was no family to reach out to, no friends she'd mentioned. Maybe Juliet wanted to disappear. He had to respect her decision but he wanted to know she was alright and not planning to jump off Waterloo Bridge in despair at losing her home and job.

'Was she upset when she left, do you know?' Phil asked.

'I was told she was her usual self. She said to say thanks to all of us in the team, smiled as she said goodbye. Just Jools.'

Phil felt only a little comforted, knowing how good she was at pretending to be OK.

He reluctantly drove to the Cross International headquarters. He walked through the revolving door and recognised the security guard he'd spoken to before.

'Detective?'

'Bernie.' Phil was glad there was a name badge pinned to his chest and offered his hand. 'I'm looking for Juliet Russell. Do you know where she is?'

'Has he reported her then?' Bernie asked.

'Has who reported what?'

'Jools left after sharing a video with the rest of the organisation. New guy's spitting.'

'A video? Of what?' Phil asked.

'Him trying it on with her in that flat of hers. Losing his rag when she wouldn't play. He got a bit nasty. But it was all caught on camera.'

'Harrison tried it on with her? Is she alright?' It was his worst fear.

'She was OK enough to come in this morning and play the video on the TV monitors around the office. Everyone saw him for what he was.'

'And where's she gone?' Phil asked.

'Dunno. After the video started, she went into his office, told him to stick his job then walked out. Best thing I've heard in ages, but don't quote me,' he said and winked.

'Were you there when it happened?' Phil asked.

'No, someone filmed the video on their phone and sent it to me.'

'Can I see it?'

'Be my guest.' Bernie pulled up the video and held his phone so Phil could watch it.

It was worse than he'd imagined. 'And where's Harrison now?'

'He left the office just after it all kicked off. Not a great start to the takeover, eh? Couldn't happen to a nicer guy, from what I've heard,' Bernie said.

'Thanks for your help. I need to find Jools,' said Phil.

'I hope she's alright. She was good, kind. Always bothered to ask about the family. I'll miss her.'

Phil nodded a thank you then went through the revolving door and into the cool of the day. With no phone number, he had no way of contacting Jools. He couldn't use WhatsApp anymore and she didn't use Facebook or Twitter. He was sure she mentioned something about Instagram in the past. He took out his phone and opened the app. He searched for her name but nothing came up.

'Damn,' he muttered to himself. He thought again about his rejection of her and closed his eyes, praying she was OK. All he could do was wait and hope she got in touch with him. She'd promised to visit Elsie at the weekend. Would she keep her promise, he wondered. He was reminded of that feeling he'd so often had about Juliet, that he knew very little about her.

Roadworks forced him a long way round to get out of the city. He ended up driving down the Embankment and towards Millbank. He noticed large posters adorning the lampposts, advertising a Pre-Raphaelite art exhibition. He remembered Jools telling him she loved the Pre-Raphaelites.

His phone rang. 'Hey, Elsie. You alright?'

'Are you coming back tonight?' she asked.

'Yeah, just on my way back now from London. Shouldn't be too long. Everything OK?'

'Yeah, just something I need doing. It can wait,' she said.

'Make sure it does. No bloody climbing.'

'I'm not a child, Phil.'

'Sorry. You haven't heard from Jools, have you?'

'No messages, no. She said she'd be around at the weekend,' Elsie said. 'Why'd you ask?'

'I'll explain when I get there. See you shortly.' He finished the call and spent the rest of the journey trying to remember what he knew about Jools. He was sure, if he thought hard enough, he'd be able to work out where she was. He was almost tempted to contact Daniel Cross. Maybe Jools had flown to Cyprus to be with him.

Chapter 30 – Daniel

Daniel was sitting on the veranda of his villa, eyes closed so he could enjoy the warmth of the late afternoon sun. It was lovely, just relaxing with nothing to do but worry about his tan. Kind of. It still felt like a holiday, not real life, and he wondered how quickly he'd get bored. He'd already identified a couple of business opportunities in Paphos that were worth considering. Nothing serious. Nothing that would cost a lot to set up. Just something to keep his hand in.

Giselle came to join him after a post-swim shower. 'You alright? Have you topped up on the suncream? Don't want you going leathery on me, like some of the old guys on the beach.'

'Right back at ya, girl. Some of the old birds out there look like you could make a handbag out of them.'

'Dan!'

Daniel looked up to see Pat waving from the next balcony. It had been a mistake to install Pat in the villa next door. Giselle had always got on with Pat but it turned out she didn't get on with Pat's wife, Jackie. Despite her own humble beginnings, Giselle looked down on Jackie. Daniel had to admit he shared her misgivings. Jackie had lost none of her "salt of the earth" behaviours, particularly towards the locals, shouting at them in exaggerated English and generally being an entitled pain in the arse. Giselle said she felt she'd elevated herself from her humble beginnings but Jackie seemed to revel in her lack of class. Pat and Daniel had spent the last few evenings in a quiet bar, swapping stories about what each wife had said about the other. Jackie thought Giselle was putting on airs and graces, pretending to be something she wasn't. Giselle thought Jackie was as common as muck, more suited to a holiday camp in Skegness than a luxury villa in Paphos.

A shared dinner had become an impossibility. The bitchy comments going across the table reminded Daniel of Wimbledon, where your head turned from one end of the court to another, as each ball of venom was lobbed at the opponent.

Pat came onto the veranda, thankfully alone. 'You got your phone with you?'

Daniel shook his head.

Giselle opened one eye. 'I've taken it off him, Pat. He needs to relax,' she said.

'Harrison's trying to get hold of you. He's raging,' said Pat.

Daniel sat up. 'What about?'

'This.' Pat handed his phone across. 'Press Play.'

Daniel watched a video, showing Jeremy Harrison slapping and kicking Jools, her taunting him about his bedwetting and him threatening her. 'Holy shit, where did you get this?' Daniel felt anger rising in his throat. He'd told Harrison to treat Jools well. What sort of a man kicks a defenceless woman?

'What is it?' Giselle asked.

Pat handed the phone across to her so she could watch it for herself. 'I got it from Bernie. It was played on all the screens in the office this morning.'

She watched it. 'Jools has always been volatile,' Giselle said.

'I'll fuckin' kill him,' said Daniel.

'She's brought it on herself, Dan. You know what she's like.'

Daniel felt his eyes flash with annoyance at Giselle's dismissal of the situation. 'Keep your nose out of my business, Giz. Is Jools safe, Pat?'

231

'No-one knows where she's gone. She resigned. Left the flat, left her car and phone behind. No-one has any contact details for her.'

'If Harrison's got her, I'll break everyone bone in his fuckin' body.'

Giselle stood up. 'Dan, what the bloody hell's got into you? Why are you acting like this? You've left all of this behind. You left Jools to Jeremy. He wanted her and she's his to do with whatever he wants. If he wants to punish her, that's his concern. Not yours.'

Daniel gritted his teeth and could feel the side of his temple throbbing with rage. He had to be careful what he said in front of Giselle. She'd started to get very jealous of Jools in recent weeks and it had swayed his decision to accept the takeover. He'd had enough of the tension he felt between work and home life. But Giselle was right. He had left Jools to fend for herself with Harrison. She'd been nervous of his successor's motives towards her and Daniel had brushed them aside. But he'd known that Harrison wanted to punish her for their earlier encounter before making her dance to his tune. He'd as good as said that to Daniel. Daniel's emotional reaction to Harrison's threat had been jealousy, not concern for Jools. He was jealous that Harrison would get to have Jools where he could not. He felt, for the first time in a very long time, ashamed of himself.

'Has she gone to ground? Or do you think Harrison has her?' Daniel asked.

'He's a better liar than I give him credit for if he has got her,' said Pat. 'He's been trying to ring you to find out where she is. He wants to get hold of her. He's spitting with rage from the humiliation.'

Daniel thought for a while, aware that both Pat and Giselle were watching his expression. 'We need to get hold of the old biddy, Pat. I bet she knows where Jools is.'

'How? We don't even know her name,' said Pat.

'Elsie,' Daniel said. 'Same as my mum.'

Pat turned his palms skyward. 'What use is that? Anyway, Bernie said that detective just came into the office, trying to find Juliet. If Elsie knew where she was, she'd have told PC Plod.'

'Not if Jools told her not to. They'd split up, hadn't they? It's worth a try.' He went into the villa and retrieved his phone. There were seven missed calls from Harrison. He rang Michael Collinson's number. 'Mikey. Need a favour.' He walked out onto the veranda. 'Your DI Haywood. I need his home address. Well, I can't really say but it's not for a bad reason. I need to speak to his landlady. I think she might know the whereabouts of a colleague of mine who's gone missing. I'm concerned for this girl's welfare and I just want to make sure she's OK. I really appreciate it, Mikey. Of course, won't say it came from you.' He ended the call. 'The Chief Constable's gonna get me that address,' he said to Pat.

Giselle stood up from her sun lounger and walked into the bedroom without saying anything.

'Pat, can I have a word?' Daniel took Pat to a corner of the veranda where neither Giselle nor Jackie would be able to hear.

'What is it? Do you want me to go back? See if I can find her?' asked Pat.

'No, nothing like that. But I need a win with Gizzy. I'm gonna have to move you and Jackie to a different villa. This tension between her and Giz is doing my head in.'

'Me too,' said Pat.

'Go and book yourself in at the golf resort and I'll cover the cost for a few days while I sort you out a villa in the next complex.'

'Do you want me to do anything about Jools?' Pat asked.

'Once I get the address, can you track down the old biddy's surname and contact number?'

'Sure. You know, Dan, Jools'll be OK. She's a smart girl. Harrison's all piss and wind.'

'I hope you're right,' said Daniel.

Pat left via the outside stairs. Dan walked into the bedroom, knowing he had some grovelling to do.

Giselle was laying on their bed. 'How dare you talk to me like that! And in front of that bitch.'

'Giz, I'm sorry. I lost my head. I feel responsible for what happened to Jools and what might happen if Harrison gets hold of her,' he said.

'How many times did you screw her?' Giselle's face was full of bitterness.

'Never, on my mother's life.' He put up his hands in a surrender posture.

'But you wanted to,' she said.

'I admit she's an attractive girl and I liked the idea. But I never did anything about it. Honest.'

She looked at him for a long time, wearing an expression of disdain. 'I want you to promise me you'll stop this ridiculous idea of her coming out here, even for a holiday. And promise me you'll never contact her. Ever. Otherwise...'

He was tempted to ask "Otherwise, what?" but realised she was making it easy for him to be forgiven. 'I will scrub the idea of her coming here, if that's what you want. I just have to make sure she's safe. Once I know she's alright, that'll be it.'

'Pat can speak to her. You don't have to talk to her to find out she's safe,' she said.

'Alright. I won't contact her again.' His phone beeped as the text came through from Collinson with the address. He forwarded it to Pat. 'By the way, Pat and Jackie are moving to the golf resort for a couple of days.'

'That's a bit posh for them, isn't it? Jackie won't really fit in with the class of people there. She's far too common,' she said.

He bit back a laugh. She couldn't resist getting a dig in at every opportunity. 'It's just while I sort out a different villa for them. Somewhere a little bit away from here. Want to keep you happy, my love.'

'Thank you. I warn you, though, Dan. You ever behave like this again and I'll get one of my brothers to teach you a lesson.'

He shivered. Giselle's family were small-time villains in the East End and he could tell she meant what she said. She might not dirty her hands in seeking revenge, but her brothers were nasty pieces of work who'd be only too pleased to do what their big sister asked. 'I hear you, Giz. And I'm sorry.'

Giselle arranged to have a late dinner with her golf instructor that night. While she got herself ready, Daniel had time to liaise in private with Pat.

After Pat had taken Jackie to their room at the golf resort, Daniel met him in the resort bar.

'I've got the number for the landlady. Her name's Elsie Tucker,' Pat said.

'Thanks. Is there somewhere we can go, somewhere a bit quieter?' Daniel asked.

'Come to the room. Jackie's having a swim in the pool.'

They walked in silence along the corridor and Pat opened the door.

'This is nice,' Daniel said, as he took in the view of the golf course through the large picture window.

'Jackie's very happy with it. Thankfully.' Pat raised his eyebrows skywards.

'Right, let's get this done.' Daniel found himself feeling uncharacteristically nervous.

Pat called the number, put it on speaker and handed it over to Daniel.

'Hallo?'

Daniel was taken by surprise by a man's voice. 'Hi. I'm trying to get hold of Elsie Tucker.'

'Who's speaking?'

'It's Daniel Cross.'

'And what do you want to talk to Elsie about?' The voice was steely.

'I'm enquiring about a mutual friend. Sorry, who is this?'

'It's Detective Inspector Haywood.'

Daniel raised his eyebrows at Pat, not sure what to say.

'I assume you're talking about Juliet?' asked Phil.

'Yes,' said Daniel.

There was no response.

'DI Haywood, it's Pat, Patrick Malcolm. I work for Daniel. We want to know that Jools is OK. We've heard about an incident at the office and we're genuinely concerned for her. That's all.'

'I'm doing everything I can to locate her. Elsie doesn't have any further information.'

'Would you keep us updated on your search?' Daniel asked.

There was a pause.

'Please,' Daniel wondered if Phil was waiting for him to beg.

'I'll text you when I know she's safe,' said Phil.

'Thanks. Appreciated,' said Daniel.

Pat hung up.

'Why did you end the call?' Daniel asked.

'He's not going to tell us anything more. You're not exactly his favourite person,' Pat said.

'But we barely asked him anything.'

'What's to ask? He doesn't know where she is. And he'll let us know when he finds her. End of,' said Pat.

'I wonder if she's on her way here,' Daniel said.

'Doubt it. She'd have called us if that was her plan.'

'It's probably just as well she's not, given how Gizzy feels about her. Where the fuck would she go?' Daniel asked.

'No idea. But if anyone's going to find her, it's that DI. You're going to have to wait it out. Why don't you phone Harrison?'

'Yeah, let's see if he knows anything.'

Pat dialled the number on speaker.

'Patrick.' Jeremy was curt.

'It's Daniel.'

'Cross, you bastard. Where the fuck is the bitch? Did you put her up to it?'

'Course I bloody didn't. Do you know where she is?' Daniel asked.

'Why the fuck would I have been ringing you if I knew where to find her?'

'In that case, Jeremy, and I'm only going to say this once, Jools would have been fine if you'd treated her alright. This is your fuck-up and you need to deal with the consequences. But I'm warning you, when

Jools surfaces, I will be keeping a very close eye on her. And if you go anywhere near her or do anything else to her, I swear I'll cut your balls off and serve 'em up to you on toast. And you know I'm a man of my word.'

There was a long silence.

'Do you understand, Jeremy?' Daniel could hear the menace in his own voice.

'Do you think I'm frightened of you, Daniel?' Jeremy asked.

'Well, if you're not, you're fuckin' stupid. Do you think I got where I am today without being able to make people sorry for their actions? You privileged classes think you own everything; think you can buy anyone. But I can arrange for some very unpleasant things to happen to your family. Your girlfriend, Fenella, your children, Darius and Hugo, your parents, brother, sisters. I know where they all live. And all the money and privilege in the world won't stop me. So, I'll say again. You go anywhere near Jools again, ever, there will be consequences. Understand?'

'Yes, I understand. You bully boys never change. Can't escape your violent low-life roots.'

'That's what you posh fuckers don't get. We don't want to escape. We're proud of our roots. And we look after our own. So just make sure you keep away from her or you won't have a dick to piss out of.'

'I don't ever want to see that bitch again,' Jeremy's voice dripped with bitterness.

'Glad to hear it. Oh, and good luck with the bedwetting.' Daniel ended the call and looked at Pat. 'Fuck, that felt good.'

'I think you enjoyed that a little bit too much,' said Pat.

They looked at each other and laughed.

'Right, I need to get back to the villa. Gizzy's going to spend the evening with that golf pro, so I need to be there to watch them flirting to make her think I'm being punished.'

'Does it not get to you?' Pat asked.

'It's quite a turn-on. It always makes her horny so I get the benefit. Adds a bit of variety under the covers.' Daniel winked.

'You're shameless,' Pat said.

'You say that like it's a bad thing.' Daniel felt himself beginning to laugh. 'Let me know the moment you hear from that copper, won't you?'

'Of course. Have a good evening, Dan.'

'You too. And thanks, Pat. I appreciate your loyalty.'

Chapter 31 – Phil

'Well, that was the last person I expected.' Phil shook his head with disbelief.

'So, Daniel Cross is worried about her too?' Elsie asked.

'Apparently.'

'And does that make you more or less worried about her?' she asked.

'More. I was sure she'd have made contact with him, maybe even flown out there to get away. But no. I just keep wishing I'd gone to see her last night. Where the hell would she go, Else?'

'Beats me, lovey. She doesn't seem to have much connection with anyone or anything. There's that boy Cameron she used to date, but he's engaged now, so she wouldn't get in touch with him.'

'There's no family. I'm not even sure where she grew up. She did mention a place where she lived. But there'd be no-one there, not been anyone there for ages. Jools said she moved out when she was eighteen.'

Phil spent three days trying to work out where Juliet might have gone. He checked hospitals and police stations, homeless shelters and refuges. He hadn't yet gone as far as getting her bank account transactions checked out. He was tempted but he'd have to have serious justification for that and right now, he didn't have, not when it was clear she'd planned her departure from both office and home. But it didn't stop him exploring the avenues that were open to him. He tried to work out where it was that Juliet had grown up with her family, but he wasn't absolutely sure that Russell was the surname of her adoptive parents. Even if it was, it was a common name so any searches he carried out brought up too many possible matches.

'Any luck?' Elsie asked, when he got home that night.

'Nothing. If only I could work out where she used to live.'

'I don't see why she'd go back there. If there's only bad memories for her, it doesn't make sense.'

'I'm all out of ideas. This is my last resort, so it's got to be worth a try. Have you had any luck remembering the name, Else?'

'It was a pretty name, I've remembered that.' She turned her head slightly sideways. 'Do you know, when she talked about it, it reminded me of a film.'

'Which one?' He watched as Elsie stared into the distance, trying to remember.

'It had that lovely actor in it. Oh, what's his name?' She thought for a while. 'Lionel Jeffries.'

'Right, which film then?'

There was a pause. 'The one with the flying car,' she said.

He frowned. '*Chitty Chitty Bang Bang*?'

'That's the one,' she said. 'A song in it.'

'Right,' he said and searched on his phone to get the song list. He ran through them one by one.

'*Toot Sweets*.'

'No.'

'*Chu-Chi Face*?'

'Course not,' she said.

'*Hushabye Mountain*.'

'That's the one,' she said. 'Only it wasn't Hushabye…'

He felt his shoulders slump.

She tapped her forehead for inspiration. 'Lullaby, not Hushabye. Lullaby Cottage,' she said.

'Yes. Yes, I remember now,' he said. 'You star, Else.' He gave her a hug. He did a rudimentary search online. A property with the name came up on Airbnb. 'Do you know where the cottage was?'

'I thought she said Surrey somewhere. Or maybe it was Sussex,' she said.

'Maybe this is it, then.' He showed her a picture of the cottage on the website.

She shrugged. 'Could be. I suppose it's worth a try, like you say. You going to check it out?' she asked.

'Nothing to lose, have I?' he said.

'And everything to gain. But lovey,' she said.

'What?'

'You know you have to accept the possibility that she's gone. That she's decided to vanish. She could have gone anywhere. And she probably doesn't want to be found,' she said.

'You're right. I keep saying to myself it's enough to know she's safe. But I want more than that. The chance to explain, to tell her how I feel.'

'Better get on, then,' she said.

'You'll be alright?' he asked.

'Of course.'

'No climbing while I'm out.'

She rolled her eyes. 'If you insist.'

He picked up his jacket and wallet from the hallstand and dashed out to his car. The satnav said it would take forty minutes. His mind was buzzing with possibilities about what he might find, if anything. On a whim, he rang his DS.

'Tom, need a favour if you can, mate,' he said.

'Course. What is it?'

'Can you get me some details on a property? Need to get a contact number for the owner,' Phil said.

'Do what I can. What's the address?'

Phil read it out.

'I assume it's urgent?' Tom asked.

'Yes and no.'

'So, yes,' Tom said.

'Not life or death, but the sooner I can speak to them, the better,' Phil said.

'I'll let you know.'

Twenty minutes into the journey, Tom rang him back. 'I'll text you the name and number.'

'I owe you one, matey,' said Phil.

'You owe me several, Guv.'

Phil laughed. 'You're right. I'll take you out for a curry and a few beers next week.'

'Look forward to it. Good luck with whatever it is.'

'Cheers.' Phil dialled the number and it was answered almost immediately.

'Portia Stansley.'

'Good evening. This is Detective Inspector Haywood.'

'The police?' she asked.

'That's right. It's regarding Lullaby Cottage.'

'I'm afraid it's let until the New Year,' she said.

He rolled his eyes. 'I'm not ringing about a booking. It's in connection with an ongoing investigation. I'd like to know if you get anyone enquiring at the cottage,' he said, 'or just hanging around.'

'At the cottage itself? Well, I'm not there. I'm in Berkshire. It'll be the guests who answer the door,' she said.

'Would you be able to ask them, when they book in, to let you know if anyone comes to call? It's someone we're trying to find for her own safety. It's a long shot but she has a historical connection to the property, so we have to explore every avenue.'

'This person. They're not dangerous, are they?' she asked.

'Not at all.'

'Jolly pleased to hear that. There's someone booked in from tomorrow after the current guest leaves, so I'll let them know to give me a ring if they have any callers. What's the name of this person?'

He hesitated. 'She's unlikely to use her own name, so it really doesn't matter.'

'And do we tell her the police are looking for her?' she asked.

'No. Don't want to alarm her.'

'Absolutely understood,' she said.

'If you can use this number to contact me,' he asked.

'What was the name again?'

'Detective Inspector Haywood.' He spelt out his surname.

'Very well. How do I know you are who you say you are?' she asked.

He gave her the name and contact number for his station. 'You can check the station number online. But you can ask them to confirm my identity and verify my number.'

'I'll do it in the morning. Must go. Need to walk the hounds,' she said.

'Thank you, Portia. I appreciate your help.'

Ten minutes later, he pulled up on the road a few doors down from Lullaby Cottage, which stood on its own with a pretty garden at the front and lawn either side of the building. The village itself was small and quiet, a little bit chocolate-boxy with the odd modern house spoiling the impression of a place untouched by time. He'd passed a pub on his way into the village so he'd check in there too. There was a light on in the right-hand window of the cottage, so he might as well go and ask whoever was staying there if they'd seen Jools.

He lifted the door knocker and gave three sharp raps. He stepped back and saw one of the upstairs curtains move, as though someone was trying to see who was knocking.

He waited.

Eventually, he heard footsteps coming down the stairs and the door was unlocked then opened.

'Hallo, Phil. Sorry it took me a while to answer, come in. I've just got out of the shower. I tried to go for a run but I'm a bit tender.'

'Jools. Oh, thank fuck. I didn't know where you were. No-one did. Elsie was worried.' He felt relief flood over him that she was safe and gave her a bear hug.

She groaned.

He pulled away. 'Sorry.'

'It's fine.' She closed the door behind him and frowned at him. 'I'm confused. If you didn't know where I was, how come you're here? Didn't you read my email?'

'Your email?' he asked.

'I sent it to your home account.'

'I never got it.' He hadn't looked at his emails since Juliet had disappeared if he was honest. 'It doesn't matter. The important thing is you're OK.'

'I'm alright, apart from some bruising,' she said.

'I heard about what happened at the flat with Harrison and your film show at the office.'

'You know about that? My God, it was sweet, to give that wanker his comeuppance,' she said.

'Why did you disappear?' he asked.

'I didn't. I emailed Elsie saying I was going away for a few days. I copied you in, just in case she didn't see it. I can't believe neither of you got it.'

'Even Daniel Cross is worried about you,' he said.

'Daniel? How do you know that?'

'He rang Elsie, trying to track you down,' he said.

'Wow. Do you want a cup of tea?' she asked.

'I…yeah, why not?' He followed her into the kitchen, head still muzzy from the feeling of relief. 'Has this place changed much since you moved out?'

'Completely refurbished inside but the room layout is just the same. Garden's still the same. I thought they might have done something different with it. Even the pond that never was is still there.'

'The what?' he asked.

'Did I not tell you about that? Dad dug a big hole and said he was going to build me a pond, talked about getting some fish and how newts and frogs would be drawn to it. Then he filled it in and said he'd changed his mind. So, it's just a random circle of concrete over in the corner. It was one of the many times he promised something and didn't deliver, and blamed his failure to deliver on me being undeserving. He was just so sad and angry all the time after Mum left.' The kettle boiled and she poured water into the waiting teapot. 'I've realised, while I've been here, that his attitude has been at the root of my problems. I've spent the last five years trying to please Daniel, just like I did my dad. All to make me feel like he wanted me, like I belonged to him. You'll understand, being a foundling. You must have had that same urge to belong somewhere? To feel valued?'

He nodded. 'I had my family though. A good, kind, loving mum and dad who made me feel like I belonged to them. And the military is kind of like a family. They break you down and put you back together again, but you go through that process with your buddies and you become part of that whole. Police too. I found my tribe.'

'I'm still looking for mine.' She poured their tea and handed him a mug. They walked through to the sitting room.

He sat down. 'Jools, I want to apologise. For being an arse.'

'What do you mean?' she asked.

'When I finished our relationship. I hurt you and I'm sorry for that.'

'Thanks.' She took a sip of her tea.

'Will you come back to Elsie's tonight? I know she misses having you about the place. And I think I'd rather know where you are, while the Harrison thing is still bubbling.'

'Tonight? I…well, I suppose I could leave here early. I've done what I came here to do.'

'What was that?' he asked.

'Just to remember.' She looked around the room. 'And give myself permission to forget. Stop everything that happened here being a barrier to my future. Hold on. The Harrison thing? What do you think is going to happen?'

'He's obviously a nasty piece of work. Thought he might want to take his embarrassment out on you,' he said.

'No. He's a bully, just like my dad. Which also means he's a coward. I don't think he's got the bottle for retribution.'

Phil wasn't so sure.

She took a drink from her mug. 'Bet you've been dying to say "I told you so".'

'I take no satisfaction from what happened. But I did warn you,' he said. A tiny smile flickered on his lips.

'I knew you couldn't resist rubbing it in,' she said.

He grinned. 'Come on. I'll give you a lift back.'

'I've got a car,' she said, gesturing outside.

'How come? You left yours at the apartment.'

'I...well, let's just say this one is a Cross International pool car that the company has given me to use during my notice period,' she said.

He looked sideways at her. 'Does the company know they've given it to you?'

'There is paperwork supporting the sign-off of the car to me. Not sure, if you were to ask anyone, whether they'd remember it happening.' She smiled and then pressed her lips together.

'You are something else,' he said and shook his head.

'It'll take me ten minutes to wash up and get my things together. You go ahead and I'll see you back at the house.'

'Let's travel in convoy,' he said. He didn't want to lose sight of her, now he'd found her. 'What's your new number, so I can keep in contact while we travel?'

'I'll text it to you. Though it is in that email if you'd bothered to read it.' She rolled her eyes at him.

His phone beeped at the text's arrival.

'Who's leading this convoy?' she asked.

'Me,' he said. 'You drive more quickly than Lewis Hamilton, according to Elsie.'

'What's wrong with that?' she asked, smiling.

Twenty minutes later, they were on the road. When they got onto the motorway, Phil was only a little surprised when Juliet sped off in front of him. He rang her. 'Don't think I won't ring my mate in Traffic and get him to pull you over for speeding.' He was pleased when she laughed. It was good to hear her laugh. He watched her slow down so he could overtake.

He rang Portia to update her so future guests at the cottage didn't have to look out for a mysterious stranger. She sounded irked that he'd bothered her in the first place.

As he turned off the motorway, he remembered he'd said he'd update Daniel so he dialled Pat's number.

'Detective,' Pat said. 'Hold on, I'll just put you on speaker.' There were muffled sounds. 'Go ahead.'

'Jools has been found. Safe and well. I said I'd let you know.'

'Can I speak to her?' It was Daniel.

'She's not with me. But I can pass on a message,' Phil said.

'Perhaps you could tell her I'm sorry I didn't take her concerns about Harrison seriously. And that I'll pay that retention bonus I offered her, because of what happened. I'll get it transferred in the next couple of days.'

'I'll let her know,' Phil said. 'Do you think Harrison will try and do anything to Jools?'

'Nah. I've made it very clear to him there will be consequences if he goes anywhere near her. He understands.'

Phil shook his head in disbelief. Cross was openly discussing intimidation. But he couldn't have been happier that Daniel had put the frighteners on Harrison. He knew it was far more of a deterrent than a word from the police. 'Good to know.'

'Thanks for updating us about Jools. I know we're not friends so it was good of you to call,' said Daniel.

'Yeah, it was,' said Phil, 'considering the photos you sent me.'

'That was a cheap trick. I'm sorry,' Daniel said.

At least he'd admitted it. 'I'll say goodbye, then.' Phil ended the call.

Phil went to ring Juliet to pass on Daniel's messages, but changed his mind. He'd prefer to see her reaction and to hear any future conversations she might have with Cross. For her own safety. Or maybe for his own sanity.

Chapter 32 – Juliet

Juliet followed Phil into the house. He knocked on Elsie's door.

Elsie opened the door and he went in. 'Any luck?'

Juliet walked in.

'Oh, lovey, it is so good to see you. I thought you'd gone forever.'

Juliet gave her a long hug. 'Can't get rid of me that easily, Else.' It felt good to be back.

'I'm dying to hear the story behind it all. Phil, get us a drink, would you?'

'What do you want?' he asked.

'A drop of red wine would be nice. Will you join me? And you, Jools?'

Juliet sat down on the sofa opposite Elsie's chair. 'Not for me, Else. Water'll be just fine.'

Phil came back in with their drinks.

Juliet began her story when Phil sat down. 'I was back in the flat watching TV when the door opened. Harrison had got himself a set of keys and started by being friendly, pleasant. Asking me about the board and telling me about the takeover. I was tense at first but I calmed down a bit and we carried on chatting, but then he said he wanted to have sex with me. Obviously, I said no but he said he owned me now and could do whatever he wanted.' She stopped to take a drink of water. 'He grabbed me and told me he'd turned off the security cameras. I tried to throw him off guard by taunting him about this medical issue he's got.'

'The bedwetting?' Phil asked.

She nodded. 'It was good because it brought him up short and he stopped to think, but once he'd realised I knew his secret, it made him really angry. He slapped my face, pushed me onto the ground then kicked me several times.' She showed them the picture she'd taken of the bruises he'd inflicted.

'The bastard,' said Phil.

'It looks bad but it could have been worse. And at least it took his mind off anything sexual. He left the flat after that, threatening to make my life hell.'

'That's a serious assault. I should arrest him,' Phil said.

'What would be the point?' Juliet asked. 'He's a lawyer. He'd weasel his way out of it somehow. You know what these people are like. It's not worth the effort of trying to prove it.'

'But you have proof. You showed the footage at the office,' Elsie said.

'I do. I did.'

'But you said he turned off the cameras at the fuse box,' Phil said.

'He turned off the fuses that said they were for the camera system, but I'd switched the labels, just in case. I had to hope he wouldn't notice.'

'Clever.' Elsie smiled at her. 'But are you alright, after what he did to you?'

'Just a bit sore. Getting better every day,' Juliet said.

'And you arranged for the video to be shown in the office?' Elsie asked.

'Not all of it. The sexual threats, the bit about the bedwetting, the violence and the threat that followed, all on a loop. I emailed Harrison a copy and told him if he ever came near me, I'd send the full tape to the police. Add that to the embarrassment that most people in head office saw his true colours and heard about the bedwetting. I think that's enough punishment for someone like him.'

'And what are you going to do? I can't imagine Cross International will give you a glowing reference,' Phil asked.

'I already got a reference from Daniel. Well, I got him to sign what I'd written. I did that before he left for Cyprus, just in case.'

'So, did you resign? Or were you sacked?' Phil asked.

'I resigned. When I left Jeremy's office, I went via HR. I'd already sent my resignation to them. They'd seen the video and said they would arrange three months' pay in lieu of notice. I've known the HR Director a long time. She knows I could sue them for something, probably constructive dismissal but to be honest, I just want a clean break.'

'So, you've got three months to find a new job,' he said, 'or maybe longer. I'd agreed to ring Daniel when I found you and he's just told me he'll pay your retention bonus, despite or rather because of what's happened.'

'Did he? That will be very helpful. I'll still need to find a new job at some point but it'll give me more time. And of course, I need to sort out somewhere to live,' Juliet said.

'You know I'd like you to move in here, lovey,' Elsie squeezed her hand. 'I like having you about the place.'

'That's very kind of you, Elsie. I wasn't fishing for an offer but it's good to know I can stay here for a bit. I do though, owe you both an apology. You warned me what might happen and you were right. I shouldn't have gone back, but at least your warnings made me plan for the worst-case scenario.'

'Are you sure you don't want to report this? I assume you have a copy of the tape?' Phil asked.

'I have several copies in different formats and places. But I just want to forget it and move on.'

'One thing I'm more confident about now is that Harrison won't come looking for you,' Phil said.

'What's changed your mind?' Juliet asked. 'You looked decidedly sceptical when I said that at the cottage.'

'Daniel assured me he's spoken to Jeremy and is confident you won't get any further trouble from him,' Phil said.

Elsie laughed. 'Well, there's a turn-up.'

'If you'd told me a week ago, I'd be having that sort of conversation with Daniel bloody Cross, I'd have thought you were nuts,' Phil said.

'I joked about having access to a heavy mob on our first date,' Juliet said and laughed. 'I thought I was joking at the time.'

Phil gave her a smile as he shook his head.

Juliet took a sip of water. 'You know, I've done a lot of thinking since I was last here. Phil, I know you don't want to go out with me, but now, I get why. I've spent so long having to fend for myself, feeling rejected because no-one gave me love, that I've held everyone at arm's length. I mean, my adoptive Mum did love me to start with, but the fact she never came back, never checked to see if I was OK, that still hurts. Life's been easier if I don't open up to anyone, so I've been faking it for as long as I can remember, pretending to be something I'm not. You really made me think when you asked when I got to be me. Do you remember?'

He nodded.

'I thought about that for a long time. Then I realised why it was so hard to answer. How can I be myself when I don't know who I am? I've become so practised at being a chameleon, saying whatever the client wants to hear, doing whatever the boss wants me to do, that I lost sight of the real me. I also lost sight of the line between right and wrong.' She looked at Elsie. 'Meeting you both made me put everything in perspective and I knew I couldn't do my job anymore. Once I'd escaped that, I had to work out who I really was. That's why I went away.'

'Two secs.' Phil left the room. When he came back, he handed an envelope to Juliet. 'You might as well have these. Not sure I want them.'

She opened the flap and took out the pictures. She felt sick when she realised what they were. 'Where did you get these?'

'Daniel had them sent to me,' he said.

'When?' She looked at each one in turn then looked up at him. 'Was this when… was this why you suddenly stopped seeing me?'

He nodded.

'I reckon Daniel was jealous,' Elsie said. 'He must have wanted Phil out of the picture so he could have you all to himself.'

'What a bastard,' Juliet said. She looked at Phil. 'These aren't real, you know.'

'I know. Detective Tucker here pointed out how obvious it is these are staged,' he said.

'Yes, not my best work. I would say "let me show you what good looks like" but I'm not sure that's a sensible thing to share with a police officer.' She met Phil's gaze. 'I suppose you're going to want to know more about all of this, officially. About the things I was doing.'

'Tell me unofficially,' he said.

'I'm reluctant to tell you for so many reasons.' It wasn't the consequences Juliet feared as much as his disappointment in her for behaving the way she had.

'You need to trust me,' he said, holding her gaze.

'You should, lovey. He's a good man,' said Elsie. 'One of the best.'

Juliet took a deep breath. 'I liked to think what I did was industrial espionage, spying on the baddies. I'd bring the guy to the flat, give him a drink with a tablet in it, stage the photos, go through his pockets and his phone. Go to his hotel room and check out the contents of his suitcase.'

'Did you take anything?' he asked.

'Only photos.'

'But you were drugging people,' he said.

She could feel herself colouring with shame as she nodded.

'Where did you get the drugs?' he asked.

'They were delivered to the flat.'

'By who?' he asked.

She shook her head. 'I'd rather not say.'

'And how were the photos used?' he asked.

'I don't remember them ever being used. Daniel liked to have them as insurance, in case he needed to bring people around to his way of thinking.'

'Were you ever involved in threatening people?' he asked.

'No. I'm hardly the menacing type, am I?'

Phil nodded. 'What about those dates and times when Daniel said he was in the office?'

She wasn't sure how much to give away, but Daniel had left her to deal with Harrison and had sent the pictures of her naked to Phil. 'There was some fudging of timings, fiddling of clocks and computers to make the people giving him an alibi think it was a different time. There were recorded phone calls that would be played from the next room so it would sound like he was around when he wasn't, as well as distraction techniques that meant people wouldn't notice his absence.'

'So, the alibis people were giving were genuine?' he asked.

'As far as they were concerned, yes. They were giving a true account of what they think happened. No-one outside of Daniel's inner circle was lying.'

'And did you, do you know what Daniel was doing while he was away?' he asked.

'He never shared any details with me. I assumed at first, he was cheating on his wife,' said Juliet.

'At first?' he asked.

'Well, when you started asking questions, I realised it must be more than him having an extra-marital fling. As to what exactly, I was never told. I'd hazard a guess, based on how some people's behaviour changed, that Daniel must have paid them a visit. But what he did or what he threatened to do, I've no idea.'

'You know, Jools, there could be a case for you being an unwitting part of all this. Groomed and coerced into criminal activities.'

'Groomed? That's not really true, is it? I don't think you can make me out to be innocent,' Juliet said.

'It's likely Daniel chose you for the role because you don't have any family. And he's probably discouraged you from having too many friends by keeping you so busy, isolating you from the rest of the world. He wanted you and I to split up, didn't he? What about your previous boyfriend? Did he get him out of the way, too?'

Juliet shook her head. 'Cam left me of his own accord.'

'And paid the price,' Elsie said. 'Ended up in a wheelchair.'

Juliet frowned at her. 'How do you know that?'

'I heard your conversation at the hospital as I was waking up. You were talking to someone. Pat, was it? You asked him if it was Daniel who arranged for Cam to be hurt. And he confirmed it, said it was because you were upset at Cam leaving. I thought I was dreaming.'

'I felt so stupid. It never occurred to me, not till Cam said something,' Juliet said.

Phil looked shocked. 'What? Are you saying this ex of yours, Cam, is in a wheelchair and it was Cross that did it to him?' Phil asked.

'Daniel didn't do it. He'd never dirty his hands. But apparently, he was responsible, though there's no proof, no audit trail. The police have never been able to find out who actually inflicted the beating on Cam,' Juliet said.

'I'm going to speak to a friend of mine, a lawyer, about your situation,' Phil said. 'She's lovely. A bit disorganised but once you have her attention, she's the best.'

'Thanks. I'll definitely need a sympathetic lawyer.'

'Her name's Thelma. She's a good sounding board on cases where people have been coerced. She advocates for them, works out if they were manipulated into criminal behaviour. Sometimes, we don't take a case forward if she thinks she's got enough evidence to support someone's innocence because of coercive control.'

'Thank you. I'm not a coward. I'll take whatever's coming. I did what I did, and even if I didn't admit it to myself, I knew it was wrong,' said Juliet.

'The good thing is you're not doing these things anymore, so it doesn't have to be at the top of my in-tray. And with Daniel retired, we'll need to consider if it's in the public interest to investigate any of it. Budgets are tight these days.'

'I always thought you were Mr Black and White when it came to your job,' Juliet said.

'I like the fact you're surprised I can be Mr Grey,' he said.

She chewed her lower lip.

'I can't deny,' he said, 'that there isn't a little bit of me that wants to question you about everything that went on at Cross International so I can nail that devious bastard, but it doesn't feel like a priority right now. I'm just so glad you're safe. But Jools, you have to promise me that you'll stop all this. That you'll carve out a new life for yourself on the right side of the law,' he said.

Elsie nudged Juliet. 'He's right, lovey. Did you give any thought, while you were away, to what you're gonna do with yourself?' Elsie asked.

'I'm going to get myself an ordinary job, working with ordinary people. Try and have an ordinary life.'

'Do you want an ordinary boyfriend?' Phil laughed. 'I'm over-qualified for that.'

Juliet sighed and gave him a warm smile. 'There's nothing ordinary about you, Phil.' She gave him as big a hug as her bruises would allow.

'I think you two need some time together,' Elsie said. 'Go on.'

'Do you want anything to eat, Else?' Phil asked her.

'No, I'm good. Got my *Eastenders* to catch up on and my whisky. You go sort yourselves out.'

Phil and Juliet went into the kitchen.

'Do you want me to make you some dinner?' he asked.

'No, thanks.'

'Drink? Tonic?' he asked.

She nodded and she watched him put some ice and a slice of lemon into the glass before adding the chilled tonic.

He gave it to her before pouring himself a glass of white wine.

'Cheers,' he said and touched his glass against hers.

'Cheers.' She took a sip and looked at him. 'I thought about you a lot while I was in the cottage.'

'And what were you thinking?' he asked.

'Mainly wishing you'd change your mind about me.'

'And what else?' he said.

'Oh, idle, impossible thoughts about what it would be like if we were back together, what we'd do together.' She blushed as she looked down at her glass, not wanting to meet his gaze. She hadn't dared hope she could have a future with Phil, not with everything she'd admitted but she knew he was exactly the sort of person she should be spending time with. Someone with integrity and honour. Someone who made her heart flutter.

He put his hand underneath her chin, moving it upwards so she was looking at him. 'Will you share those idle, impossible thoughts with me?'

'I will,' she said, taking his hand and kissing the palm gently before holding it. She felt her heart beating faster. 'But before I do, would you kiss me, Phil? Please?'

Phil's mobile burst into life.

'No point in telling you to ignore it, I assume,' said Juliet.

He looked at the phone. 'Not when it's the DCS calling,' he said. 'Sir, how can I help?' He put the call on speaker.

'Phil, hoping you can provide some reassurance for me,' DCS Pidgeon said.

'I'll certainly do my best, Sir,' Phil said.

'No doubt you're aware of the recent events at Cross International?'

'Yes, Sir. I have heard about the situation.'

'Unfortunate business. I'm hoping there won't be any further repercussions, that there's no intention of charges being brought against Jeremy Harrison by this person,' the DCS said. 'Are you able to provide any insight on the matter?'

Phil raised his eyebrows at Juliet, who shrugged. 'As I understand it, Sir, as long as Mr Harrison keeps away from this person, there'll be no charges brought,' he said. He mouthed 'OK?' at Juliet and she nodded.

'That's good news, thank you Phil. And I do want to congratulate you and your team on the successful conclusion to the Johnstone case. It's about time your career took an upward trajectory. This success won't go unnoticed,' the DCS said.

Juliet gave Phil a silent round of applause.

'Thank you, Sir. I'll pass on the congratulations to the team,' Phil said.

'Good. I'll leave you to your evening, then.' The DCS hung up.

Juliet smiled. 'An upward trajectory, eh?'

'I'm not going to read too much into that,' Phil said. 'He'll have forgotten by next week.'

'I hope not, for your sake. Now, are you ever going to kiss me?'

'There's nothing I'd rather do.' He pressed his lips against hers and she felt her stomach erupt with butterflies. He put his arms around her as he kissed her and she knew there was nowhere she'd rather be than in the arms of this ordinary, extraordinary man. This is where she belonged.

Epilogue

Juliet walked upstairs to the office of her boss, Thelma Morris.

'I've prepared the paperwork for the meeting you've got with Davison's tomorrow,' Juliet said and handed over a folder. 'Soft copy sent on email as I bet you want to look at it tonight.'

'Too right,' said Thelma. 'What's your gut feel? Will they settle out of court?'

Juliet nodded. 'I reckon. There's too strong a case on our side and I'm sure Tim Davison is, to put it crudely, shit scared of you.'

'As he should be.' Thelma let out a throaty laugh.

'Now you're up for that Lawyer of the Year award for the BSN, the whole world will be afraid,' Juliet said.

'I cannot tell a lie. I love it, having a reputation as a force to be reckoned with.' Thelma chuckled. 'How long have you been here now, Jools?'

'Six months tomorrow. It's gone really quick.'

'You've done wonders. I'm so glad you took the job.'

'Me too,' Juliet said.

'You're still enjoying it? Not getting bored?'

'Not at all. I love the daily challenge of keeping you on track. And it's so good to be a part of something that's helping people out, righting wrongs. Making a difference to people. Just like you did for me,' said Juliet.

'Thank goodness. You've made my working life so much less stressful now you've got me organised. Anyway, why don't you get off home? Oh, and please don't forget the barbecue on Sunday. I'm relying on you and Phil for the salads,' Thelma said.

'I won't.' Juliet went back to her office and switched off her computer. She put on her jacket, switched the office answerphone on, and walked the twenty minutes home.

'Hi,' she shouted as she walked into the hallway. She put her keys in a bowl on the hall table and kicked off her shoes. She put her head around Elsie's door. 'Evening, Else. You OK?'

'Never better. Got my poker ladies coming over tonight. Wanna join us?'

'And get fleeced again? You gotta be kidding. What's for dinner?' asked Juliet.

'It's a chicken stew, very nice. Yours is on the stove. I had mine early,' Elsie said.

'Cuppa tea?'

'No, thanks. I've already started on my pre-game tipple. Get myself in the mood.' Elsie lifted up her glass.

'Well, you have a nice night.'

'I assume you already heard the news about your old firm.'

'No. What?' Juliet asked.

'Daniel Cross is taking back over.'

'Really? I'm not surprised. I thought he'd get bored doing nothing. He always liked to keep busy,' Juliet said.

'Do you think he might contact you? Ask you to go back and work for him?'

'Wouldn't matter if he did, Else. I'm not going anywhere near Cross International.'

'Glad to hear that,' said Elsie.

'Right. I'm going up to the allotment before I have my dinner. Lots to do.'

'See you later, lovey.'

Jools dashed upstairs and changed into some old jeans and a sweatshirt. She picked up her house key then walked to the allotment.

The shed door was ajar. She pushed on it and saw Phil cutting lengths of string from a ball.

'Hiya,' he said and leant forward to kiss her.

She put her arms around him and they embraced for a few seconds.

'Good day at work?' he asked.

'Yes. How about you?'

'It's pretty quiet at the moment. Touch wood.' He tapped the wooden bench for luck.

'Long may that continue,' she said, 'then I'll keep coming home to a cooked meal.'

'I'm just a slave to you, aren't I?' he said.

She smiled. 'You're the man who taught me how to be honest with myself. How to love. And even if I told you every day, I could never make you understand how grateful I am.' She kissed him again. 'By the way, Thelma reminded me again about the salads for Sunday. And I've been thinking about my birthday. I've decided where I want to go.'

'Let's hear it,' he said.

'Malta,' she said.

'Jools, you don't have to do that.'

'Do what? I've never been there and I want to go. It's a nice place, so you keep saying. You can see the boys and I can finally meet them. We'll get an Airbnb that's big enough for the boys to stay in, too.'

'Sal would hate her boys being away from her,' he said.

'Then we get a big enough place for her and her bloke to stay.'

'I gather her bloke has left her,' he said.

'Has he? Even more reason for her to join us. You don't want her stewing at home, feeling sorry for herself when she's been dumped, while we go off and have fun with her children. It'd be good for the boys to see us all co-existing happily. Good role models. You're always saying about youngsters need good role models. At least think about it?' she asked.

He sighed. 'OK. I will. But it seems like you're thinking of everyone but yourself here, for what is supposed to be your 30th birthday treat.' His phone rang. He walked out of the shed and Juliet wondered why. She couldn't hear the conversation. He came back in, looking worried. 'I need to talk to you about something.'

A look of panic crossed her face. 'What is it?'

'I need to take you to a police station tomorrow.'

'What? Why?' she asked.

'Best to wait till we're there so you can hear the whole thing.'

'Am I going to be arrested? I thought you'd agreed with Thelma it wasn't worth pursuing,' she said.

He put his hands over his eyes and grimaced before looking at her. 'Sorry, I'm an idiot. You're not in trouble. It's nothing like that.'

'What is it then? Tell me or I'll spend all night imagining. I won't sleep,' she said.

'A body's been found, a historic murder and…' He stopped.

'What?'

'The body was found in the garden of Lullaby Cottage. Under the pond that never was,' he said.

'What?' Her voice went wobbly.

'It's always puzzled me how a loving mum like yours never got in touch with you. And when I tracked you down there and you told me

265

about that pond, I started wondering. And I talked to a friend who works at the station near there and he was sympathetic, reckoned it was worth investigating. But it was hard to get traction. Between us, we got someone senior to take the possibility seriously, spoke to the owner and the digging started a few days ago. They're pretty certain it's a woman they've found, from the bones and the clothing fragments. Blunt force trauma to the skull, so she was murdered. She was wearing a crucifix and a locket.'

Juliet's knees buckled but she managed to guide herself onto one of the stools in the corner. 'That's what she always wore.' She thought for a moment. 'I'd be able to recognise the jewellery. The crucifix had a nick out of one part of the cross. And the locket. I know what pictures are inside, if they've survived. One of me and one of her and my dad.'

'We'll go in the morning so you can talk to the investigation team.'

'If it is her, it would explain why she never came back. Murdered?' She shook her head. 'Of all the things I imagined, that was never on the list.' She stared into space for a while.

He held her hand. 'You were only young, so you didn't question what your father told you. And being a kid, you thought about it only in terms of her rejecting you.'

'He'd torment me sometimes when he was drunk. That it was my fault that Mum had left. That I was a bad daughter and that it was me who drove her away. I cried myself to sleep so often about that.'

'Are you OK to carry on here?' He gestured with his head toward the allotment outside. 'Or would you rather go home?'

She nodded. 'I can cope with anything as long as you're by my side.'

'I promise I will be. Always.'

Printed in Great Britain
by Amazon

29326105R00158